My W(

By Brann

My Wedding Contract Too

Branny Smith

Published by Banny Joma Enterprise, 2024.

This is a work of fiction. Similarities to real people, places, or events are entirely coincidental.

MY WEDDING CONTRACT TOO

First edition. December 7, 2024.

Copyright © 2024 Branny Smith.

ISBN: 979-8227391766

Written by Branny Smith.

Also by Branny Smith

Series 1
How to Live in Happiness and Peace

Standalone
How to Negotiate, Present and Solve Problems
A Handbook for Stoma Care Management
Her Lover is Gone
The Professor's Descent
My Wedding Contract Too

I dedicate this book to my lovely friends who know me across the sea and in my own country and family members.

I wish that life will treat you better as you all dwell into the road to be loving and to be loved.

The questions of justice and morality don't always come with clear answers.

Preface of this book

There is too much trust, loneliness and love among friends and certain things are not said, they remain the secrets.

"My Wedding Contract Too is a book that brings elements of drama, moral questioning, and social commentary. It invites readers to think critically about their own values and how they would respond to complex situations.

Through the exploration of friendship, betrayal, legal complexities, and moral dilemmas, the story provides valuable insights into the human condition and the intricacies of relationships.

Acknowledgements

I acknowledge the presence of my colleagues in the film industry, my extended professional friends, spouse's motivation and love, which carry me through to write daily, and my family; they are all the pillars of strength to continue telling these stories.

By Branny Smith

Copyright © 2024 Branny Smith.

The book author retains sole copyright to his contributions to this book

More information: brannysmithsa@gmail.com

Banny Joma Enterprise Publishers Johannesburg
South Africa
@Branny Smith
@Branny Mthelebofu
Copyright © 2024, December, Banny Joma Enterprise
All rights reserved.

No part of this publication may be reproduced or transmitted in any form or by any means, electronic or mechanical, including photocopy, recording, or any information storage and retrieval system, without permission in writing from the publisher.

© South Africa, Pretoria.
Banny Joma Enterprise Publishers

Dedication

I dedicate this story to all the people who need love, courage, and hope daily to reach their destiny.

I dedicate this story to those women and men who lost their partners, soulmates and close friends and family members.

The Author

The author of How to 'Negotiate, Present and Solve Problems", " Her Lover is Gone", and The Professor's Descent", he was born and raised in Limpopo Province, in a small town, Mokopane in South Africa.

Branny Smith is a holistic therapist, and filmmaker who is producing feature films and feature documentary films and is a musician. He has worked as an investigative journalist and a researcher for more than 15 years in medical research and creative industry years of experience.

His films have been shown in the UK and currently, his feature film will be shown all over the world in film festivals. He has published scientific articles in different publications.

He enjoys watching movies, cheers, and going out to the bush to watch nature.

Wedding

A tangled web of deceit and unexpected revelations unfolds as Onica navigates through a maze of marriage certificate mix-ups, business turmoil, and personal crises after the sudden death of her husband, Peter.

My Wedding Contract Too

The morning sun filtered through the lace curtains of Onica's modest apartment, casting a deceptive serenity over a life that was anything but calm. She sat at the edge of her bed, the weight of the legal document in her trembling hands. Her late husband's name, Peter, stared back at her from the top of the page like a ghost demanding acknowledgment. The marriage certificate, once a symbol of love and security, now felt like a cruel joke—its legitimacy questioned, its implications tearing her world apart. The past few months had unraveled with a cruel intensity: Peter's untimely death, the battle for his business empire, and now this—her very identity as his wife was being challenged.

The world outside moved on, blissfully unaware of the storm raging within her. But Onica knew she couldn't let this mistake define her. The stakes were high—not just for her but for everyone connected to the company Peter had worked so hard to build. The whispers of doubt among employees, the probing questions from lawyers, and the relentless rumors in the media painted her as an opportunist rather than a grieving widow. Each accusation chipped away at her resolve.

Downstairs, the sound of clinking cups echoed as her best friend, Lizer, prepared coffee. She had insisted on staying over, knowing Onica wasn't in the right frame of mind to be alone. Lizer was the only person Onica could trust, though even her unwavering support couldn't shield her from the harsh realities that awaited.

At the heart of it all was a sinister question: Could it be true? Could this "mistake" in the paperwork be more than an error—a deliberate act orchestrated by those who wanted her out of the picture? As Onica gazed at the certificate, she felt the familiar sting of betrayal, and her thoughts drifted to Jersey, the woman who seemed to take pleasure in her misery. Jersey's smugness during the court hearings suggested she knew more than she let on.

But there was no time for self-pity. Onica was no stranger to adversity. She had clawed her way through life before meeting Peter, and she wasn't about to let his legacy—and her future—be snatched away. She placed the document on the desk, determination replacing fear in her eyes. Whatever the truth behind the marriage certificate, she would uncover it.

My Wedding Contract Too isn't just Onica's fight against a legal technicality. It's a labyrinth of deception, friendships tested to their limits, and the insidious lengths people go to secure their ambitions. In this tale of suspense and betrayal, love is questioned, trust is shattered, and the pursuit of justice comes at a cost.

The cemetery was cloaked in a somber stillness, the kind that seemed to draw the color from the world and weigh down the air. Rows of weathered tombstones stretched out in precise lines beneath a sky thick with gray clouds. A cold breeze rustled the nearby oaks, their bare branches clawing at the heavens. Among the gravestones, a lone figure stood, her presence striking in its solitude against the desolation.

Onica, her shoulders hunched beneath a simple black coat, clutched a bouquet of lilies—Peter's favorite. Her face, pale and drawn, bore the unmistakable traces of sleepless nights and tears shed in anguished solitude. She stepped forward, her heels sinking slightly into the damp earth, to the freshly dug grave that had been the source of her sorrow for weeks.

Kneeling slowly, as though the weight of her grief might crush her entirely, Onica placed the flowers gently on the mound of soil that marked the end of the life she had built with Peter. Her trembling fingers brushed against the engraved stone, tracing the name that once brought her so much joy.

"Peter," she murmured, her voice raw and fragile, carried away almost immediately by the cold wind. "I can't believe you're gone... I miss you so much."

She swallowed hard, her breath visible in the crisp air, and leaned closer to the grave, her words barely more than a whisper. "We had so many dreams together. Remember? We were going to grow old, travel to Paris in the spring, buy that little beach house... all the things we used to talk about. You promised me forever, Peter."

Her hand rested on the stone as though hoping to feel some trace of warmth, some reassurance that this was all a mistake. But the cold granite offered none. The finality of it loomed over her like a shadow, deepening the ache in her chest.

"It's not fair," Onica whispered, her voice breaking. "You didn't deserve this. We didn't deserve this."

The distant caw of a crow broke the quiet, and for a moment, Onica's tear-filled eyes lifted to the overcast sky. She closed them, inhaling deeply to steady herself, though the weight of grief pressed harder with each breath.

Kneeling there, alone in the cemetery, Onica knew she had reached a crossroads. The life she had envisioned with Peter was gone, buried beneath the soil along with him. Ahead lay uncertainty—battles she hadn't anticipated, betrayals she couldn't foresee.

But for now, in this moment, she allowed herself to grieve. To mourn the man who had been her partner, her love, her future. She wiped a tear from her cheek, whispering her last promise to him.

"I'll make things right, Peter. Somehow, I'll fix this. For us."

The wind carried her words away as she rose slowly, her knees trembling under the strain. With one last glance at the grave, she turned and walked back to the car, her head held high, though her heart weighed heavier than ever before.

The wind whispered softly through the trees, stirring the brittle leaves that clung stubbornly to their branches. The quiet melody of a bird's song echoed faintly in the distance, a stark contrast to the heaviness of the moment. Onica stood motionless at the graveside, her figure framed by the muted colors of the overcast sky and the solemn gray stones surrounding her.

Her voice quivered as she spoke, each word trembling under the weight of her grief. "I don't know how to do this without you."

ONICA (sobbing)

I don't know how to do this without you. I feel so lost.

The wind rustles the leaves of nearby trees, and the distant sound of a bird's chirping echoes through the cemetery. Onica takes a deep breath and composes herself.

ONICA (resolute)

But I promise, Peter, I'll find a way to move forward. I'll make sure your memory lives on.

Onica stands, takes one last lingering look at the tombstone, and begins to walk away from the gravesite, her heart heavy with sorrow.

Onica is sitting at a small wooden table, a cup of tea growing cold in front of her. She's going through a box of documents, seeking solace in her husband's memory.

Among the papers, she pulls out a sealed envelope with a certificate inside. Her fingers tremble as she carefully opens it.

The quiet of the room was broken only by the rustle of paper as Onica carefully unfolded the certificate she had cherished for years. Her fingers trembled slightly as she smoothed the document, her eyes gliding over the words that should have been a testament to her love.

"Peter," she whispered, her voice soft and reverent, as though speaking directly to the memory of her late husband. "This is the marriage certificate we signed on our wedding day. It should be a reminder of our love."

Her gaze lingered on the elegant script, and for a moment, her expression softened with nostalgia. But as her eyes caught a detail she hadn't noticed before, her body stiffened. Her breath hitched audibly in her throat.

"No..." she gasped, the word barely escaping her lips. Her heart began to race as her hand darted back to the paper, her fingers tracing the name printed where her own should have been.

Jersey.

"Jersey's name?" she murmured, her voice shaking with disbelief. "No, this can't be right... this can't be!"

Her knees felt weak as she clutched the certificate tighter, as if gripping it would somehow force it to change. The walls of the room seemed to close in, and a sharp chill crept down her spine.

The camera zoomed in on the certificate, capturing the damning detail—"Jersey Collins" scrawled where "Onica Daniels" was supposed to be. The trembling of Onica's fingers became more pronounced as she hovered over the name, unable to look away.

Her voice cracked as she stumbled backward, her mind spiraling into chaos. "How could this happen? How could Peter let this happen?"

The once-cherished document now felt like a betrayal in her hands.

Onica's breath hitched as she stared at the document in her hands, the name glaring back at her like a taunt. Her fingers traced over the bold, official lettering that read: *Jersey Collins*.

Her voice came out trembling, barely above a whisper. "Jersey... why is your name here?"

The words tasted bitter on her tongue. Her grip on the paper tightened, her knuckles whitening. "This is *our* marriage certificate!" she said, her voice cracking, the weight of disbelief pressing down on her chest.

Her hands began to tremble, the paper quivering in her grip. She flipped through the pages, frantically scanning for an explanation—an amendment, a correction, *something* to explain this absurdity. But the error remained, sharp and unyielding.

"No," she muttered, shaking her head as though the motion could shake loose the truth. Her vision blurred with unshed tears. "No, this has to be a mistake."

She lowered the paper, her eyes drifting upward, unfocused as her thoughts raced. "Oh, Peter..." she murmured, her voice thick with emotion. "How could this happen? How could *you* let this happen?"

Her body sagged as though the weight of the revelation had drained the strength from her limbs. She slumped into the chair behind her, the document still clutched in her hands. The pages, once a treasured keepsake, now felt like a betrayal.

Tears welled in her eyes, spilling over as the enormity of the situation settled in her chest. Each drop felt heavier than the last, a mix of heartbreak, confusion, and anger she could scarcely contain.

The room was silent, save for the rustle of the paper as her hands trembled. She looked at the document again, desperate to understand. But there was no explanation—only the cruel finality of the name staring back at her.

Her voice cracked as she whispered, "This can't be real. It just... can't be."

The discovery had shaken her to her core, leaving her grappling with a truth she wasn't ready to face. Her world, already fragile, felt like it was crumbling beneath her.

The room was dimly lit, shadows dancing across the walls as the faint glow of a single lamp cast a warm, intimate light over the space. Peter sat on the edge of the couch, his elbows resting on his knees, his hands clasped tightly together. His expression was a storm of emotions—guilt, conflict, and something deeper, something darker that he couldn't fully suppress.

The door creaked open, and Jersey stepped in. Her presence was magnetic, her movements deliberate. She was dressed in a way that left little to the imagination, her confidence radiating as she crossed the room. The soft click of her heels echoed, each step drawing her closer to him.

Peter looked up, his eyes meeting hers, and for a moment, the air between them felt heavy, charged with unspoken words and undeniable tension.

"Jersey..." he started, his voice low and strained. He exhaled sharply, looking away as if he couldn't bear the sight of her. "This is wrong. I'm about to marry Onica." His words hung in the air, a desperate attempt to remind himself of the lines he shouldn't cross.

Jersey tilted her head, a faint smile playing on her lips as she moved closer. She knelt slightly, her hand resting on the arm of the couch, bringing her face level with his. "But don't you want one last memory before you tie the knot?" she whispered, her voice soft, almost like a caress. Her eyes glimmered with a mix of mischief and determination. "Just between us."

Peter's jaw tightened as he clenched his fists, his resolve visibly wavering. His heart raced, each beat louder than the last as he wrestled with his conscience. He opened his mouth to protest, to say *no*, but the words never came. Instead, he remained frozen, trapped in the web Jersey was weaving.

Jersey leaned in closer, her presence overwhelming, intoxicating. "Peter," she murmured, her voice dropping to a sultry whisper. "No one has to know. Just one last moment... one last secret."

Peter closed his eyes, his breath unsteady. His thoughts were a whirlwind—Onica's laugh, her trust, her dreams for their future. But then there was Jersey, here, now, igniting something he couldn't name. He looked at her again, his expression softening as temptation began to override reason.

He hesitated, his lips trembling with words unspoken. And then, slowly, he reached out, his hand brushing against hers. Jersey's smile deepened as she closed the gap between them, and in an instant, the line was crossed.

Their kiss was intense, fueled by a mix of forbidden desire and reckless abandon. The room seemed to close in around them, the dim light casting their shadows against the walls as they gave in to the moment.

But even as they succumbed, a flicker of doubt lingered in Peter's eyes—an unspoken acknowledgment that this fleeting indulgence could unravel everything he held dear.

The wedding venue was alive with joy and celebration, a cascade of laughter and music filling the grand hall. Strings of fairy lights twinkled above the crowd, casting a soft golden glow on the dancing guests. The air was thick with the scent of fresh flowers—roses, lilies,

The questions of justice and morality don't always come with clear answers.

and jasmine—and the clink of champagne glasses added a symphony of elegance to the evening.

Onica stood at the center of the room, resplendent in her flowing white gown, her face glowing with happiness. Beside her, Peter looked dashing in his tailored suit, his grin wide and boyish as he held Onica's hand tightly. Their love was palpable, radiating like an aura that drew everyone closer to share in their joy.

Peter turned to Onica, his dark eyes shimmering with excitement. "Can you believe it?" he said, his voice carrying above the cheerful chaos. "We're finally getting married, Onica."

Onica looked up at him, her smile soft and full of emotion. "It's a dream come true, Peter," she replied, her voice trembling slightly with joy. "And having Jersey by our side makes it even more special."

As if summoned by her name, Jersey approached the couple, her emerald-green bridesmaid dress catching the light as she moved. Her eyes glistened with unshed tears, and her lips quivered in a mix of happiness and sentiment. She clutched her bouquet close, the vibrant blooms a striking contrast against her dress.

"I'm so honored to be part of your special day," Jersey said, her voice thick with emotion. She glanced between Peter and Onica, her gaze lingering on each of them. "You two deserve all the happiness in the world."

Peter reached out and placed a hand on Jersey's shoulder, his smile genuine and warm. "We wouldn't have it any other way, Jersey. You've been there for us through everything."

Onica nodded, her expression one of heartfelt gratitude. "We couldn't have done this without you."

The trio stood together, a moment of shared understanding passing between them, as though sealing a bond forged long before this day. Around them, the celebration carried on, oblivious to the quiet connection they shared.

Jersey's eyes flickered briefly with an emotion she quickly masked, her smile growing brighter as she raised her glass. "To love, loyalty, and lifelong friendships," she toasted.

"To forever," Peter added, raising his own glass with a laugh.

Onica joined in, her voice steady and full of hope. "To forever."

The glasses clinked, the sound ringing out like a promise in the midst of their perfect day, oblivious to the shadows that would later haunt their lives. For now, it was a day of unbridled joy, the first chapter of a story they couldn't yet imagine.

The ceremony was an exquisite affair, a symphony of love and commitment woven together in the golden glow of the afternoon. The sun streamed through the tall arched windows of the chapel, casting ethereal light on the trio at the altar. Onica, Peter, and Jersey stood together, their bond radiating an intimacy that seemed unbreakable.

Onica's white dress shimmered as she turned to face Peter, her hands trembling slightly as she held his. Her eyes, glistening with unshed tears, locked onto his, and the room seemed to fade, leaving just the two of them in the moment.

"I promise to love and cherish you, Peter, for all the days of our lives," Onica said, her voice steady yet brimming with emotion. Her words carried a weight that echoed through the chapel, touching the hearts of all who listened.

Peter squeezed her hands gently, a reassuring smile spreading across his face. Dressed in a crisp black suit, he looked every bit the picture of a groom deeply in love. "I promise to be your partner in every adventure, Onica," he replied, his voice firm yet tender. "To share your joys, your sorrows, and everything in between."

Jersey, standing just behind them, clutched her bouquet with a mixture of pride and sentiment. The soft emerald of her bridesmaid dress complemented the glow in her eyes. Stepping slightly forward, she addressed the couple with a sincerity that resonated deeply. "And

I promise to stand by your side," she said, her voice thick with emotion, "as your friend and supporter, through thick and thin."

The audience of family and friends sat captivated, the air charged with the beauty of the moment. The vows were not merely words; they were declarations of a connection that had been built over years of laughter, challenges, and unwavering loyalty.

As the officiant pronounced them husband and wife, Peter leaned forward to kiss Onica, sealing their vows with a gentle yet passionate embrace. The chapel erupted into applause and cheers, the sound echoing joyfully against the high ceilings.

Jersey stepped closer, enveloping them both in a hug that was as much a promise as it was a celebration. In that moment, they were not just a bride, a groom, and a witness—they were a family bound by more than blood, a shared history and a future they all believed would be bright.

The flashback lingered on their intertwined hands, capturing a fleeting yet eternal moment of unity, unaware of the trials that would one day test the strength of their promises. For now, it was a scene of untainted joy, a memory etched in the fabric of their lives, glowing in its perfection.

The sterile scent of the hospital room hung heavy in the air, mingling with the quiet hum of machines that had fought valiantly to sustain Peter's life. The dim light cast long shadows on the walls, making the space feel cavernous and cold. Onica stood by the bedside, her trembling hand clutching Peter's pale one, her other hand brushing back strands of his damp hair. Her love for him was etched across her face, in the furrow of her brow and the tears brimming in her eyes.

"Hang in there, my love," Onica whispered, her voice barely above a breath. "We'll get through this."

Peter's eyelids fluttered open, his hazel eyes dull with exhaustion but still carrying the faint glimmer of love. With the last vestige of strength he could gather, he squeezed her hand weakly. His lips curled into a ghost of a smile, one filled with both devotion and resignation.

"I love you, Onica," he whispered, his voice hoarse, the words fragile as glass. "Promise me... you'll be happy."

Her heart shattered at his words, the enormity of what he was implying striking her like a blow. Tears spilled freely down her cheeks, dripping onto the bedsheet as she shook her head, refusing to let go of hope. "I promise, Peter," she said, her voice breaking. "But I need you by my side. I can't do this without you."

The room fell silent save for the faint, irregular beeps of the heart monitor. Then the nurse entered, her expression solemn, eyes filled with compassion. The moment her gaze met Onica's, the truth hit with the force of a tidal wave.

"I'm so sorry..." the nurse said softly. "Peter has passed away."

Time seemed to stand still. Onica's knees buckled, and she gripped the edge of the bed to steady herself. Her world crumbled in an instant as she stared at Peter's lifeless face, his hand now limp in hers. A guttural sob escaped her, raw and unrestrained, echoing in the cold, unforgiving room. The nurse gently placed a hand on her shoulder.

"I'll give you a moment to say goodbye," the nurse murmured, stepping out quietly to leave her with her grief.

Moments later, Jersey appeared in the doorway, her usually vibrant face now pale and streaked with tears. She walked in hesitantly, her own sorrow etched in her features as she took in the devastating sight of her best friend crumpled beside Peter's still form.

"Onica," Jersey said, her voice trembling. "I'm so sorry."

Onica turned her tear-streaked face to Jersey, her eyes filled with a depth of pain that words could never capture. "It's all falling apart, Jersey," she choked out, her voice breaking. "The pastor is gone, and now Peter. What am I going to do?"

Jersey crossed the room in a heartbeat, wrapping her arms tightly around Onica. The two women clung to each other amidst the weight of unspeakable loss, their shared sorrow the only solace in a moment defined by heartbreak.

The church was alive with joy and celebration, sunlight streaming through the stained-glass windows to cast colorful patterns across the floor. The air buzzed with the happy chatter of guests, all dressed in their finest, as they watched the couple at the altar. Onica stood radiant in her flowing white gown, her face glowing with love and excitement. Beside her, Peter looked dashing, his nervous smile betraying the depth of his emotions. Jersey, the ever-supportive friend, stood just a step behind them, a mixture of pride and happiness lighting up her features.

The pastor held the official marriage certificate in his hands, his eyes darting over the names before he looked up, beaming at the couple. His voice carried warmth and authority as he addressed the congregation.

"We are gathered here today to celebrate the union of Peter and Onica in holy matrimony," he announced, his tone imbued with solemnity and joy.

The guests fell silent, their eyes fixed on the couple. The pastor turned back to Peter, the marriage certificate momentarily forgotten in the excitement of the occasion.

"Do you, Peter, take Onica to be your lawfully wedded wife?" he asked.

"I do!" Peter replied without hesitation, his voice strong and filled with conviction.

The pastor smiled and turned to Onica. "And do you, Onica, take Peter to be your lawfully wedded husband?"

"I do!" Onica said, her voice trembling with emotion, tears sparkling in her eyes.

The room erupted in applause, guests clapping and cheering as the pastor prepared to conclude the ceremony. His gaze dropped briefly to the certificate, a formality he performed out of habit rather than scrutiny.

"By the power vested in me, I now pronounce you husband and wife," he declared, his voice ringing with finality. "You may kiss the bride!"

Peter stepped forward, pulling Onica into a loving, passionate kiss as the audience cheered louder, some whistling and shouting words of encouragement. The moment was perfect, filled with the kind of joy that seemed untouchable, unassailable.

But as the couple basked in the glow of their newfound union, the marriage certificate remained clutched in the pastor's hand. The names on it, a glaring mix-up that no one noticed in the heat of the moment, went uncorrected.

The celebration continued unabated, a whirlwind of laughter, music, and dancing. No one thought to double-check the details, swept up as they were in the ecstasy of the day. It was a small oversight, a detail lost in the happiness of the moment—but one that would have far-reaching consequences, altering lives in ways none of them could have foreseen.

Night had settled over the city, the distant hum of traffic and the occasional bark of a dog the only sounds breaking the stillness. In the dimly lit living room of her apartment, Jersey sat on the edge of her worn leather couch, the crumpled marriage certificate clenched tightly in her hands. Her usually composed demeanor had given way to frustration and desperation, etched in the tight set of her jaw and the restless tapping of her foot against the hardwood floor.

The phone was pressed to her ear, her voice sharp and trembling as she spoke.

"I understand the mistake," Jersey said, her words cutting through the silence. "But I can't wait any longer. I need this resolved!"

On the other end, the marriage official's voice was calm but tinged with weariness. "We're doing everything we can to rectify the error, Jersey. But these things take time."

Time. The word rang hollow in Jersey's ears. She sprang up from the couch, pacing the small space like a caged animal. The dim light of a table lamp caught the glint of unshed tears in her eyes.

"Time is the one thing I don't have!" she exclaimed, her voice rising in pitch. "I'm in love with someone, and we want to get married. But I can't, because of this mess!"

Her frustration spilled over, her movements becoming more erratic as she clutched the certificate to her chest, a cruel symbol of the bureaucratic nightmare that had upended her life. She stopped pacing and pressed her free hand to her forehead, as if trying to contain the chaos swirling inside her.

The official sighed on the other end of the line, their tone softening. "I know this is incredibly difficult, but we must follow the legal process. These corrections involve formal steps—paperwork, reviews—it's not something we can expedite overnight."

Jersey let out a bitter laugh, shaking her head. "Legal process?" she repeated, her voice thick with disbelief. "I've done everything right, and now I'm being punished for someone else's mistake."

Her vision blurred with tears as her grip on the phone tightened. The official's continued reassurances faded into background noise. She couldn't listen anymore. With a shaky breath, she pulled the phone away from her ear and ended the call.

The apartment was quiet again, but the stillness offered no comfort. Jersey sank back onto the couch, the certificate still in her hand. She stared at it, her mind racing through a hundred scenarios, none of which offered an easy solution. The paper crinkled under her fingers as she fought back a wave of hopelessness.

She was trapped—bound by a mistake that wasn't hers, yet held her future hostage. And as the tears she'd been holding back finally spilled over, Jersey realized she was fighting more than just a legal error. She was fighting for her life, her love, and her chance at happiness.

The soft glow of the table lamp cast long, flickering shadows across the living room, creating an intimate cocoon of light amidst the dark chaos of scattered papers. Onica and Jersey sat side by side on the worn couch, their shoulders almost touching. The coffee table in front of them was a battlefield of bureaucracy—documents, envelopes, and the offending marriage certificate from Home Affairs lying conspicuously in the center like a smoking gun.

Onica's face was flushed with exasperation, her hands gripping the edge of the couch as though steadying herself against the weight of her frustration. Her voice, though soft, was sharp enough to cut through the suffocating silence.

"I can't believe this, Jersey," she said, her words dripping with disbelief. "How did they mess up our marriage certificate? This is supposed to be the most straightforward thing!"

Jersey leaned forward, her elbows on her knees, her fingers combing through her hair in an effort to calm herself. Her expression mirrored Onica's—a mixture of anger and disbelief that simmered beneath the surface. She shook her head, letting out a huff of breath that was more of a growl.

"I have no idea, Onica," she said, her voice tight with frustration. "We followed all the procedures, submitted the right documents, and now we're stuck with this mess. A mistake like this—it's not just embarrassing; it could ruin everything."

Onica reached for the certificate with trembling hands, her eyes scanning the glaring error that turned their lives into a bureaucratic nightmare. Her gaze flickered to Jersey, searching for some reassurance amidst the turmoil. "Do you think this can be fixed?" she asked, her voice cracking under the weight of uncertainty.

Jersey leaned back, letting her head hit the cushion as she stared at the ceiling. "Fixed?" she echoed bitterly. "Do you know how long these things take? Appeals, corrections, legal processes—it's a nightmare! And all because someone couldn't do their job properly."

Onica pressed the certificate against her chest, as if trying to shield herself from its damning words. "This isn't just about paperwork, Jersey," she whispered. "This is about Peter. About us. About everything we built together. How can they reduce our life to a clerical error?"

Jersey turned to her friend, her frustration softening into empathy. She placed a hand on Onica's shoulder, squeezing it gently. "We'll figure this out, Onica," she said, her voice steadying. "It's a mess, but it's not the end. We'll get lawyers, go to Home Affairs, whatever it takes. We'll fight this."

Onica looked at her friend, the tightness in her chest loosening ever so slightly. "You really think we can fix this?" she asked, the vulnerability in her voice stark and raw.

Jersey's lips twitched into a faint, determined smile. "We have to," she said simply. "Because giving up isn't an option."

The two women sat in silence for a moment, their resolve slowly building like the faint glow of dawn breaking through the night. The papers scattered around them were no longer just symbols of chaos—they were reminders of what was at stake. Together, they would face this battle, one step at a time.

The dim light of the table lamp cast flickering shadows across the room, highlighting Onica's trembling hands as she held the marriage certificate. Her brows were knit tightly together, disbelief etched into her face. Jersey sat across from her, tapping her fingers nervously on the edge of the coffee table, her own anxiety bubbling just beneath the surface.

"What are we going to do now?" Jersey finally asked, her voice trembling. "We can't get married if the certificate is wrong."

Onica's eyes darted to the document, her fingers tightening around the paper. "I know, I know," she said, her voice thick with agitation. "But this—this is beyond infuriating. We've been planning our wedding for so long, and now it's all up in the air because of their incompetence."

Jersey leaned forward, her face pale with worry. "We should call the Home Affairs office first thing in the morning," she suggested, trying to sound calm. "They need to fix this. We need that certificate for the wedding, Onica."

Onica let out a deep, exasperated sigh, nodding slowly. "Yes, we should. But what if they can't fix it in time? What if—" Her words faltered, and she sank deeper into her chair.

Jersey reached over and put a comforting arm around her friend. "Let's not panic just yet," she said soothingly. "We'll call them, explain the situation, and see what they can do. We still have time to sort this out."

Onica inhaled deeply, trying to steady herself. Jersey's reassurance was comforting, but the sinking feeling in her chest remained. "You're right," she said reluctantly. "Let's not jump to conclusions. We'll make those calls first thing in the morning. Hopefully, they'll have a solution for us."

The room fell into an uneasy silence, broken only by the soft rustling of papers as they began gathering the scattered documents. The tension was palpable, and Onica's mind raced with questions she couldn't suppress any longer.

Her voice broke the silence like a thunderclap. "Jersey, you need to explain this to me," she said, her tone sharp and accusing. "Why is your name on my husband's marriage certificate?"

MY WEDDING CONTRACT TOO 25

Jersey froze, her hands halting mid-motion. Her face flushed as she stammered, "Onica, I... I didn't know. It must be a mistake—a terrible mistake."

Onica's eyes blazed as she stood, the certificate clutched tightly in her fist. "A mistake?" she repeated, her voice rising with every word. "This is *our* marriage certificate, Jersey! How could it be a mistake? We all signed it on our wedding day!"

Jersey rose to her feet, her voice trembling as she tried to explain. "I swear, I had no idea," she said, her words coming out in a rush. "I thought we were just signing as witnesses."

"Witnesses?" Onica's voice cracked as tears welled up in her eyes. "This is not some casual mix-up, Jersey. It says I'm not his wife—it says *you* are!"

Jersey's eyes widened in horror as the weight of Onica's words hit her. "I don't know how this happened, Onica," she said, her voice thick with guilt. "I would never do something like this intentionally. You have to believe me."

Onica's legs buckled, and she sank back into the chair, her shoulders shaking as the sobs she'd been holding back finally broke free. "My husband is gone," she cried, her voice raw with pain. "And now this... this nightmare. What are we going to do?"

Jersey knelt beside her, her own eyes glistening with unshed tears. "We'll fix this," she said, her voice firm despite her own doubts. "I don't know how yet, but we'll fix it. I promise."

But as the two women sat in the dimly lit room, the weight of the error pressed down on them like an unrelenting storm, threatening to sweep away everything they held dear.

Jersey sat on the edge of the couch, her fingers clutching the marriage certificate as though it might crumble in her grasp. Her boyfriend, Mabella, sat beside her, his hand resting gently on her shoulder, offering silent support. Despite his comforting presence, her frustration was palpable, the tension in the room almost tangible.

"Babe, you won't believe the mess I'm in," Jersey began, her voice sharp with exasperation. She thrust the certificate toward Mabella, her hands trembling. "This—this thing is all wrong."

Mabella took the paper, his brow furrowing as he scanned the text. "What's wrong?" he asked, his tone calm but concerned. "Tell me."

Jersey let out a bitter laugh, leaning back against the couch. "Look at it!" she exclaimed. "It says I'm married to Peter. To Peter, Mabella! And now I can't marry anyone else until this ridiculous mess is fixed."

Mabella's face darkened as he examined the certificate more closely. "That's messed up," he said, his voice firm. "How did this even happen?"

Jersey shook her head, her expression a mixture of anger and disbelief. "The pastor misread the names during the ceremony," she explained. "It was just a stupid mistake, but now it's turned into a nightmare. Onica thinks I did this on purpose, and I don't even know how to make it right."

Mabella handed the certificate back to her and reached for her hand. "I can only imagine how hard this is for you," he said softly, his eyes filled with sympathy.

Jersey's shoulders slumped, and she looked down at their intertwined hands. "It's more than hard, Mabella," she said, her voice breaking. "I'm in love with you. I want us to be together, to build a future, but I can't even think about that until this mess is fixed."

Mabella leaned closer, his voice steady and resolute. "We'll find a way, Jersey," he said, his words like a lifeline in the storm of her emotions. "Whatever it takes, we'll get through this together. You're not alone in this."

Jersey looked up at him, her eyes glistening with unshed tears. "You mean that?" she asked, her voice barely a whisper.

"Of course I do," Mabella replied, cupping her face gently with his hands. "I'm with you, no matter what. We'll fight this, and we'll win."

For the first time that night, a flicker of hope crossed Jersey's face. She nodded, taking a deep breath to steady herself. "Okay," she said. "We'll call Home Affairs in the morning. We'll figure this out."

Mabella smiled, his confidence contagious. "That's the spirit," he said. "One step at a time."

As they sat together, the weight of the situation still lingered, but Jersey felt a little lighter with Mabella's unwavering support. Together, they faced a mountain, but together, they would climb it.

Jersey turned to Mabella, her eyes shimmering with unshed tears, but this time, there was a glimmer of hope beneath the sorrow. His steady presence, the warmth of his gaze, and the reassurance in his touch anchored her in the chaotic storm of her emotions. She felt a flicker of resolve take root.

"I don't know how," she began, her voice soft but edged with determination. "But I need to fix this." Her fingers tightened around the crumpled marriage certificate in her lap, the paper now a symbol of her entrapment. "I can't let a piece of paper determine my happiness."

Mabella reached for her hand, entwining his fingers with hers. His touch was gentle, but his grip was firm, a silent promise that he would stand by her through whatever lay ahead.

"You're right," he said quietly, his voice a blend of encouragement and calm certainty. "That paper doesn't define who you are or what you deserve. We'll fix this, Jersey. Together."

She let out a shaky breath, a small smile breaking through the tension on her face. "You always make it sound so simple," she murmured, her tone lightening just enough to hint at her gratitude.

Mabella tilted his head, a playful smirk dancing on his lips. "Simple? No," he replied. "But possible? Absolutely."

Jersey chuckled softly, the sound like a balm to her frayed nerves. "I don't know what I'd do without you," she admitted, the weight of her gratitude reflected in her gaze.

"You'll never have to find out," Mabella said firmly. "We'll call Home Affairs first thing tomorrow. And if they can't fix it, we'll escalate. Whatever it takes, Jersey. We'll figure it out."

Jersey nodded, her resolve solidifying with each word. For the first time since discovering the error, she felt a sense of agency, a belief that the situation wasn't entirely insurmountable. With Mabella by her side, she could see a way forward, even if it was still shrouded in uncertainty.

"I just want this nightmare to end," she said, her voice softer now, a mix of weariness and determination. "I want to be free of this... of everything tying me to a past that's not mine."

"And you will be," Mabella assured her. "One step at a time."

As the night deepened, Jersey leaned into Mabella's embrace, finding solace in the steady rhythm of his heartbeat. For now, she allowed herself to rest, knowing that tomorrow would bring another battle—but also knowing she wouldn't have to face it alone.

The dim glow of the security monitors cast a muted light over Mabella and Joseph as they sat side by side in the small, quiet room. The low hum of the cameras was the only sound breaking the silence, punctuated by the occasional click of a keyboard. Both men were dressed in the same standard security guard uniforms, their faces tired but resolute. Yet despite the stillness of the night, there was an unmistakable tension hanging in the air around Mabella.

Mabella sighed heavily, leaning back in his chair and running a hand through his hair. His fingers drummed nervously on the table before he turned to Joseph, his expression frustrated.

"Man, Joseph, I've got a big problem," Mabella muttered, the weight of his thoughts clear in his voice.

Joseph, his face marked by concern, glanced over at his friend. "What's eating at you, my friend?"

Mabella hesitated, staring down at the security monitors in front of them, as though the blinking cameras might offer some form of comfort. Finally, he let out a long breath, the words slipping out with a mix of frustration and vulnerability.

"It's Jersey," he began, his voice low and unsure. "We're deeply in love, and I want to marry her, but I'm flat broke."

Joseph raised an eyebrow, leaning forward slightly. "I get it, man," he said, his tone sympathetic. "Times are tough. But you're a hard worker, Mabella. Things will turn around."

Mabella shook his head, his eyes distant. "It's not about that," he admitted, his voice tightening with frustration. "It's about her. She deserves the world, Joseph. She's smart, beautiful, and ambitious. But I can't even afford a decent ring, let alone a wedding."

Joseph sat back in his chair, his expression softening with understanding. He knew Mabella, knew the way his friend wore his heart on his sleeve, especially when it came to Jersey. He had watched him fall for her, seen the way she had changed him, brought him hope in ways he hadn't thought possible.

"I've been there, too," Joseph said quietly, his voice thoughtful. "Money doesn't define our worth, man. I get where you're coming from, but you know Jersey loves you for who you are. Not for what you can give her."

Mabella sighed again, his hand clenching the edge of the table. "I know, I know," he replied, voice tinged with worry. "But she's amazing. She deserves a wedding to remember. She deserves everything I can't give her."

Joseph studied him for a moment, his eyes steady and knowing. "Maybe you should talk to her," he suggested gently. "Be honest about what you're going through. If she loves you, she'll understand. And if she's the one, it won't matter what kind of ring you give her. It'll be about you two—together."

Mabella bit his lip, uncertainty clouding his expression. "I don't know, Joseph. What if she decides I'm not enough? What if she thinks I can't provide for her?"

Joseph's voice was firm now, filled with conviction. "Mabella, you're more than enough. Trust me on this. You're a good man. You've got heart, and you've got love. That's all that really matters. Love isn't about how much money you have or the grand gestures you can make. It's about the connection, the partnership. If she truly loves you, that's enough."

Mabella let out a slow breath, the tension in his shoulders easing slightly. He looked at Joseph, gratitude flickering in his eyes. "Thanks, Joseph. I needed to hear that."

The two friends shared a quiet moment, the hum of the monitors filling the space between them. Mabella's thoughts drifted to Jersey—the way she smiled, the way she made him feel like he was enough, even when he had nothing.

As the night shifted on, he felt a little lighter, the weight on his shoulders not quite as heavy. Joseph was right. Maybe it wasn't about the ring or the wedding—it was about the love they shared. That was something money could never buy.

"Let's just get through tonight," Mabella muttered, more to himself than to Joseph.

Joseph chuckled softly, a glimmer of humor in his eyes. "One shift at a time, my friend. One shift at a time."

Onica stood at the counter in the Home Affairs office, her hands gripping the incorrect marriage certificate so tightly her knuckles had turned white. The sterile, fluorescent lighting above did nothing to ease the heaviness in the air around her. She could feel her frustration building, the injustice of it all gnawing at her insides.

She took a deep breath before stepping forward, her voice steady but firm as she addressed the marriage official behind the counter.

"Excuse me, Mr. Anderson," Onica began, her tone leaving no room for confusion. "There's been a mistake on my husband's marriage certificate."

Mr. Anderson, a middle-aged man with glasses perched at the edge of his nose, glanced up from his paperwork and gave her a polite but distant smile. "A mistake? Let me see, ma'am."

Onica handed him the certificate, her fingers shaking slightly, though she refused to show any more weakness. Mr. Anderson took the document, scanning the information printed neatly on the page. His brow furrowed as his eyes moved from one line to the next, and his expression shifted from neutral to one of concern.

"This is... unusual," he muttered under his breath. "I'll have to look into it."

"Unusual?" Onica's voice raised slightly, her patience fraying. "Mr. Anderson, this is my husband's certificate, and it says I'm not his wife! Jersey's name is here!"

The words seemed to hang in the air for a moment, heavy with disbelief. Onica felt the walls of the office closing in around her, her heart racing as she realized just how deep the mistake ran. Her voice trembled with anger as she spoke again, her hands trembling with the weight of the situation.

Mr. Anderson blinked, clearly taken aback by the revelation. He looked down at the certificate again, his expression growing more perplexed with each passing second.

"That... that's not right," he said slowly, his words fumbling with uncertainty. "Let me investigate this further."

But before he could say anything more, the sound of footsteps approached. Onica turned, her stomach tightening as she saw Jersey walking toward them. Her best friend's face was a mask of concern, and Onica's heart sank. The last thing she needed was Jersey to be part of this nightmare.

"Onica, what's going on?" Jersey asked, her voice filled with worry as she stopped next to her. "Is there a problem with the certificate?"

Onica's anger boiled over, and she snapped, turning sharply to face Jersey. "Jersey, there's a *big* problem. According to this certificate, we're married, and I'm not Peter's wife!" Her voice broke slightly as the words left her mouth, the shock of it all flooding back in waves.

Jersey's face went pale at the revelation. Her eyes moved to the certificate in Onica's hand, and she swallowed hard. She looked between Onica and Mr. Anderson, the confusion clear on her face.

"I... I don't understand," Jersey stammered, her voice trembling with disbelief. "This must be a mistake. How could this happen?"

Onica's chest tightened. She didn't know if Jersey was speaking out of confusion or guilt, but it didn't matter anymore. The truth was written right there in front of them—*Jersey's name* was on the certificate, not hers.

Mr. Anderson looked uncomfortable, his eyes darting between the two women. "It seems there's been an error," he said awkwardly. "I'll need to escalate this. We'll sort it out as quickly as we can."

Onica's frustration reached its peak. She stepped closer to the counter, her eyes narrowing as she looked Mr. Anderson in the eye. "You better sort this out, Mr. Anderson. I want answers. I *deserve* answers."

Her voice was steady, but there was an underlying tremor of desperation in it. Peter was gone. Her world had already shattered, and now this. It was too much to bear. She could already feel the tears threatening to rise again, but she refused to let them fall. Not here, not in front of Jersey.

"I'll take this up with my supervisor," Mr. Anderson said, backing away slightly, clearly eager to avoid any further confrontation. "Please, allow me a moment."

As he walked away to make the necessary calls, Onica stood there, the weight of the moment pressing down on her. Jersey stood beside her, still silent, her face a mixture of confusion and guilt. Neither woman knew what to say next. The mistake had been made, and no one seemed to know how to fix it.

Onica's mind raced. The implications of the error were far worse than she could have imagined, and now there was only one thing left to do: demand answers, no matter the cost.

The door creaked open, and Jersey stepped into the dimly lit office, her eyes searching for any sign of comfort or understanding. The room was quiet, the air thick with a stillness that matched the heaviness in her heart. She stopped just inside, her gaze landing on a man sitting behind a worn desk, engrossed in the pages of a Bible. His features were strong, his posture impeccable, and though he was not the man she sought, there was something undeniably comforting about his presence.

"Excuse me," Jersey said, her voice wavering with uncertainty. "I'm looking for Pastor Paul."

The man lowered the Bible, his eyes meeting hers with a solemn, knowing look. "Ah, my dear," he replied softly. "Pastor Paul is with our Savior now, standing face to face with Jesus. Who are you?"

Jersey's heart plummeted at the words. A cold wave of disbelief washed over her, and before she could control it, the tears began to fall. She stumbled forward, her shoulders shaking as the grief she had been holding in for so long finally broke free. Her vision blurred as she covered her face with her hands, consumed by the sudden wave of despair.

Pastor Leena, who had been standing nearby, quickly stepped forward with a box of tissues. He handed one to Jersey gently, his eyes filled with compassion. "Here, child, take this. Wipe your tears."

Jersey took the tissue, dabbing at her eyes, but her voice was choked with sorrow as she spoke. "So I have lost... He was my only key witness. So... who killed him?"

The words hung in the air, as heavy as the silence that followed. Pastor Leena sighed deeply, his gaze softening with understanding. "We all knew Pastor Paul struggled with that tumor, a cruel and sudden ailment that took him from us. It was God's will. He had a plan for his life, a purpose he served faithfully."

Jersey's hands trembled as she clutched the tissue, her mind spiraling. "He left me with misery," she muttered, voice breaking. "He left a curse upon my life."

Pastor Leena's eyes widened with concern, his voice steady but gentle. "Pastor Paul was a great man, my dear. He served his Lord with love and devotion. What is it that troubles you so much? Is there something we can do?"

Jersey shook her head slowly, her chest tight with grief and frustration. "If he's dead, there's nothing you can do to solve this. He was supposed to be my key witness. And now... he's gone. Everything's gone." Her words spilled out in a rush, each one laced with the weight of all the unanswered questions that haunted her.

Pastor Leena paused, taking in the depth of her words. Then, with a glimmer of realization, he nodded slowly. "Ah, I see now. You were the couple Pastor Paul often spoke of, the one he held so dear. What a beautiful wedding ceremony you had... Hallelujah."

Jersey stood in stunned silence, the mention of the wedding stirring up memories of a time when everything had seemed perfect—before the storm had come crashing down. She turned away, her mind reeling with confusion, hurt, and a deep sense of loss.

Without another word, she walked toward the door, each step heavy with questions that no one could answer. As she reached for the handle, she paused, casting one last glance at Pastor Leena. His gaze followed her, his eyes filled with something she couldn't quite decipher.

"Goodbye," Jersey whispered softly, the word lingering in the still air. "I don't know what to do anymore."

And with that, she stepped out of the office, the weight of her troubles pressing down on her like an unbearable burden. The world outside was still, but within her, a storm continued to rage.

A sharp knock echoed through the apartment, and Mabella, still clad in his security uniform, stood up from the couch to answer the door. As he opened it, a tall man dressed in a dark suit stood on the doorstep, a suitcase in hand. He looked every bit the professional—his posture rigid, his expression serious, as if he had a purpose that couldn't be delayed. Mabella stepped aside, allowing the man to enter, but not before casting a questioning glance at him.

"Jersey, someone's here for you," Mabella called out, his voice carrying just enough weight to prompt Jersey to get up from the chair where she had been sitting, lost in her thoughts. Mabella gave the man a polite nod before stepping away, retreating to a corner of the room where he remained standing but half-hidden behind a wall, eager to listen without intruding.

The man's gaze swept the room as he stepped inside, taking in the surroundings with a faint nod of approval. There was something about the way he looked at everything—a detached, almost clinical assessment that didn't sit quite right with Jersey.

"May I see Jersey, please?" he asked, his voice smooth and confident. "I assume I'm in the right place?"

Jersey felt a strange unease settle in her stomach as she walked toward him, her hand instinctively moving to straighten her clothes.

She had no idea who this man was, but she could already tell something about him felt off.

"Yes, I'm Jersey," she said cautiously, her eyes narrowing slightly. "How can I help you, sir?"

"I'm Mr. Taller," the man introduced himself, his tone flat and formal. "I'm the legal representative of Peter Collins, your late husband. I've been entrusted with delivering some important documents regarding your inheritance."

Jersey's heart skipped a beat. The mention of Peter sent a rush of conflicting emotions flooding through her. *Peter...* she thought, her throat tightening at the mere mention of his name. He was gone, but now this man, with his cold, calculated demeanor, was here to discuss what Peter had left behind. Jersey instinctively felt a ripple of suspicion, but she said nothing, waiting for him to continue.

"Apparently, you've been delegated all of your late husband's assets, including both properties and his company," Mr. Taller continued, opening his briefcase with a deliberate motion. "I will read through the will, and if everything is in order, you'll need to sign."

Jersey's mind raced, trying to process his words. She'd heard nothing about this—no one had warned her that Peter had left behind such a large legacy. A mixture of shock and curiosity settled in her chest as she listened intently.

Mr. Taller began reading aloud, his voice cold and matter-of-fact, as if reciting the terms of a business deal.

"I, Peter Collins," he read, "give all rights and shares of my assets, including the company operations, to my only wedded wife. In the event of my terminal illness or death, she will assume full control over these assets. She will also be responsible for the care of my mother."

Jersey's heart raced as she absorbed the gravity of his words. *Peter had left all of this for me?* she thought, still processing the magnitude of what was being presented to her.

Mr. Taller glanced up from the will, his eyes briefly locking with hers. "You may sign here, after you've read the document. The value of the company shares and the amount in the offshore accounts have been included as well. Everything is yours now, Jersey. This will be your responsibility."

She felt the weight of his words sinking in. The company. The shares. The bank accounts. Everything Peter had worked for. She could hardly fathom it.

"And the cars?" she asked, her voice barely a whisper, her mind still reeling.

Mr. Taller didn't miss a beat. "They are included as well. All part of your inheritance."

Jersey nodded slowly, still grappling with the enormity of the situation. "Thank you, Mr. Taller," she said, her voice quiet but steady. "I appreciate your help."

Mr. Taller didn't seem to react to her gratitude. He simply handed her his business card with a practiced gesture. "If you need assistance, I would recommend you make use of my services. I'm happy to guide you through the company operations and draft your own will, should you need it."

Jersey glanced down at the card, her fingers brushing over the embossed text. "I'll be in touch," she said, though she had no intention of relying on him more than absolutely necessary. The last thing she needed was to get tangled deeper into whatever web he was spinning.

Without another word, Mr. Taller closed his suitcase with a snap and turned to leave, his steps echoing in the quiet apartment. Jersey watched him go, the door clicking shut behind him with an unsettling finality.

She stood in the center of the room, the weight of the documents in her hands feeling heavier than she had ever imagined. *What now?* she wondered. There was so much to process, so many things to figure out. And yet, as the silence pressed in around her, one thing became glaringly clear—her life had just changed in ways she couldn't yet understand.

Jersey could hardly contain herself as she paced around the apartment, her heart racing with excitement. She picked up the phone, unable to stop herself from shouting into it. The weight of the will, the assets, everything Peter had left behind, still felt surreal, but in the best possible way.

"So today I'm a millionaire!" she exclaimed, her voice ringing with pure joy. "Wow! Oh ha, who would've thought that everything my own friend owns... I might own them now!"

Mabella's voice came through the phone, slightly amused but calm in contrast to Jersey's high energy. "What about the cars?"

Jersey froze mid-spin, her thoughts abruptly shifting gears. "Okay, I should lay low on the cars," she said, her tone turning thoughtful. "Maybe take one house, leave her... I need a strategy. A good one."

Mabella chuckled, his voice becoming more playful. "We need a strategy too. Remember, we're a big team now. We're millionaires! Can I give my millionaire lady a massage to thank her in advance for everything you're going to do for me?"

Jersey rolled her eyes, though a smile tugged at the corners of her mouth. She could practically hear Mabella's smirk.

"Sure," she teased, her energy still sky-high. "But only if you promise not to take it too far."

She felt his presence behind her before she saw him. Mabella stood there, his hands gently resting on her shoulders, massaging her slowly, with a calm confidence that contrasted Jersey's excitement. She let out a soft sigh, grateful for his grounding presence.

As Mabella worked the tension out of her shoulders, Jersey couldn't help but count the possibilities on her fingers, her mind racing. She was juggling it all—Peter's estate, the company, the houses, the cars, everything. A wealth she had never imagined was now within her grasp, but the magnitude of it all made her think twice.

She pulled away from Mabella, standing up abruptly, her feet planted firmly as she looked out the window. Her thoughts were intense, calculating. *What's my next move?* she thought, her mind running through every scenario, every detail.

"What are you thinking now, without telling me?" Mabella asked, sensing the shift in her mood, his voice laced with curiosity.

Jersey turned to face him, her gaze focused but distant. "Okay, I'm calculating my moves," she said, her voice low and purposeful. She wasn't sure what the future held, but one thing was for certain—she wasn't going to let this fortune slip through her fingers. There was power now, and it was hers for the taking.

Mabella smiled knowingly, stepping back to give her space to think. "I trust you, Jersey," he said softly. "Just remember, we're in this together. Whatever you decide, I've got your back."

Jersey nodded, her mind already in motion. It wasn't just about the money anymore—it was about taking control of her life. And for once, she wasn't going to let anything or anyone stop her.

Jersey sat on the couch, her body slumped as if the weight of the world had settled on her shoulders. The marriage certificate mix-up, the mounting legal pressures, and the constant swirl of uncertainty had drained her, leaving her feeling like a shell of the person she once was. Her face, pale and etched with signs of sleepless nights, seemed distant, as if she were looking through the present into a future she couldn't quite grasp.

Mabella, standing a few feet away, held a thick wad of cash in his hand. The faint glimmer of the bills caught the soft light from the apartment's lamp, and it was as if the money itself was a symbol of the escape they both so desperately needed. Mabella's presence, always a comfort, now felt charged with an urgency, a need to act, to do something — anything — to break the tension in the air.

"Jersey," his voice was soft, but there was a pleading edge to it. "You've been through so much. This money could help us escape all that trauma, even if it's just for a little while."

Jersey turned her gaze to the cash, her mind spinning. She felt the temptation coil in her chest, but it didn't stop the gnawing ache that weighed on her heart. Her eyes flicked up to Mabella, her face taut with the burden of all that had happened. "I know, but it's not about the money, Mabella," she replied, her voice tight with restraint. "It's about the fact that I can't marry you. Not with all this mess."

Mabella took a slow step closer, his tone shifting, softer but more persuasive. "I understand that, Jersey," he said, almost coaxing. "But we could use this money to create wonderful memories together. Maybe even go on a trip. It might help you forget, even if just for a moment."

Jersey's thoughts churned, the image of her life for the past few weeks flickering in her mind. The stress, the confusion, the endless questions. *Maybe a break could help*, she thought. The weight of her responsibilities, the looming uncertainty, seemed almost insurmountable. *Could a temporary escape really make a difference?*

"I've been carrying so much stress lately," Jersey admitted, her voice quieter now, almost as if speaking the words aloud would make them less true. "Maybe a break could do us good."

Mabella's eyes lit up, relief washing over him in an instant. "That's the spirit, Jersey. Let's take this money, enjoy ourselves, and come back stronger. We deserve it."

Her gaze dropped to the cash again, still uncertain, but the idea of a brief reprieve from her problems, even just a small one, was increasingly tempting. The promise of a fresh start, however fleeting, whispered to her, and for the first time in a long while, she considered it seriously. *Could this be the answer?*

Later that evening, the apartment felt smaller somehow. The sounds of the bustling city outside were muffled against the walls, leaving only the soft hum of their quiet conversation. Jersey's fingers nervously traced the edges of the cash in Mabella's hand, uncertainty clouding her thoughts. She had never been one to rush decisions, especially not one like this, but tonight... tonight felt different.

"I can't believe I'm doing this, Mabella," she said, her voice faltering slightly as she spoke.

Mabella stepped closer, the warmth of his hand on her shoulder grounding her. "It's just for a while, Jersey," he said, his voice filled with gentle reassurance. "We need a break from all the stress. Let's make some happy memories together. We deserve it."

The words washed over her, and for a brief moment, Jersey felt something inside her soften, like a dam finally giving way. Her fingers trembled as they reached for the money, the decision weighing heavily on her, but also offering a glimmer of relief.

"Okay," she breathed out, a heavy sigh escaping her lips as she took the money from his hand. "Let's do it. Maybe a little escape is exactly what we need."

Mabella smiled, his eyes sparkling with a quiet joy that seemed to fill the space between them. In that moment, despite the weight of everything else, the future felt just a little less daunting. The two of them exchanged a look, an unspoken agreement, a promise that whatever happened, they would face it together, even if it was just for a little while. With the worries of the world momentarily set aside, they stepped forward, hand in hand, ready to take on whatever lay ahead — even if it was just a brief moment of peace.

Jersey sat on the couch, her posture slumped and her face drawn with the weight of everything that had happened. The events surrounding the marriage certificate, the chaos that had followed, had drained her more than she cared to admit. Each day felt heavier than the last, and the exhaustion in her eyes was a reflection of the turmoil within.

Mabella stood nearby, holding a thick wad of cash in his hand. The money shimmered in the soft light of the apartment, its presence both tempting and intimidating. His gaze was steady, his stance confident, but Jersey could see the undercurrent of urgency beneath his calm exterior.

"Jersey," Mabella's voice was soft but coaxing, as if trying to reach her through the fog of her thoughts. "You've been through so much. This money could help us escape all that trauma, even if it's just for a little while."

Jersey's eyes drifted toward the cash, her mind a whirl of conflicting emotions. She knew the weight of her responsibilities, the overwhelming sense of being trapped in a situation she couldn't control. But it wasn't just about the money—it never had been.

"I know, but it's not about the money, Mabella," Jersey murmured, her voice tight with restraint. "It's about the fact that I can't marry you."

Mabella's expression softened, and he took a small step closer, as though closing the distance between them could somehow offer her the peace she so desperately needed. "I understand that, Jersey," he said, his tone warm and persuasive. "But we could use this money to create wonderful memories together. Maybe even go on a trip. It might help you forget, even if just for a moment."

The thought of leaving everything behind, even if only temporarily, had a certain appeal. Jersey's eyes flicked from the money to Mabella, the possibility of escape like a distant horizon. She had been living in a storm of confusion, stress, and uncertainty. *Maybe a break could help*, she thought. Maybe she could just step away from it all for a little while.

"I've been carrying so much stress lately," Jersey admitted quietly, her voice barely more than a whisper. "Maybe a break could do us good."

Mabella smiled, a glimmer of hope shining in his eyes. "That's the spirit, Jersey. Let's take this money, enjoy ourselves, and come back stronger."

Jersey looked at him, the exhaustion in her body apparent, but something in his words sparked a tiny flicker of something she hadn't felt in days—hope. The idea of a fresh start, even for a brief moment, felt almost impossible to turn down.

Later, in the quiet of their apartment, the evening air seemed thick with the weight of the decision hanging between them. Jersey's gaze lingered on the wad of cash still in Mabella's hand. It seemed like such a small thing, yet it represented so much more—freedom, relief, a chance to breathe.

"I can't believe I'm doing this, Mabella," Jersey said, her voice laden with uncertainty. The decision felt heavy, like one she wasn't quite ready to make, but somehow had no choice but to.

Mabella, ever patient, offered her a reassuring smile. "It's just for a while, Jersey. We need a break from all the stress. Let's make some happy memories together."

His words, simple but sincere, eased the tightness in her chest just a little. Jersey's fingers twitched, then slowly reached out to take the money from his hand. She exhaled a breath she hadn't realized she'd been holding.

"Okay," she said, her voice soft, almost resigned. "Let's do it. Maybe a little escape is exactly what we need."

Mabella's smile widened, a spark of relief in his eyes. They exchanged a look, one full of hope and quiet determination. It wasn't a solution to all their problems, but for now, it was enough. As Jersey held the money in her hands, the future seemed just a little less heavy, and for the first time in a long while, she allowed herself to believe in the possibility of happiness, even if it was only temporary.

They stood together, ready to face whatever came next, their shared moment of hope stretching before them, even as the shadows of their troubles remained just out of reach.

Jersey sat across from the Interviewer, her hands resting nervously on the polished table, her fingers tapping a subtle rhythm that betrayed her calm exterior. She had come a long way to be here, but the nerves still lingered, gnawing at her. The air between them was thick with anticipation, the interviewer's gaze sharp, weighing her every word.

"So," the Interviewer began, leaning slightly forward, "you're highly qualified for the senior manager role. But I have to ask, why do you want to work here?"

Jersey took a breath, steadying herself. She'd practiced this moment in her head a thousand times, but now that it was happening, it felt more real than ever. She knew this interview was about more than just her qualifications. It was about proving herself—about showing that despite the unusual circumstances surrounding her application, she had what it took to excel.

"It's true, I have the qualifications," she began, her voice steady. "But what sets me apart is that I'm uniquely positioned to make significant decisions."

The Interviewer raised an eyebrow, his expression a mixture of intrigue and skepticism. "Uniquely positioned? Could you explain?"

Jersey straightened, her eyes locking with his. This was the moment to be honest, to reveal the truth she had been carrying for so long. It wasn't the most conventional path, but it was hers.

"I'm legally married to the owner," she said, her tone calm but firm. "Peter. There was an unfortunate mix-up with our marriage certificate, but that means I can sign all the necessary documents and manage the business effectively."

The Interviewer blinked, a flicker of surprise crossing his face. He leaned back in his chair, clearly processing this revelation. Jersey could almost see the wheels turning in his head, wondering if what she had said was true, or if it was just another clever sales pitch. She could feel the weight of his silence, but she didn't back down.

"So, you see this as an opportunity?" the Interviewer asked, his voice now tinged with curiosity rather than doubt.

"Yes, I do," Jersey replied, her determination clear. "I want to prove myself in this role. I believe I can bring value to the company, and I know I can help it grow. This situation, as unconventional as it may be, gives me a perspective that most others don't have. I'm in a position to make decisions that can truly impact the future."

The Interviewer studied her for a long moment, his gaze calculating but not unkind. He seemed to be weighing her words, deciding if her unique position truly made her the right fit for the job. Jersey could feel the tension in the air, but she kept her composure, holding her ground.

Finally, he nodded, a slight smile tugging at the corner of his lips. "Well, Jersey, your determination is evident. Let's see what you can bring to the table."

Jersey's heart raced, a surge of hope coursing through her. She had done it—she had earned a chance. The weight of the strange marriage certificate situation still lingered in the background, but it no longer felt like a curse. Instead, it was an opportunity, one she intended to make the most of.

As the interview unfolded, Jersey's nerves began to settle. She spoke with confidence, presenting her ideas with clarity and conviction, showing the Interviewer that despite the odds stacked against her, she was exactly the person they needed. The unusual circumstances surrounding her application had made her stand out, and now she was determined to prove that it was not just her situation that made her special—it was her drive, her passion, and her belief in what she could accomplish.

By the time the interview concluded, Jersey stood up with a sense of quiet triumph. She had come into this room uncertain, but she was leaving with something more: a chance to rewrite her own future.

The company office was sleek and modern, a blend of polished glass and contemporary design that offered a panoramic view of the city skyline. Jersey, now dressed impeccably in a tailored suit, walked confidently through the space. The high heels clicking softly against the polished floors were the only sound accompanying her steady pace as she made her way deeper into the heart of the building.

Her hands were full—clutching a small diary, a laptop, and a stack of important documents. Every few steps, her fingers would idly shuffle through the papers, making sure everything was in order, or perhaps just a habit to calm the nerves that occasionally bubbled up inside her. But for the most part, she exuded a quiet confidence, her eyes bright with excitement.

As she passed the cubicles and desks of employees, she made sure to smile at each one she met. The employees, some familiar, some new, greeted her back with curiosity and respect. Jersey was no stranger to the world of business, but this place—this new chapter—felt different. It felt like an opportunity, a chance to finally step into her own power.

When she reached the reception area, the receptionist—a friendly woman in her early thirties with an effortless smile—handed Jersey a cup of coffee with a warm greeting.

"Good morning, Ms. Jersey. Your coffee," the receptionist said, her tone cheerful.

Jersey smiled back, genuinely appreciative. "Thank you so much," she replied, accepting the cup. The warmth of the coffee in her hands gave her a sense of reassurance. It was a small comfort, but she needed it today.

She continued toward her office, her steps purposeful but unhurried. The door to her office swung open with a soft click, revealing a spacious, sunlit room with large windows that framed a breathtaking view of the city below. Jersey paused for a moment, taking in the sight—the glittering glass towers, the river winding through the city, the cars moving like tiny ants on the streets far below. This was hers now, this world.

With a soft sigh of satisfaction, she made her way to her desk. The chair was comfortable, and as she sank into it, she felt a sense of belonging settle over her. She opened her laptop, her fingers moving deftly over the keys as she began to organize her day. On the desk, her diary lay open, filled with notes and plans, sketches of ideas she hoped to implement. She quickly jotted down a few reminders, her smile never wavering.

Her co-workers, those passing by her office, couldn't help but peek in through the glass walls. They nodded to her respectfully, some with smiles, others with admiration for her apparent dedication. Jersey's energy was contagious. There was something in her that seemed to radiate, a warmth and purpose that made everyone around her feel as though anything was possible.

As the hours passed, Jersey moved effortlessly from one task to another. She checked emails, met with various team members, and made decisions with clarity and focus. It was clear to everyone around her that she was not just here to fill a role—she was here to lead, to make things happen.

By midday, the office was buzzing with activity, but Jersey's presence seemed to calm it, like a steady anchor in the storm of deadlines and meetings. She was taking full advantage of this opportunity, and the energy in the office seemed to shift with her joy. She wasn't just making the most of her chance—she was thriving.

Jersey paused at her desk for a moment, looking out over the city. The future was uncertain, and there were challenges ahead, but right now, in this moment, she felt a sense of peace, of purpose. This was her new beginning, and she was determined to make it count.

Onica sat on her couch, her shoulders slumped as though the weight of the world had been placed upon them. Her gaze was unfocused, eyes distant as she tried to make sense of the whirlwind of events that had turned her life upside down. Beside her, her friend Lizer sat, leaning forward with concern, her face etched with empathy.

"Onica," Lizer said softly, her voice gentle but filled with worry, "you won't believe the chaos that's unfolded. First, my husband's death, then the messed-up marriage certificate, and now, Peter's sudden passing. It's like my life has spiraled out of control."

Onica's voice wavered as she spoke, the exhaustion clear in every word. The turmoil she was facing had worn her down, leaving her feeling like a stranger in her own life.

Lizer, her eyes full of sympathy, nodded slowly. "I can't even begin to imagine how tough this must be for you, Onica. You've been through so much."

Onica let out a frustrated breath, her hands gripping the edge of the couch as she shook her head. "And now, there's this business mess. I can't manage it because I don't have the right marriage certificate," she said, her tone tinged with helplessness. "Everything seems impossible. Everything feels wrong."

Lizer reached out, placing a comforting hand on her friend's arm. "That's a lot to handle all at once. But we'll figure it out together. You're not alone in this, Onica."

Onica swallowed hard, fighting back tears as they welled in her eyes. She wiped them away quickly, not wanting to let Lizer see her so vulnerable, but the raw emotion was hard to hide. "I appreciate your support, Lizer," she said, her voice thick with frustration. "It's just overwhelming, and I feel so unprepared to deal with it all."

The tears continued to flow, each drop a reflection of the fear and uncertainty she felt about the future. Her life, once so certain, now seemed like a house of cards, ready to collapse at any moment.

Lizer, never one to falter in her commitment to her friends, gave Onica a reassuring squeeze. "We'll find a way, Onica. We'll get through this together. And who knows, maybe there's a solution we haven't thought of yet."

Onica looked up at her friend, her tear-streaked face softening slightly as she allowed herself a small sliver of hope. Maybe there was a way out of this storm, a way forward through the chaos. With Lizer by her side, she felt a flicker of strength. Perhaps they could still find a solution, even in the face of everything that had happened.

Onica sat at her dining table, her hands trembling slightly as she shuffled through a stack of unpaid bills and job applications. The cluttered table, filled with reminders of everything she couldn't seem to fix, seemed to mock her every attempt to find a way out. She sighed deeply, her face etched with worry, and ran a hand through her hair, frustrated beyond measure.

"This is impossible," she muttered under her breath. "The bills just keep piling up, and I can't find a job anywhere." Her voice cracked with the weight of the frustration she felt. It had been weeks—no, months—since things had started to spiral, and she was running out of options.

Just as the thought of her bleak situation began to close in on her, her phone rang, breaking through the fog of despair. She glanced at the screen, seeing Jersey's name flash across it. She answered, her voice a mix of curiosity and exhaustion.

"Onica," Jersey's voice came through, sounding urgent but composed, "We need to talk. Can you meet me at Peter's company office?"

Onica's brow furrowed in confusion. "What's going on, Jersey?" she asked, a sense of unease settling over her.

"You'll find out when you get here," Jersey replied, her voice laced with a hint of something she couldn't quite place.

When Onica arrived at the office, the familiar building that once felt like a symbol of stability now seemed distant, almost foreign. As she walked through the doors and into Peter's former office, she was greeted by the sight of Jersey, sitting behind the large desk, flipping through paperwork with an air of casual authority.

"Jersey?" Onica's voice shook slightly, concern flooding her chest. "What's all this about?"

Jersey looked up, a smirk playing at the corner of her lips. She leaned back in the chair, her posture confident, as if she had been in charge all along. "Onica," she said slowly, enjoying the moment of surprise, "I've taken over Peter's company. I have the authority to sign all documents and make decisions now."

Onica's heart skipped a beat. "What?" she gasped, the shock registering in her features. "You can't do that! This is Peter's legacy!" Her voice rose in disbelief. She wanted to shout, to demand answers, but all she could manage was the weight of the injustice sinking deep into her chest.

Jersey's smirk didn't falter. Her tone was cold, calculated. "I legally can, Onica," she said with an almost mocking calm. "And I have."

The words hit Onica like a slap, the reality of the situation crashing down on her. The company that had once been her husband's—and now, in her mind, a lifeline—was no longer within her reach. She had no control, no say in the decisions being made, not when it came to Peter's legacy.

Onica stood frozen for a moment, her mind scrambling for something to hold onto. "Jersey," she said, her voice tight with a mix of frustration and desperation, "You can't just take over. I need that company to support myself!" The words tumbled out, unfiltered, as though this were her last hope.

Jersey only shrugged, her expression indifferent as she continued rifling through the papers. "Well, Onica," she said, her tone dripping with satisfaction, "it's in my name now, legally. You should have thought about that before."

The room seemed to shrink around Onica. Her heart pounded in her chest, the weight of her financial struggles now compounded by the loss of everything she thought she could rely on. The company—her last hope—had slipped away from her grasp, leaving nothing but a gaping void.

"Jersey, please," Onica whispered, a plea hidden beneath her words. "I don't know what to do."

Jersey sat at the conference table, her hands clenched tightly under the surface, as her gaze flickered between the papers in front of her and Onica, who sat across from her. The room was filled with the murmurs of colleagues, the usual hum of a business meeting, but the tension between Jersey and Onica was almost tangible. Every word spoken felt loaded, every glance shared was laced with something unspoken.

Onica's voice broke the silence, calm and assertive. "As the legal owner, I'll need to make some decisions for the company moving forward."

Jersey's jaw tightened, her fingers digging into the table beneath her, a surge of frustration flooding through her. *This should be my company,* she thought bitterly. *I should be the one running things. But because of some ridiculous mistake with a marriage certificate, here I am, sidelined.* She tried to keep her expression neutral, but the bitterness rose, and it was a struggle to keep it in check.

"I should be the one managing this company," Jersey muttered under her breath, her voice barely audible, but sharp, filled with a quiet venom. "But because of a ridiculous mistake, I can't."

Onica, ever the composed one, didn't flinch at Jersey's words. She kept her voice steady, almost unnervingly calm. "It's not my fault, Jersey. I didn't ask for this either."

Jersey's fists tightened, her nails digging into her palms as she fought the urge to shout. How could Onica sit there so calmly, like none of this was her fault? Jersey's entire life had been upended, and yet Onica was playing the victim, as if she hadn't been handed everything on a silver platter because of a clerical error.

Onica continued, her tone unyielding. "I didn't want this responsibility. It's not like I planned any of this." She paused, letting the words sink in. "But we have to move forward. The company needs stability."

Jersey wanted to argue, wanted to scream, to demand what was rightfully hers. But the nagging reality of her situation kept her silent. She couldn't take control—not legally. Not unless she could somehow fix the mess the marriage certificate had caused. And time was running out.

Her thoughts raced, but she forced herself to focus, to listen to Onica, to pretend as though everything was okay for the sake of the team. *For now, just for now,* she told herself, *I'll play along.*

But deep down, Jersey knew one thing: *This wasn't over. Not by a long shot.*

The soft hum of the apartment felt distant, as Jersey sat on the couch, her hands resting nervously in her lap. The weight of her newfound control over Peter's company hung heavy in the air, and she couldn't shake the unease that settled in her chest. Mabella sat beside her, exuding a quiet confidence, the kind that came with a sharp mind and a strong will.

"I can't believe I'm in charge of Peter's company," Jersey muttered, her voice betraying her internal struggle. "It doesn't feel right."

Mabella turned toward her, his eyes sharp, focused. "Jersey, you're in a position of power now. Think about what we can gain from this."

Jersey's gaze lingered on Mabella, the sense of ambition in his voice unmistakable. She knew him too well. He had always seen the world through a lens of opportunity, constantly seeking ways to rise above. But this... this felt different. It wasn't just about the money anymore.

"What do you mean, Mabella?" Jersey asked, her voice filled with a mix of curiosity and caution.

Mabella leaned in, his tone low and persuasive. "Well, now that you control the company, we can make it work for us. We can live a comfortable life, move out of this place, and never worry about money again. Imagine that, Jersey—no more stress, no more struggling."

Jersey's breath caught in her throat, her mind racing at the possibilities. She had been buried under stress, under bills, under the crushing weight of everything that had gone wrong in her life. Mabella's words were seductive, offering a way out, a way to change everything. But still, something gnawed at her conscience.

"But what about Onica?" she asked, her voice uncertain, a trace of guilt tugging at her heart. "She needs the company to support herself."

Mabella's expression hardened, a flicker of irritation passing over his face. "Onica had her chance, Jersey. She can find another job. You're the one in control now. Don't let this opportunity slip away."

Jersey's fingers tightened around her diary, her thoughts swirling. Onica had been a part of her life for so long. How could she just take away the company from her? It wasn't right. Was it?

She shook her head slightly, conflicted. "I don't want to hurt Onica, Mabella," she whispered, almost to herself.

Mabella's eyes softened, but his voice remained steady, calculated. "You won't be hurting her, Jersey. You'll be helping us. Helping *you*." He placed his hand gently on hers, a subtle but firm gesture. "This is your chance to finally take control. Don't let it go to waste."

Jersey's heart raced as she processed his words. She knew Mabella was right about one thing—this was a rare opportunity. But it felt wrong to take everything from Onica, someone who had been there for her when things got tough.

She looked down at her hands, trying to reconcile the two parts of herself—the part that wanted a life free from financial worry, and the part that still cared about her friend's well-being. For a moment, the weight of the decision felt too much to bear.

"I need time to think," she said quietly, her voice thick with emotion. "This is all happening so fast. I can't just... make this decision without considering everything."

Mabella sighed, but there was no frustration in it, only patience. "Take all the time you need, Jersey. But remember—this is your life now. You don't have to share control with anyone. You've earned it."

As Jersey sat there, torn between the future Mabella was offering and the loyalty she felt to Onica, she couldn't help but wonder if this decision would be the one that changed everything. And if it would be for better or for worse.

Jersey sat at the head of the long, polished conference table, her posture straight and confident, a stack of contracts neatly arranged in front of her. The room was silent except for the sound of the occasional shuffle of papers as the employees around her waited for her to speak. Her eyes scanned the documents before her, each page a potential turning point for the company.

"Alright," she began, her voice clear and steady, cutting through the silence. "Let's go through these new contracts one by one. Time is of the essence, and we need to keep the business moving forward."

Her words were met with a chorus of nods. The employees sitting around the table, a mix of executives and senior managers, exchanged looks of anticipation. They knew that Jersey's decisions now held the weight of the company's future in her hands, and each one was eager to hear what she would decide.

The first employee, a man in a well-tailored suit, leaned forward slightly. "Jersey, what do you think about the deal with XYZ Corporation?"

Jersey didn't hesitate. Her eyes flicked to the contract in front of her, scanning it once more, and then she met the employee's gaze with a level of certainty that left no room for doubt.

"I've reviewed it, and I believe it's a sound opportunity for us," she said, her tone matter-of-fact. "We should proceed with it."

A few murmurs of agreement rippled through the room. The decision was swift, calculated, and most importantly—right.

Another employee, a woman sitting across from Jersey, tapped her pen against the table as she spoke. "And the partnership agreement with ABC Inc.?"

Jersey didn't even need to glance at the papers this time. She had already weighed the pros and cons of the deal.

"It aligns with our goals," she replied, her voice firm and resolute. "I see potential in that partnership. We should sign it."

As she moved from one contract to the next, her focus never wavered. Each decision was made with precision, and her ability to think quickly, yet thoughtfully, left the room in awe. She was no longer the uncertain woman who had once hesitated at the helm of Peter's company. The uncertainty was gone, replaced by a commanding presence that made the employees trust her judgment implicitly.

The final contract was placed in front of her, and Jersey looked up, scanning the room.

"Excellent work, everyone," she said, her voice calm but authoritative. "We've made some important choices today. Let's move forward and keep the company thriving."

There was a pause, followed by the sound of chairs scraping back as the employees stood and began to file out of the room. Their expressions were a mix of admiration and respect for the woman who had once seemed an outsider but was now their leader, steering the company toward new heights.

As the last of the employees left, Jersey remained seated for a moment, the weight of the decisions she'd made sinking in. She had done it—she had taken control, and in that moment, she knew she had earned her place at the top.

The soft glow of the laptop cast faint light on Jersey's face as she sat at the dining table, surrounded by a sea of work documents. Her focus was absolute, eyes scanning over contracts, financial reports, and emails, all of it blending together in a blur of opportunity and pressure. The room was dimly lit, the only other light coming from the streetlights outside, but Jersey barely noticed. Her mind was elsewhere—on the deals that could change everything, on the future she was working so tirelessly to secure.

Mabella, stretched out on the bed in the adjacent room, watched Jersey with an expression that wavered between admiration and something darker. Her eyes traced the movements of Jersey's fingers on the keyboard, and a small sigh escaped her lips.

"You've been working all day and now into the night, Jersey," Mabella complained, her voice laced with a pouting tone. "Can't you take a break?"

Jersey didn't look up from her laptop. Her fingers continued to fly over the keys, her concentration fierce. "I wish I could, but I can't afford to miss this opportunity," she replied, her voice steady but urgent. "It's a big contract that could change everything for us."

MY WEDDING CONTRACT TOO 57

She felt Mabella's eyes on her, but it didn't break her focus. She had worked too hard, fought too many battles, to let this slip away now. This was her chance to pull them both out of the grind and into something better. But Mabella's words lingered in the air, thick with the tension that had been building between them for weeks.

Mabella shifted on the bed, the rustle of sheets the only sound breaking the quiet. "It's always about your work, Jersey," she muttered, her voice tinged with jealousy. "You're obsessed with it. What about us? What about me?"

Jersey paused, her fingers hovering over the keys as a pang of guilt flickered in her chest. She hadn't meant to neglect Mabella, but she couldn't let this moment slip away. The future they both dreamed of was within her reach, but to get there, she had to push through the long hours, the endless days of paperwork, and the sacrifices it took to secure it.

"I'm sorry," Jersey said, her voice softer now, but still firm. "I know it's hard, but you know I love you. We both need this. We need financial security. And this... this is the way for us to have a better life."

She could see the way Mabella's face twisted, the hurt in her eyes even as she turned away, burying her face in the pillow. "It's like I'm not even a part of your life anymore," Mabella mumbled, her voice muffled but still sharp with emotion.

Jersey felt the weight of it all—the guilt, the responsibility, the pressure. She loved Mabella, but she couldn't afford to stop now, not when the finish line was so close. She glanced at Mabella, her heart torn. There was love there, but also the cold truth that they needed more than love to survive.

Her fingers resumed their steady typing, even as her thoughts swirled between the woman she loved and the future she was building. She was caught between two worlds, each pulling her in opposite directions. And as the night stretched on, the weight of her choices hung heavily in the dim room, the only sound the quiet clicking of keys.

Dim light flickered above as Mabella trudged through the narrow hallway of the run-down apartment building. The peeling wallpaper, worn-out carpet, and the faint smell of dampness seemed to press in on him as he made his way down the hallway. His security guard uniform, slightly askew, clung to his tired frame, the weight of a long night shift settling in his bones. He checked his watch: 3:00 AM. His shift was over, but his night wasn't quite done.

With a weary sigh, he adjusted the envelope tucked under his arm, taking a moment to steady himself. His eyes flicked to the faded door in front of him, the one that marked the end of his long walk. Vertina's door. He gave a quick knock, heart beating faster than he expected. This was his chance, his way to give her something better.

The door opened, and there she was. Vertina. Standing in a simple nightgown, her face alight with a mixture of surprise and excitement. Her dark hair fell in soft waves around her shoulders, and her eyes sparkled as soon as they locked onto his.

"Mabella! You're here!" she said, her voice thick with excitement. She looked so beautiful, standing there, as if nothing in the world could be wrong.

Mabella grinned, the exhaustion fading as he handed her the envelope filled with cash. "You won't ever have to worry about a thing, Vertina," he said, the promise ringing in his words.

Vertina's eyes widened as she took the envelope from him, her hands trembling slightly. "This... this is so much," she whispered, her voice full of wonder and disbelief. "You really did it, Mabella?"

He smiled, his thumb gently brushing her cheek. "For you, anything."

Without another word, they embraced, and the world outside seemed to fall away. The cramped, dingy apartment faded into the background as their lips met in a kiss full of urgency and longing.

They held each other close, their bodies finding comfort in the warmth of each other's arms.

Mabella pulled back for a moment, tracing a finger down her cheek, his gaze soft. "With this money, we can have a good life together, Vertina. No more struggling."

Her eyes sparkled as she looked at him, a soft laugh escaping her lips. "I can't believe this is really happening. No more living like this. No more worry. We can finally be free."

Mabella felt a weight in his chest. There was hope, yes, but something gnawed at him. He could see Vertina's happiness, but it only reminded him of the things he'd left behind, the life he was still tethered to.

He sighed, the words slipping out before he could stop them. "But you know... Jersey. My woman. She's so focused on her company. She's forgetting about me. I'm just a security guard to her."

Vertina's expression softened, her smile dimming for a moment. She placed her hands on his chest, rubbing gently, as if to soothe the storm brewing inside him. "I understand, Mabella. It's hard. I can see how much you care about her. But don't forget, you matter too. We'll figure this out, together."

Mabella looked at her, searching her eyes for the comfort he so desperately needed. He nodded, taking in her words, though doubt still lingered.

"I just... I don't want to lose myself, you know? I want more than just being the guy who watches over things."

Vertina gave him a small smile, her voice soft but firm. "Promise me one thing, Mabella. Promise me that no matter what happens, we'll never let money come between us."

Mabella swallowed hard, his gaze softening. "I promise, Vertina. We're in this together."

And for a moment, there was nothing but the sound of their breathing, the warmth of their bodies pressed close. In a world that often seemed so bleak, they found solace in each other, holding onto the love that might be the only thing that could carry them through.

Jersey sat hunched at the dining table, her eyes scanning the jumble of legal documents scattered across its surface. Her laptop glowed in the dim light of the room, its screen filled with more articles and legal jargon than she cared to decipher. But she had no choice. If there was any hope of overturning this situation, of protecting what was rightfully hers, she had to understand the law. She had to fight.

"I can't believe it's come to this," she muttered, her voice thick with frustration. "But I have to find a way."

Her fingers clicked through pages and pages of legal websites, each search more desperate than the last. The words blurred in front of her eyes as she skimmed through clauses, terms, and conditions that only seemed to deepen the knot in her stomach. Every sentence felt like another dead end.

"It's not just about my rights," she said to herself, her tone growing more determined. "It's about justice. I can't let her take everything from me."

Jersey stood up abruptly, the chair scraping loudly against the floor as she made her way to the study. The weight of the situation was settling in, pressing on her chest with each step. The study was quieter than the dining room, the only sound the faint hum of her laptop. But it felt colder, more isolated. She could almost hear the echoes of her frustration bouncing off the walls as she combed through more papers—contracts, business forms, letters—anything that might hold the key to unlocking her next move.

She flipped through them one by one, a growing sense of helplessness creeping in. Her hands trembled as she shuffled the pages, her mind racing. She couldn't afford to miss a single detail, but every paper felt like a dead weight. She glanced at the bookshelves stacked with volumes of legal textbooks, their spines collecting dust, and pulled a few down. She skimmed the pages, flipping through the chapters with a sharp, agitated pace.

Nothing.

She let out a frustrated sigh and dropped the books onto the floor, the thud of them hitting the carpet loud in the silence of the room. The darkness outside pressed in against the windows, adding to the oppressive feeling that had settled over her.

Jersey walked back to the dining table, rubbing her temples in an attempt to ward off the growing headache. Her thoughts were a tangled mess of legal terms and strategies, none of which felt quite right. But she couldn't stop. Not now. Not when everything she had worked for was at stake.

She resumed her search, typing fervently into the laptop. Her gaze flicked from the screen to the papers around her, her mind never still. She wasn't going to stop until she found a way to protect her future.

Jersey leaned back in her chair, her eyes narrowing as she scanned a new article that had caught her attention. Maybe this was the answer she had been looking for. Maybe—just maybe—there was still hope.

Her fingers hovered above the keyboard, steadying her breath. She could do this.

Onica sat in the sleek, modern office, her fingers nervously drumming against the edge of the polished wooden table. The weight of the battle ahead felt heavy on her shoulders, but today, there was a glimmer of hope. Morgan, her attorney, sat across from her, his brow furrowed as he carefully examined the phone records that could turn the tide in her favor.

Morgan's voice broke the silence as he flipped through pages on his desk. "We've been reviewing your husband's phone conversations and wedding photos," he said, his tone focused yet calm. "Let's see if there's anything that can help your case."

Onica leaned forward, her chest tightening as she watched Morgan sift through the records. Every moment felt like an eternity. The past few weeks had been a blur of legal battles, uncertainty, and the sinking feeling that her marriage—her life with Peter—was slipping through her fingers.

"Please, Morgan," she said, her voice barely above a whisper. "There has to be something here that proves my rightful marriage."

Morgan nodded, his eyes scanning the records. He suddenly stopped, a small smile tugging at the corner of his lips. "Wait a minute, Onica. Look at this phone conversation from the day of your wedding."

He hit play on the recorder, and the room was filled with the voice of Peter—Onica's heart leaped at the sound of it. The familiar warmth of his voice was like a wave crashing over her, stirring memories she had tried to hold on to.

The recording played out, the voice of Peter speaking to his best friend, James. "Yeah, James, I can't wait to marry Onica today. She's the love of my life."

Onica's breath caught in her throat. Tears welled in her eyes as she heard Peter's words. His love for her—his devotion—was unmistakable. She couldn't stop the emotions that rushed over her. *That was Peter's voice,* she thought. *He truly saw me as his wife.*

"That's Peter's voice," she murmured, her voice thick with emotion. "He called me the love of his life."

Morgan looked at her, his expression softening. "It's powerful, Onica. It's evidence that speaks to your marriage—your bond."

With a gentle movement, Morgan slid a folder toward her. "And look at these wedding photos."

Onica's heart skipped a beat as she gazed at the images in front of her. They were beautiful, raw moments of joy—her in the bridal gown, Peter by her side, his eyes filled with love and devotion. The photos told the story of a wedding, of a life built on shared dreams and promises. There was no mistaking it. She was the bride.

"These photos," she whispered, her voice trembling. "They prove we were meant to be together."

Morgan smiled, his eyes sharp with determination. "With this evidence, we have a strong case to prove your rightful marriage. This isn't just about legalities; it's about your truth. We'll take this to court."

Onica nodded, feeling a surge of relief and hope she hadn't allowed herself to feel in so long. For the first time in weeks, she felt like she had a chance—like she could fight for what was hers, what was *rightfully hers*. The pain of losing Peter had been unbearable, but now, with this evidence, she could honor their love, secure her future, and reclaim what had been taken from her.

As she stood up from the table, a new strength settled within her. She wasn't just fighting for a piece of paper or a title; she was fighting for her life with Peter, for the love they had shared. And with Morgan by her side, she felt ready to face whatever came next.

Onica left the attorney's office, the weight of the world still on her shoulders but a newfound sense of hope lighting her way. The road ahead wasn't easy, but now, she had something solid to stand on. And for the first time in a long time, she believed she could win.

JERSEY sat across from the lawyer, her hands trembling slightly as she adjusted the papers in front of her. Mabella sat beside her, watching intently, though there was an undercurrent of tension in the room. The lawyer, a sharp-eyed woman with a no-nonsense demeanor, scanned through the documents before looking up, waiting for JERSEY to speak.

JERSEY took a deep breath, her heart racing. This wasn't going to be easy, but it had to be done. "I need to tell you something important," she said, her voice steady but carrying the weight of what she was about to reveal. "I'm three months pregnant."

The lawyer didn't flinch, though her brow lifted in surprise. She set her pen down, folding her hands on the table as she focused entirely on JERSEY. "That's a significant piece of information, JERSEY. Is this relevant to the case?"

Mabella, who had been leaning back in her chair, suddenly sat upright. Her eyes widened in shock. "You're pregnant?" She turned to JERSEY, her voice a mixture of disbelief and hurt. "Why didn't you tell me?"

JERSEY flinched at the question, feeling the weight of her secrecy. She had never been sure how to bring it up, especially not in the midst of everything else going on. "I wasn't sure how to bring it up, Mabella," she said quietly, her gaze falling to her lap. "Things are complicated enough already."

The lawyer nodded thoughtfully, her expression unreadable. "Let's focus on the legal matters here," she said, her voice returning to its usual professionalism. "This pregnancy might have implications for the case, and we'll need to address them."

JERSEY felt her nerves settle slightly as the lawyer's practical tone anchored her back into the reality of the situation. Her personal life was no longer just hers—it was now entwined with the legal battle, and everything she did seemed to add another layer of complexity. But at least she wasn't alone in this. The revelation of the pregnancy felt like a weight lifting, even as it complicated matters.

Mabella remained quiet, her face unreadable, but the silence between them was charged with unspoken words. JERSEY wasn't sure how this would change things—if it would change things—but she knew it would.

In another office across town, Onica sat in a sterile, windowless room, a different kind of tension hanging in the air. She sat at a table surrounded by her lawyer, Morgan, and Sarah, a private investigator who had been helping with the case. There were stacks of evidence before them, photos and documents that Onica knew held the key to her fight.

Morgan looked over the papers with a critical eye. "Onica," he began, his tone serious, "the evidence we have is crucial for your case. We need to keep it secure at all times."

Onica's hands clenched in her lap, her mind buzzing with worries. "I know," she said, her voice tight. "But it's been hard to sleep with all this stress. It feels like everything is falling apart."

Sarah, who had been quietly reviewing some of the surveillance reports, looked up at her with understanding. "We'll make sure the evidence is safe, Onica," she said reassuringly. "You don't need to worry about that right now."

But even with Sarah's comforting words, Onica could feel the weight of everything pressing down on her. The legal battle, the loss of Peter, the constant fear that everything could slip away. It was overwhelming, and despite the assurance that the evidence was safe, she couldn't shake the feeling that it might not be enough.

Morgan's gaze softened as he placed a hand on the table. "You've come this far, Onica," he said gently. "We're going to get through this. But you need to take care of yourself too."

Onica nodded, though the doubt lingered. She had to fight—for Peter, for the future, for the truth. But she was beginning to realize that this fight was more than just about legal documents. It was about finding a way to live with the loss of her husband, with the mess of everything that had followed, and with the hope that, somehow, she could still win.

The room fell into a quiet, contemplative silence as Onica looked down at the pile of documents before her, steeling herself for what was to come. The weight of the case was unbearable, but with Morgan and Sarah by her side, she knew she couldn't give up. She wouldn't let Peter's legacy be taken from her without a fight.

The archive room smelled of old paper and dust, the dim light casting long shadows over the rows of file cabinets. Sarah stood at one of the large, metal filing cabinets, her fingers sifting through the documents with precision. She was deep in concentration, her eyes scanning each folder before moving on to the next. She had learned long ago to be thorough, to make sure that nothing was overlooked.

The weight of the task wasn't lost on her. This evidence could mean the difference between victory and defeat in the battle for Peter's company.

"I'll put the evidence in a secure place here," Sarah murmured softly to herself, more out of habit than necessity. She had been entrusted with the sensitive documents, and she wasn't about to let anyone, especially not Onica's rivals, get their hands on them.

She slid the final file into the safe—an old but sturdy steel contraption tucked away in the far corner of the room. With a deliberate twist, the heavy lock clicked into place, sealing the evidence inside.

But as Sarah turned, she caught a flicker of movement in the corner of her eye. It was quick—just a shadow in the farthest reaches of the room. Her heart skipped a beat. She instinctively reached for the drawer handle, her pulse quickening.

There was someone else in the room.

A chill ran down her spine as she cautiously scanned the dim corners, her instincts on high alert. The shadow had disappeared, but she couldn't shake the feeling that she wasn't alone.

Her hand hovered near the flashlight on the desk. She flicked it on, the beam slicing through the darkness, revealing nothing but the rows of files and boxes stacked meticulously on the shelves.

Sarah exhaled slowly, forcing her body to relax. It was probably just her imagination, the weight of the case and the pressure getting to her. But she couldn't ignore the feeling that something—or someone—was watching her.

She took a few steps back toward the safe, making sure everything was in place. Still, she felt the prickling sensation on the back of her neck, as though someone was just out of view, lurking in the shadows.

Her breath quickened as the door to the archive room creaked ever so slightly, a subtle sound that echoed in the silence. It was faint, but enough to make her pulse race again.

She froze. Someone was definitely here.

Sarah's grip tightened on the flashlight as she slowly edged closer to the door. Her mind raced. Was it an employee? An intruder? The stakes were too high for her to take any chances. She had to be careful.

A soft, almost inaudible footstep echoed in the distance, and her blood ran cold.

The door slowly began to swing open, the faint squeak of the hinges making Sarah's heart hammer in her chest. The light from the hallway spilled into the dark room as she braced herself, the flashlight now illuminating the figure standing in the doorway.

There, in the dim light, was someone watching her.

Sarah walked briskly to her car, the cold night air biting at her skin. She had spent hours in the company archive room, organizing the final pieces of evidence. It had been a long day, but she was satisfied with the progress. All that was left was to drive home and get some rest before the next round of strategy meetings.

But as she approached her car, her heart dropped into her stomach.

The door was ajar.

Her fingers trembled as she reached for the handle, the unmistakable feeling of dread settling over her like a thick fog. She swung open the door and her eyes scanned the interior in disbelief.

It was gone.

The safe.

Her breath caught in her throat, panic bubbling up from deep inside. "No!" she hissed, slamming the car door shut in a rush. She looked around the parking lot, her mind racing. Who would have done this?

She pulled out her phone, hands shaking as she dialed the number she knew all too well.

The atmosphere in the law office was tense. The air was thick with frustration and disbelief as Sarah paced back and forth in front of the group. Onica sat at the conference table, her face pale, her hands clenched into fists. Morgan, the lawyer, stood by the window, arms crossed, lost in thought.

Onica's voice cut through the silence. "How could this happen? It's our only chance! All of our work, everything we've gathered... it's gone."

Morgan turned slowly to face Onica, his gaze sharp and unwavering. "We can't give up. We'll find out who did this. We have resources, and we're not without options."

Sarah stood at the side, biting her lip as the weight of the situation pressed down on her. "I have a lead," she said, her voice steady despite the storm raging in her chest. "I saw someone suspicious in the parking lot last night."

Onica and Morgan both looked at her, hope flickering in their eyes.

"Tell us everything," Morgan urged.

The walls of the private investigator's office were lined with monitors, each displaying grainy images of security footage. Sarah sat with a tense focus, her eyes locked on the screen as her team played back the video from the night of the break-in. A faint click echoed as they adjusted the footage, trying to make out any distinguishing details.

Sarah's finger hovered over the mouse, zooming in on a figure in the distance. "There," she said, pointing at the screen. "That's the person who broke into my car."

The camera angle shifted, showing the figure moving quickly across the parking lot, their face obscured in the shadows. Sarah leaned in, her heart pounding. "Can you enhance it?"

One of the team members worked quickly, fingers flying over the keyboard. The image sharpened, revealing the blurry outline of a man in a dark hoodie. A flicker of recognition passed through Sarah's mind, but she couldn't place it yet.

"Wait a minute," Sarah muttered to herself, squinting at the screen. "I've seen him before."

The investigator leaned in, peering at the screen. "Who is he?"

Sarah's pulse quickened as the pieces began to fall into place. "I think he works for Peter's company," she said, her voice laced with growing suspicion. "He's an employee. I've seen him around the office a few times, but never really paid attention."

"Let's get a closer look at him," Morgan said, stepping forward. "If he's involved, then we need to know everything about him."

They enhanced the image further, zooming in on his face. The blurry outline now became a clear portrait of a man with sharp features and dark eyes.

"We'll need to dig into his background," Morgan continued, his tone now full of authority. "Find out who he is, where he's been. This could be our way in."

Sarah nodded, her heart still racing. They had a lead. It wasn't much, but it was a start. And with it, they might just find the person who stole everything they had fought for.

Sarah walked into Detective Rodriguez's office, holding the small evidence bag carefully, her fingers trembling slightly from the weight of everything that had happened. The detective, a no-nonsense type with sharp eyes and a calm demeanor, looked up from his desk. His expression softened when he saw the evidence she was holding.

"Detective Rodriguez," Sarah said, her voice steady but carrying the relief of finally having something to show for all her hard work. "This is everything. The evidence, the security footage, and everything we've gathered."

Rodriguez nodded, his expression serious but acknowledging the gravity of the moment. "I'll take it from here. We'll do our best to track down the thief and recover the stolen property. You've done well, Sarah."

She handed over the evidence with a firm, determined gesture. "I just want to make sure we have a chance to put this all behind us. Onica deserves to get what's rightfully hers."

Rodriguez gave a curt nod. "We'll make sure justice is served. You've done your part. Now, let's make sure the thief doesn't slip through the cracks."

Sarah walked into the law office, her steps quick, her face beaming with relief. The moment she stepped into the room, Onica, Morgan, and the rest of the team turned toward her, anticipation on their faces.

"Good news," Sarah said, her voice excited but with a touch of exhaustion from the whirlwind of the past few days. "Detective Rodriguez found the thief, and we got the evidence back!"

Onica's face broke into an expression of pure relief. She stood up from her chair, her eyes wide. "Thank goodness! Now we can finally move forward with the case."

Morgan, ever the professional, let out a small, approving nod. "Well done, Sarah. This evidence is our lifeline. We can't afford any more setbacks."

Sarah smiled, the tension finally easing from her shoulders. The battle was far from over, but they were back on track. "We're not out of the woods yet," she said, though the weight of her words felt lighter. "But this is a huge step in the right direction."

The scene was serene. The sun hung high in the sky, casting a warm glow over the outdoor pool area. Jersey and Mabella were sprawled out on lounge chairs, sipping chilled wine and nibbling on berries and grapes. Their sunglasses glinted under the sun's rays, and their laughter mingled with the gentle lapping of the pool water.

"This is the life I always wanted," Jersey said, her voice laced with contentment. She stretched her arms wide, taking in the beauty of the moment, her eyes squinting against the sunlight. "Onica, though... I think she can only have this life alone."

Mabella leaned in, his expression softened by the warmth of the day. "Nothing lasts forever. We got it, my love. We've worked for it."

Jersey turned her gaze to him, a hint of something bittersweet lingering in her eyes. "I'm made to succeed. This should stay this way."

She stood up, stretching her arms again, feeling the cool air on her skin. She walked around the pool, savoring the feeling of the sun against her skin and the peace that came with it. Mabella followed her, a playful smile tugging at his lips. Jersey, in a moment of pure joy, ran toward the edge of the pool and dove in, the splash echoing through the tranquil setting.

Mabella jumped in after her, laughing as they both emerged from the water, their hands finding each other in the cool embrace of the pool. They clung to one another, blissful in their shared moment.

Just then, Jersey's phone rang, interrupting the tranquility. She swam out to the edge of the pool, the phone still ringing in her hand.

"Hello," Jersey said, a hint of annoyance in her tone.

The voice on the other end was formal, professional. "This is Bennet, the mediator from the local court. I'm handling your case, and I must warn you, this could cost a lot of money if it doesn't get resolved soon."

Jersey's expression hardened, her grip tightening on the phone. "Okay."

"I suggest we meet in person to discuss this further," Bennet continued. "I'll check my calendar and have my secretary email you the details."

Jersey let out a frustrated sigh, her eyes narrowing slightly as she glanced at Mabella, who watched her with growing concern. "I'm not ready for any war," she muttered under her breath, the peaceful bubble she had created now feeling threatened.

Bennet's voice was calm, almost too calm. "This will benefit everyone," he said before hanging up.

Jersey switched off the phone, tossing it onto the lounge chair as she returned to the pool with a frustrated sigh.

Mabella raised an eyebrow. "What now?"

Jersey stood still for a moment, her gaze distant as she took in the stillness of the water. "It's a call that will resolve my problems," she said, her voice thick with a mixture of unease and determination. "But it's going to disrupt my peace."

Mabella reached out, taking her hand, a silent understanding passing between them. "We'll figure it out," he said softly.

The room is sterile, its white walls giving off an air of neutrality, yet the tension between Jersey and Onica is palpable. They sit across from each other at a long, sleek table, the mediator seated in the middle, trying to maintain order as the two women glare at each other.

MEDIATOR
(calm, yet firm)
"Ladies, I understand the complexity of your situation. We're here to find a solution that benefits both parties. Let's try to open up a dialogue."

Onica, her face tight with frustration, shifts in her seat, clearly unable to mask her exasperation.

ONICA

(gritting her teeth)

"Dialogue won't change the fact that my marriage certificate was messed up, and now I'm stuck in this legal mess. I want what's rightfully mine."

Jersey leans forward, her eyes flashing with determination, not ready to let go of what she believes is rightfully hers.

JERSEY

(defensive, her voice rising slightly)

"I've worked my ass off to keep this company afloat. I've made the tough decisions and handled the finances. Legally, I have the authority to make the calls. You can't just waltz in and take it all away from me."

The mediator, sensing the growing hostility, tries to deescalate the situation, his voice smooth but firm.

MEDIATOR

(diplomatic, trying to soften the tension)

"Perhaps we can discuss a compromise. Onica, you deserve recognition for your role in the company, but Jersey has been running it. Is there a middle ground we can find?"

Jersey's jaw tightens, her hands resting firmly on the table. She's unwavering.

JERSEY

(adamant, her tone final)

"I won't share this company with anyone. It's mine. Legally. End of discussion."

Onica's face falls, her shoulders sagging under the weight of Jersey's refusal. The mediator looks between them, his expression one of concern, but the room feels like it's closing in on all sides.

ONICA

(voice strained, almost breaking)

"Mediator, I don't see how we can resolve this. Jersey won't budge, and I can't just give up my rights. This isn't just about money or power—it's about my future."

Jersey crosses her arms, her gaze cold. The silence between them is thick, like an unspoken wall that neither can breach. The mediator sighs quietly, realizing that a solution is far from reach.

MEDIATOR
(sighing, but still trying to find a way forward)
"We can't keep going in circles like this. I understand the stakes are high, but you both need to consider what's best for the future—not just for yourselves, but for the company and everyone involved."

Onica looks down, her hands clenched into fists on the table. Jersey's expression softens for a brief moment, but only for a flash, before her resolve hardens again.

ONICA
(whispering to herself, almost defeated)
"I just want what's right... what was promised to me."

The mediator watches both women carefully, knowing that the road ahead won't be an easy one, and it might take more than just a few words to bridge the chasm between them. But for now, the dialogue hangs in the air—unfinished, unresolved.

MEDIATOR
(calm, but resolute)
"Let's take a break. I think both of you need some time to think before we continue."

The room falls into an uneasy silence as Jersey and Onica sit, each staring straight ahead, lost in their thoughts.

The courtroom is silent, the weight of the moment pressing down on everyone in the room. Onica sits at one end of the table, her expression tense but resolute. Her attorney, Morgan, stands beside her, confidently presenting their case to the judge. The air is thick

MY WEDDING CONTRACT TOO 75

with anticipation as they lay out the evidence that could determine the future of the company—and Onica's rightful place in it.

MORGAN

(passionate, commanding attention)

"Your Honor, these phone conversations and wedding photos provide irrefutable evidence that Onica is the rightful wife of the late Peter. The marriage certificate may have been tampered with, but the truth is clear in the way Peter spoke of Onica, in his words, in his actions. We demand justice for her."

The judge, an older man with sharp eyes, leans forward slightly, examining the documents before him with deliberation. His fingers tap lightly on the edge of the desk as he processes the information.

JUDGE

(thoughtful, measured)

"This is a complex case, and we will need time to review the evidence. The implications of these claims are far-reaching, not only for the parties involved but for the future of the company. We will reconvene next week."

The gavel strikes, and the court session adjourns. Onica, despite her lawyer's impassioned plea, feels a knot of anxiety tighten in her chest. This battle isn't over yet—not by a long shot.

The sunlight blazes down as Onica exits the courthouse, her heels clicking sharply on the pavement. Morgan walks beside her, glancing at her from time to time, but Onica's mind is elsewhere—focused, determined.

ONICA

(to Morgan, barely containing her frustration)

"We can't just wait for the next hearing. I need more. I need something that will force Jersey's hand."

Morgan pauses, hesitating before replying, sensing the shift in Onica's tone.

MORGAN

(warning, but understanding)
"Onica, pushing too hard could backfire. The legal process is delicate. We've presented our evidence; now we wait for the judge's decision."

But Onica isn't listening. She's already walking toward her car, her jaw clenched, her mind racing. She doesn't have the patience for this drawn-out battle. She needs something more tangible, something Jersey won't be able to deny.

ONICA
(muttering to herself, determined)
"I can't wait. I won't wait."

The office is dark, save for the dim glow of the desk lamp. Onica moves quietly through the familiar space, her eyes scanning the shelves, the filing cabinets—anything that could hold the evidence she needs. She knows Jersey's likely to be somewhere else tonight, and that gives her the perfect window of opportunity.

Her heart pounds in her chest as she pulls open drawers, rifling through files. The silence of the office feels oppressive, almost suffocating. Each document she flips through brings her one step closer to the truth she's desperate to uncover.

ONICA
(whispering to herself, almost breathless)
"There has to be something—anything—that can give me leverage."

She pauses, her eyes falling on a folder tucked away at the back of a filing cabinet. With a sharp intake of breath, she pulls it out, her fingers trembling as she opens it. Inside are more phone records—private conversations between Jersey and a mysterious figure, someone who might hold the key to everything. Onica's eyes widen as she scans the pages, realizing the significance of what she's found.

ONICA

(softly, to herself)
"This... this could change everything."

She quickly snaps a photo of the records with her phone, slipping the documents back into the folder. As she closes the drawer, she hears a noise—a creak from the hallway outside the office. Her heart skips a beat.

Someone's here.

Onica hurries out of the building, her pulse racing, her phone clutched tightly in her hand. She glances over her shoulder, half-expecting someone to appear from the shadows. But the lot is empty, save for the dim light of the streetlamps.

As she gets into her car and drives away, her mind races with thoughts of what she's just uncovered. This new evidence could be the turning point she needs to secure her place in the company—and to prove that Jersey has been hiding things all along.

ONICA
(to herself, determined)
"This isn't over. Not by a long shot."

The house is eerily quiet, a stark contrast to the storm of emotions brewing inside Onica. She stands at the door, her heart pounding in her chest. The faint moonlight filters through the dusty windows, casting long shadows on the floor. She holds a crowbar in her hand, the metal cold and unfamiliar as she pries at the lock.

Her breath comes in shallow, hurried gasps. She knows this is a risky move—if anyone finds out, it could destroy everything. But she has no choice. The evidence she needs to win the case, to reclaim her place in Peter's legacy, might be buried somewhere inside these walls. And she's willing to do whatever it takes to find it.

ONICA
(whispering to herself, determined)
"I just need one thing. One thing to prove it."

The lock gives way with a soft click, and she steps inside. Her eyes adjust to the dim light as she slowly moves through the house, avoiding the creaky floorboards that could betray her presence. The house feels like a ghost, a relic of a life that once was. It doesn't feel like Peter's anymore. But it's still his, and for Onica, that means everything.

She moves quickly, heading straight for the study, where Peter used to keep all his important documents. The drawers are locked, but she knows where he hid the spare key. Her hands tremble as she searches through the drawer, finding the small brass key tucked away beneath a pile of old letters.

ONICA
(muttering to herself, anxious)
"Come on, come on..."

The key slips into the lock with a satisfying turn, and she pulls the drawer open. The smell of paper and dust fills the air as she rifles through the files, her eyes scanning each document with growing desperation. Then, just as she's about to give up, she spots a file tucked in the back, its name barely visible in the dim light.

Her fingers curl around it, and she pulls it out. She flips it open, her heart racing. Inside are photos of Peter's business dealings—contracts, legal documents, and something else. A handwritten note that makes her blood run cold. It's a letter, addressed to Peter's lawyer, discussing the legitimacy of their marriage.

ONICA
(whispering, shocked)
"This... this is it."

But before she can fully process the weight of what she's found, a sharp voice cuts through the silence.

MABELLA
(from behind her, cold and accusing)

"Well, well, well. What do we have here?"

Onica freezes, her blood running cold. She slowly turns around to find Mabella standing in the doorway, her face a mask of fury and disbelief.

ONICA
(caught off guard, defensive)
"Mabella, I—"

MABELLA
(interrupting, voice rising)
"You've got some nerve, Onica. Breaking into Peter's house? Are you really that desperate?"

Onica tries to gather her thoughts, but Mabella's presence is like a suffocating force, pressing in on her. She can feel the tension thickening in the air as Mabella pulls out her phone and begins dialing.

MABELLA
(into the phone, calm but seething)
"I've caught an intruder at Peter's house. Please come quickly."

Onica's stomach drops. She knows she's been caught, and there's no escaping the mess she's just stepped into. She takes a step back, her eyes darting around the room, searching for any way out. But she knows there's nothing she can do now. Mabella has already made the call.

ONICA
(pleading, trying to reason)
"Mabella, please. I wasn't here to steal anything. I was just looking for the truth. For evidence. You don't understand—this isn't just about the company. It's about what's rightfully mine."

Mabella's face hardens, her grip on the phone tightening.

MABELLA
(coldly, without sympathy)

"Your truth doesn't matter here. You had no right to come into this house. This is Peter's home, and you have no place here anymore."

Before Onica can respond, the sound of sirens wails in the distance, growing louder. Her heart sinks. The police are on their way.

ONICA
(desperate, voice trembling)
"Mabella, don't do this. You don't understand—this evidence could change everything. I need it."

But Mabella simply shakes her head, her lips curling into a tight, unforgiving smile.

MABELLA
(firmly, coldly)
"I understand perfectly, Onica. And I'm done with your games. The only thing you're going to find here is trouble."

Onica stands frozen, the file clutched in her hands, the weight of her situation crashing down on her. She knows there's no turning back now. The police are on their way, and she'll be forced to face the consequences of her actions.

Onica stands before the judge, her hands trembling slightly as she grips the edge of the wooden podium. The courtroom is silent, save for the rustle of papers and the occasional cough from the audience. Her attorney, Morgan, stands at her side, eyes narrowed with concern. The judge, a stern and composed woman with sharp eyes, gazes down at Onica with unwavering authority.

The air is thick with tension as the judge looks at the documents in front of her, reading the final ruling aloud.

JUDGE
(firmly)
"Ms. Onica, you are hereby issued a restraining order. You are not allowed to go near any of the properties belonging to the late Peter or

his company. You are to remain at least five hundred feet away from these locations at all times."

Onica's heart sinks into her stomach. The words seem to echo in her mind, a brutal finality that she can't escape. Her body stiffens, the fight she has left in her burning in her chest, but she knows—this is a heavy blow, one that could shatter everything she's been fighting for.

ONICA
(desperate, her voice wavering)
"Your Honor, I need to find evidence to prove my rightful marriage. This is unfair! I can't just walk away. I—"

She stops herself, her voice catching in her throat. Her eyes flicker to Morgan, who watches her with a mixture of sympathy and concern, but he remains silent, knowing there's little more he can do.

The judge's gaze sharpens, and she interrupts Onica with a measured tone.

JUDGE
(resolute)
"The law is clear, Ms. Onica. You must abide by this order. Any further violation will result in serious consequences. This court has made its decision, and it is final."

Onica stands frozen, the weight of the decision crushing her. She had hoped for a different outcome, something that would allow her to continue the fight, but now, it feels like the walls are closing in. Her mind races, her thoughts a blur as the reality of her situation settles in. She can no longer pursue the evidence she so desperately needs.

ONICA
(softly, to herself)
"This isn't over... it can't be."

Morgan places a gentle hand on her shoulder, his voice calm yet laced with the knowledge of the uphill battle ahead.

MORGAN

(quietly)
"We'll find another way, Onica. This isn't the end, but you need to follow the court's order for now."

Onica nods, though she knows the road ahead is more complicated than ever. The restraining order feels like a shackle, a prison that keeps her from the one thing that could clear her name. But as the judge's gavel strikes down with a resounding thud, Onica's heart hardens with determination.

The fight isn't over. She refuses to let it be.

The courtroom empties, the silence heavy with unspoken words as Onica walks out, her head held high despite the storm raging inside her. Her mind is already working, already searching for the cracks in the system where she can push through.

She will find a way. No matter what it takes.

The room is dim, scattered with papers—legal documents, photographs, and notes that Onica has painstakingly sorted through in her pursuit of justice. Her laptop screen glows faintly, its contents unfinished, much like the thoughts racing through her mind.

Onica sits cross-legged on the floor, her back against the couch, her hand clutching her chest. Her face is contorted in discomfort, a sharp pain radiating through her ribs. Her breath is shallow, each inhale more difficult than the last. She winces, closing her eyes, trying to push through the agony, but the pain only intensifies.

ONICA
(whispering, struggling to breathe)
"Oh, my chest... it hurts..."

Her grip on the papers weakens, and they begin to slip from her hands, fluttering down to the floor like discarded fragments of her hopes. She tries to steady herself, but her vision blurs, her body trembling from the strain.

And then, without warning, the world around her tilts. Her breath catches in her throat, and she collapses, her body crumpling to the floor, unconscious.

The front door bursts open, and Jersey enters, her footsteps hurried and frantic. Her eyes scan the room before landing on Onica, crumpled on the floor in a heap of papers. Her heart stops for a moment, panic flooding her chest.

JERSEY
(panicked, rushing to Onica's side)
"Onica! Wake up! Oh my God!"

Jersey kneels beside her friend, her hands trembling as she gently shakes Onica's shoulders. When there's no response, she pulls her phone from her pocket, dialing the number of the doctor she trusts.

JERSEY
(voice cracking, pleading into the phone)
"Please, you have to come right away. My friend just collapsed, and she's in a lot of pain. I don't know what's happening... please, hurry."

She hangs up quickly, her mind racing as she looks down at Onica, her face pale and her breathing faint.

Jersey carefully lifts Onica, easing her onto the couch, desperate to keep her friend comfortable. She moves with urgency, grabbing a glass of water and splashing it gently across Onica's face, hoping for some sign of life.

JERSEY
(softly, her voice trembling as she leans over Onica)
"Hang in there, Onica. Help is on the way. Please, wake up."

Onica doesn't stir. Jersey presses a cold compress to her friend's forehead, her eyes brimming with worry. Time seems to stretch endlessly as she waits for the sound of sirens, for the arrival of the doctor who will have the answers she so desperately needs.

Jersey watches Onica's still form, her own heartbeat loud in her ears. She wants to scream, to do something—anything—but all she can do is wait, her mind clouded with fear.

JERSEY
(whispering, mostly to herself)
"Please... don't leave me now, Onica. Not like this."

She clasps her friend's hand, holding it tightly as if her touch alone could bring Onica back. The tension in the room is suffocating, the silence only broken by Jersey's quiet, desperate pleas.

The parking area is dimly lit, shadows stretching long across the concrete floor. The faint hum of distant traffic seeps in through the walls, but otherwise, the garage is eerily quiet. Onica moves like a shadow, dressed in black, her large sunglasses hiding the fury in her eyes. The weight of what she's about to do hangs heavily in the air, and every step she takes is deliberate, calculated.

She spots Mabella's car—sleek, expensive, a symbol of the life he's built with Jersey. The sight of it causes a surge of anger in Onica's chest. The pain of the betrayal she's endured, the lies, the legal battles, the losses, all come crashing down in this single moment.

With a steady hand, she pulls out a gleaming knife, its blade reflecting the dim light. She presses the tip against the first tire and, with a swift motion, punctures it. The hissing sound of air escaping fills the garage, sharp and satisfying. She moves to the next tire, the next, and the next, methodically deflating each one as if she's taking revenge on every wrong they've done to her. Each puncture is a release of the fury that has been building inside her.

ONICA
(whispering to herself, her voice low and dangerous)
"This is for everything they've done."

The knife moves with practiced precision, and with each strike, Onica feels a flicker of satisfaction, a brief moment of control in the chaos of her life. By the time she's finished, all four tires are shredded, flattened beneath her knife's cruel kiss.

Just as she steps back, admiring the damage, the sound of footsteps echoes down the corridor. Mabella appears at the far end, his eyes immediately locking on his car. His steps falter as the sight of the vandalized vehicle registers in his mind. He stops dead in his tracks, shock etching across his face. His heart skips a beat as he takes in the scene—the car, once pristine, now reduced to a helpless wreck, its tires mere rubber carcasses.

Mabella's hands tremble as he pulls out his phone. His finger hovers over the screen before he dials Jersey's number, his voice thick with frustration.

MABELLA
(frustrated, voice rising in disbelief)
"Jersey, you won't believe what's happened! My car... it's been vandalized! Every tire's been slashed!"

Onica watches from the shadows, her breathing steady as she listens to Mabella's panicked voice. The rush of adrenaline still pulses through her veins. She knows this won't be the end of it—the consequences will come, but for now, she's satisfied. For now, she's made her mark.

JERSEY *(over the phone, concerned)*
"What? Are you serious? I'll be right there."

Mabella's voice is frazzled, trying to keep his cool as he responds, but Onica can't hear him anymore. The sound of Jersey's voice cuts through his words, and for a moment, it feels like the calm before the storm.

Onica pulls the knife from the last tire, steps back, and disappears into the shadows, her heart still racing. She walks away from the parking garage as the tension hangs thick in the air, knowing full well that this act of revenge has set something much bigger into motion.

Mabella stood beside his car, eyes scanning the damage with disbelief. The night air hung heavy with the scent of rubber and gasoline as he ran a hand through his disheveled hair. His frustration was palpable, his chest tight with anger and helplessness. His once-pristine car, a symbol of the life he and Jersey had worked so hard to build, was now a mess of slashed tires and deflated hope.

With trembling hands, he pulled out his phone and dialed Jersey's number. The ringing tone echoed in his ears, but his mind was already racing. He knew who was behind this. There was only one person who could be responsible for something like this.

The phone clicked, and Jersey's voice, calm but concerned, came through the line.

MABELLA
(frustrated, voice rising)
"Jersey, you won't believe what's happened. My car... it's been vandalized!"

On the other end of the line, Jersey's breath hitched, her tone immediately shifting to one of concern. She could hear the distress in Mabella's voice, and it made her stomach churn.

JERSEY
(concerned, almost whispering)
"What? Are you serious? I'll be right there."

Mabella's heart pounded in his chest. He could hear Jersey's urgency, but it wasn't enough to calm him. His mind was already jumping to conclusions, the weight of everything they had been through with Onica driving him to anger.

MABELLA
(accusingly, voice shaking with frustration)
"I knew it, Jersey. This has Onica's fingerprints all over it. She's trying to get back at us! I *told* you she wouldn't stop until she destroyed everything."

Jersey paused for a moment, the words hanging in the air between them. She could feel the tension in his voice, but something in her gut told her to be cautious. Onica was unpredictable, yes, but it was still a big leap to pin something like this on her without proof.

JERSEY
(defensive, trying to stay calm)
"Let's not jump to conclusions, Mabella. We can't be sure it's her. We don't have any evidence yet."

Despite Jersey's attempt to steady the situation, both of them were on edge, their suspicions growing with every passing second. Mabella's eyes darted to the mangled tires again, his jaw clenched tightly.

MABELLA
(determined, voice low and steady)
"We need to do something about this. We can't let her ruin everything for us."

Jersey felt the weight of his words settle in her chest. She knew how much was at stake—how fragile their success had been up until now. One slip, one wrong move, and it could all come crashing down.

She took a deep breath, steadying herself. She couldn't afford to be rattled. Not now. Not when there was still so much to fight for.

JERSEY
(resolute, with a sense of finality)
"I'll handle it, Mabella. Just give me some time. I'll figure this out."

The line went silent for a beat as Mabella processed her words. He didn't want to feel helpless, but he knew there was nothing more he could do at the moment. Jersey was the one with the power, the one who could take charge of the situation.

MABELLA
(softly, but still angry)

"Just make sure you do. We can't afford any more mistakes."

Jersey's grip on the phone tightened. She was already planning her next steps in her mind. She had to act quickly—before the situation spiraled further out of control. Onica had crossed a line, and Jersey would make sure that line would not be crossed again.

JERSEY
(firmly)
"I will, Mabella. I promise."

The call ended with a click, but the tension lingered between them, thick and suffocating. Jersey stood in the quiet of her home, her mind already working through the possibilities. She didn't trust Onica, not after everything that had happened. But she wasn't about to let her emotions dictate her next move. She would find a way to protect what was hers—no matter the cost.

Onica sat on the couch, her shoulders hunched under the weight of the world. A pile of medical bills and legal expenses lay scattered across the coffee table in front of her, the papers a constant reminder of the turmoil she was facing. Her fingers trembled slightly as she sifted through the documents, the numbers on the bills blurring together. She could feel the pressure building in her chest, a mixture of frustration and fear that seemed impossible to escape.

Lizer sat across from her, her presence a comforting anchor in the midst of the storm. She watched Onica closely, her concern evident as she noticed the deep worry etched on her friend's face. Onica's once vibrant spirit seemed drained, and Lizer could see the toll that the mounting stress was taking on her.

ONICA
(sighs, rubbing her temples)
"Lizer, I don't know how I'm going to handle all these bills. The hospital, the lawyers... it's all piling up, and I can't work because of my health. It feels like I'm drowning."

Lizer's heart ached for her friend. She knew how strong Onica was, how determined, but she also saw the vulnerability that came with the weight of the world on her shoulders. Lizer reached across the table, gently placing her hand on Onica's shoulder, offering a silent comfort.

LIZER
(sympathetic, soft)
"I understand, Onica. It's a tough situation, but you don't have to go through it alone. We'll find a way to manage the expenses. I'm here for you, every step of the way."

Onica lifted her gaze to meet Lizer's, her tired eyes brimming with gratitude. She hadn't realized how much she needed to hear those words until now. The isolation she had been feeling, the weight of her problems, had made it hard to reach out. But Lizer was always there, a steady presence in the chaos.

ONICA
(grateful, voice thick with emotion)
"Thank you, Lizer. I don't know what I'd do without you. It's just so overwhelming, and I feel like I'm carrying it all on my own."

Lizer gave her shoulder a reassuring squeeze, her voice steady and comforting.

LIZER
(supportive, firm)
"We'll figure it out together, Onica. Don't worry. We'll get through this. One step at a time."

Onica let out a shaky breath, feeling a small glimmer of hope start to form in the pit of her stomach. It wasn't much, but it was something—something to hold on to in the midst of all the uncertainty. She wasn't alone. Lizer had always been there for her, and now more than ever, that meant the world.

They sat in silence for a moment, the weight of Onica's crisis still looming, but the warmth of their shared understanding filling the space between them. It was a small comfort, but sometimes, it was enough.

Jersey sat at the head of the sleek boardroom table, her expression a carefully crafted mask of composure. The faint hum of the air conditioning was the only sound as Jones, the seasoned representative from the rival firm, leaned back in his chair, exuding an air of unshakable confidence. Beside Jersey, her business colleague shuffled a stack of papers nervously, casting occasional glances her way as if searching for a signal.

Jones broke the silence with a practiced smile, his voice smooth and commanding.

JONES
(confidently)
"Now, Ms. Jersey, let's get down to the nitty-gritty. Our proposal involves intricate data analysis, which, as you know, is pivotal in today's market. We're prepared to offer you a 24/7 data analytics service to handle the extra load. Our experts are well-versed in predictive modeling, AI algorithms, and... well, you get the idea."

Jersey's heart raced as the flood of technical jargon washed over her. She exchanged a brief, uncertain glance with her colleague, who was already scribbling furiously on a notepad. Jones's words were polished, almost rehearsed, leaving little room for rebuttal.

JERSEY
(measured, attempting to keep pace)
"That sounds... comprehensive. But our team is also quite adept at data analysis. We just need some time to evaluate the figures you've presented."

Jones's smirk deepened, the glint in his eyes signaling he had anticipated this response.

JONES
(leaning forward slightly)

"Of course, Ms. Jersey, time is money. But allow me to clarify that our offer includes not just data analysis but real-time integration, cloud-based infrastructure, and a dedicated server farm. It's a substantial investment, I must say."

Jersey felt a knot tightening in her stomach. The sheer scope of what Jones was proposing was overwhelming, and she could sense her colleague's growing unease. Despite her best efforts to project confidence, the pressure was building.

JERSEY
(forced calm, feeling the weight of the decision)
"I see... That's impressive. We'll need to consult our data team and provide you with a response within the next 24 hours."

Jones leaned forward, his tone taking on an edge of urgency, though his smirk remained firmly in place.

JONES
(intently)
"Ms. Jersey, I would advise you not to take this lightly. Our initial proposal of one million dollars is contingent on your swift decision. Anything beyond that, well, we might have to reassess."

The words hung in the air like a veiled threat. Jersey's mind raced, weighing her options. She couldn't afford to appear weak, but the pressure to make a swift decision was almost suffocating. Her colleague whispered something inaudible, but Jersey barely registered it, her focus locked on Jones.

The boardroom felt stifling, the polished walls and immaculate decor doing little to ease the tension. Jersey straightened her shoulders, determined not to let Jones see her falter.

JERSEY
(firmly, though her voice betrayed a hint of strain)
"We'll take your advice into consideration, Mr. Jones. Expect our decision within the stated timeframe."

Jones sat back, his smirk softening into a more neutral expression, though Jersey suspected it was just another tactic in his arsenal.

JONES
(pleasantly)
"Fair enough. I look forward to your response. Don't keep me waiting too long, Ms. Jersey."

With that, he rose smoothly from his chair, gathering his papers with a practiced efficiency. Jersey watched him leave, her mind a whirl of conflicting thoughts. As the heavy boardroom door clicked shut behind him, she turned to her colleague.

JERSEY
(exhaling deeply)
"We need to figure this out. Fast."

Her colleague nodded, but the uncertainty in their eyes mirrored Jersey's own. The clock was ticking, and the stakes had never felt higher.

Jones's imposing figure cast a long shadow over the boardroom as he leaned in, his gaze unwavering and his words razor-sharp. His voice cut through the tense atmosphere like a blade, each syllable calculated for maximum impact.

JONES
(assertive)
"Let me be perfectly clear, Ms. Jersey. I'm not one of those sharks trying to take advantage of your situation. We're here to do business, and we're willing to offer you a competitive edge. But let me remind you—the clock is ticking."

Jersey felt the weight of his words settle heavily in the room. She exchanged a wary glance with her team, all too aware of the delicate tightrope they were walking. Jones's veneer of professionalism couldn't hide the underlying current of pressure he was applying. Every gesture, every word, carried a calculated intent.

Levy, Jersey's senior strategist, leaned forward, his calm confidence a welcome reprieve from the tension. He adjusted his tie before speaking with measured authority.

LEVY
(stepping in confidently)
"Mr. Jones, I appreciate your sense of urgency. We understand the stakes, and I assure you, our creative team is prepared to operate 24/7 to meet your demands. We'll deliver—no question about it."

For a moment, Jones regarded Levy with an inscrutable expression. Then, a tight-lipped smile spread across his face, though it did little to mask the ambiguity of his true motives.

JONES
(nodding)
"Very well, Mr. Levy. We look forward to a prosperous partnership. I'll expect your decision within 24 hours."

As Jones gathered his materials and rose to leave, the tension in the room shifted but didn't dissipate. His presence lingered, a reminder of the high stakes and the looming deadline. Jersey watched him closely, her mind racing to parse out his true intentions.

When the door clicked shut behind him, a collective exhale swept through the team. The pressure, though momentarily lifted, still weighed heavily on their shoulders.

JERSEY
(determined)
"We understand the urgency, Mr. Jones," she had said as the meeting concluded. "We'll do our best to meet your deadline."

Now, as her team huddled around the table, her resolve only deepened.

JERSEY
(turning to her team)
"We've got 24 hours to make this work. Let's pull out all the stops and get this done."

Levy nodded, already flipping through his notes, while the rest of the team dove into their laptops and phones, brainstorming strategies to navigate the precarious situation. Yet, the questions hung in the air, unspoken but palpable: What was Jones really after? And how much were they willing to risk to meet his demands?

Outside the boardroom, the corporate battlefield loomed larger than ever. Rival companies circled like predators, and every move felt like a gamble with far-reaching consequences. For Jersey, the pressure wasn't just about sealing a deal—it was about safeguarding the future of everything she'd worked so hard to build.

As the echo of Jones's confident footsteps faded, the tension in the boardroom remained suffocating. Jersey sat at the head of the table, her usually composed demeanor cracking under the weight of the moment. She took a deep breath, scanning the faces of her team, who seemed just as daunted by the task ahead.

JERSEY
(concerned)
"Does anyone here know a data analyst we can call on? We need expertise, and we need it fast."

A heavy silence fell over the room, broken only by the faint hum of the air conditioner. Then Levy, always quick on his feet, snapped his fingers as an idea struck him.

LEVY
(decisive)
"I know someone. Jacob. He's one of the best data analysts out there. If anyone can make sense of this mess, it's him."

Without waiting for approval, Levy pulled out his phone and dialed. The room watched anxiously as he paced back and forth, the tension mirrored in his clipped tone.

LEVY
(on the phone)

"Jacob, it's Levy. We're in a tight spot here, and we need your expertise. Can you help us out?"

On the other end, Jacob sat in his dimly lit apartment, surrounded by empty coffee cups and the faint haze of cigarette smoke curling through the air. He leaned back in his chair, smirking as he took a drag.

JACOB
(cool, rapid-fire delivery)
"Tight spot, huh? Sounds like your kind of problem, Levy. What's it worth to you?"

Levy's jaw tightened. He knew Jacob didn't come cheap.

LEVY
(with urgency)
"Name your price, Jacob. We need you now."

Jacob exhaled a long plume of smoke, his fingers drumming against his desk. He glanced toward his cluttered coat rack, where his threadbare but supposedly "lucky" jacket hung, a relic of his early career.

JACOB
(with a sly chuckle)
"Double the market rate, Levy. And I'm not stepping out of this room without my lucky jacket. It's non-negotiable."

Levy pinched the bridge of his nose, his mind racing. He turned to Jersey, covering the phone.

LEVY
(low voice)
"He's asking for double the usual rate. Do we have the budget for this?"

Jersey didn't hesitate.

JERSEY
(firm)
"We don't have a choice. Do it. Just get him here."

Levy returned to the phone.

LEVY
(reluctant)
"Fine, Jacob. Double the rate. Just get here as soon as you can."

Jacob's grin widened.

JACOB
"Smart decision, Levy. Send me the details. I'll be there—lucky jacket and all."

As Levy hung up, the room collectively exhaled, though the unease lingered. Jersey clasped her hands together, her expression resolute.

JERSEY
(to the team)
"All right, everyone. Jacob's coming in. Let's make sure we're ready for him. This deal isn't slipping through our fingers."

The room stirred back to life, the team galvanized by Jersey's determination. Outside, the corporate battlefield grew ever more treacherous, but inside the boardroom, Jersey was ready to fight—and win.

Jacob sat hunched in the dim glow of his laptop screen, the only source of light in a room that seemed to thrive in controlled chaos. The soft hum of computer fans mixed with the occasional clink of a coffee mug being moved from one precarious stack of papers to another. Around him, a labyrinth of wires sprawled across the floor, connecting monitors, external drives, and a DIY server that blinked with a reassuring rhythm.

The scent of stale coffee mingled with cigarette smoke, creating a heavy atmosphere, though Jacob appeared unfazed. This was his domain, the place where chaos turned into insight. He took a long drag from his cigarette, his dark eyes narrowing as Levy's voice crackled through his phone.

LEVY

(urgent)
"We need you, Jacob. Big job. Time-sensitive. What's it gonna take?"

Jacob's lips curled into a sly smirk. His mind, ever calculating, dissected Levy's tone—desperation was a powerful negotiating tool. He exhaled, watching the smoke curl into delicate shapes before dissipating.

JACOB
(to himself, amused)
"Levy, Levy, Levy... still calling me only when your ship's about to sink."

Out loud, his voice was smooth but firm.

JACOB
"Double the market rate. And I'm not stepping foot out of this room without my lucky jacket."

Levy's frustrated sigh was almost audible even through the poor connection, but Jacob didn't flinch. He reached for the jacket draped over the back of his chair. It was oversized, its sleeves nearly swallowing his hands, but it was a relic of his first big breakthrough—a charm he swore by.

As Levy grudgingly agreed, Jacob ended the call with a decisive tap and leaned back in his chair. He rested the cigarette between his lips as he began typing furiously, pulling up databases and configuring tools he knew would be vital for the task ahead.

JACOB
(to himself, determined)
"Time to show them why they always come back to me."

Sliding into his lucky jacket, Jacob grabbed a backpack loaded with the essentials—hard drives, a laptop, and a flask of his favorite strong brew. He stepped out of his apartment and into the night, the cool air biting at his cheeks.

The faint glow of streetlights illuminated his confident stride as he made his way to the meeting that could change everything. Jacob wasn't just a data analyst; he was the wildcard they needed, and he knew it.

The park is bathed in the soft, golden light of the morning sun. Peter, a fit and energetic man in his early thirties, is jogging around the park, passing a particular area multiple times.

Each time he runs by, he can't help but notice JERSEY, a woman in her late twenties, sitting alone on a bench, engrossed in a book.

As Peter makes another round, he decides to slow down and take a break, intrigued by the mysterious woman reading her book.

JERSEY senses his presence and looks up from her book as he approaches. She watches him with curiosity in her eyes.

The morning air was crisp and fresh, the kind of early breeze that seemed to awaken the soul. A soft hum of distant birdsong filled the atmosphere, and the sun cast golden light across the park. PETER jogged past, his stride confident and easy, his attention momentarily caught by the figure sitting on the bench. JERSEY, engrossed in the pages of a book, seemed completely unaware of the world around her.

Slowing his pace, he glanced at her curiously, an amused smile spreading across his face as he slowed to a stop beside her.

PETER
(with a friendly smile)
"You know, it's a beautiful morning for a run, but I couldn't help but notice that you seem to be enjoying your book more."

JERSEY, her nose buried in the novel, lifted her head slowly, her eyes scanning his face for a moment before a playful smirk tugged at the corners of her lips.

JERSEY
(raising an eyebrow, intrigued)

"Well, sometimes a good book can transport you to another world, and this world can wait."

PETER chuckled, nodding in agreement as he took a step closer, his eyes twinkling with the kind of enthusiasm that made him seem both approachable and genuinely engaged in the moment.

PETER
(enthusiastically)
"I couldn't agree more! Books have a way of opening up new horizons. I'm Peter, by the way."

JERSEY closed her book with a soft thud, intrigued by his presence. She offered a warm, genuine smile as she stood up, stretching her arms to relieve the stiffness from sitting too long.

JERSEY
(offering a warm smile)
"JERSEY. Nice to meet you, Peter."

Their exchange was simple, but there was an ease between them—a quiet understanding, as though they both appreciated the serenity of the moment, the stillness of the world around them that was so often drowned out by the busyness of life.

Peter takes a seat next to JERSEY on the bench, and they begin to chat, their conversation filled with laughter, shared interests, and the promise of a blossoming connection. Their meeting in the park, under the bright morning sun, marks the start of something special, as they discover a genuine connection between them.

JERSEY's team navigate their way through the turbulent negotiations with Jones.

Jacob burst through the doors of the boardroom, his disheveled appearance in stark contrast to the sharp, polished suits of the corporate world around him. The oversized jacket hung off his frame like a cape, the sleeves far too long, and his thick glasses slid down his nose as he made his way to the center of the room, laptop clutched tightly in one hand. He looked less like the data analyst he was and more like someone who had wandered in from another dimension—one where style and time were irrelevant.

He placed the laptop on the table with a flourish, his fingers already dancing over the keys. His eyes gleamed with excitement as he looked up at the team, who were seated around the polished table, exchanging uncertain glances. Jacob had no time for pleasantries, it seemed. He was here on a mission.

JACOB
(excitedly, with a grin)
"You see, folks, big data is like... it's like a chaotic symphony, but I've got the conductor's wand."

His voice was animated, almost too energetic for the room, but the intensity of his words seemed to draw the attention of everyone around the table. He paused for a moment, letting the metaphor sink in before continuing.

JACOB
(grinning wildly)
"These numbers, they're the notes, and I'm here to make sweet music out of them."

He clicked a button on the laptop, and the screen lit up with a maze of graphs, pie charts, and intricate algorithms that seemed to defy comprehension to anyone outside the realm of data science. Jacob's eyes sparkled as he navigated through the slides, explaining his methods with a rapid-fire confidence that left little room for doubt—if you could follow his train of thought, that is.

JACOB
(confidently, leaning forward)
"If you use my analytics approach, we can show Jones that we're worth every cent of what he's offering. And trust me—this isn't just about numbers; it's about perception. If we don't make the data sing, then all we've got are just... numbers. But, with my approach? Well,

that's where we can really convince Jones that our proposal stands out above the rest."

He paused, letting the weight of his words hang in the air. Then, without missing a beat, he dropped the real bombshell.

JACOB
(with a sly smile, his eyes glinting)
"And I'm not doing this for cheap, mind you. I want 1.5 million dollars if you use my methods. Deal?"

The room fell silent for a moment, the offer hanging like an unsolved puzzle. Jacob, unfazed by the shocked expressions or the quiet murmurs, leaned back in his chair with a smug look of satisfaction. He knew he had just placed the team in a difficult position. There was no denying the power of his analytics, but the cost of it... that was another matter entirely.

JERSEY exchanged a glance with Levy, both weighing the pros and cons of agreeing to Jacob's terms. On one hand, his analytics could very well be the key to securing the contract with Jones. On the other, the price tag was steep, and the clock was ticking.

Jacob's eyes flicked between them, his smirk never fading as he waited for their response.

The room is filled with a mixture of astonishment and hope, as they consider Jacob's unconventional but promising solution to their complex problem.

JACOB
(confidently)
You see, folks, big data is like... it's like a chaotic symphony, but I've got the conductor's wand.

These numbers, they're the notes, and I'm here to make sweet music out of them.

You know, China and Gabon had a similar problem complex issues, big contracts, and no one thinking outside the box. They threw money at the problem, but it didn't work.

Why? Because they weren't data-oriented, and their management couldn't accept the fresh perspectives of us, the young guns.

(PAUSE) But here's the good news, JERSEY.

I've had a secret weapon up my sleeve for two years now, waiting for the right moment.

Jacob grins, his eyes gleaming with excitement.

JERSEY (relieved)

Jacob, that's incredible! We're in a tough spot here, and your experience is just what we need. I'm thrilled to have you on board.

We'll make this work, I know it.

Just one thing, Jacob, we need the report ready by tomorrow morning, before 10 am. Mr. Jones wants to see it, and your insights could be the game-changer we've been looking for.

Jacob nods, a sense of purpose and enthusiasm radiating from him.

JACOB (determined)

You've got it, JERSEY. I'll work through the night if I have to. We'll show Mr. Jones that we mean business and that we're worth every cent. It's time to make some magic with this data.

With a shared sense of determination, JERSEY and Jacob set out to work through the night, armed with Jacob's unconventional but potentially transformative approach to their complex problem.

Mabella sits on the couch, her face etched with frustration as she repeatedly dials JERSEY's number. Each unanswered call only deepens her irritation. She impatiently glances at the clock on the wall, the minutes dragging on.

MABELLA (muttering to herself)

Why isn't she picking up? This is important.

After a final, futile attempt to reach JERSEY, Mabella abruptly stands up, leaving her phone behind on the coffee table. She storms toward the door, her mood unmistakably sour.

Mabella slammed the door behind her, the sound of it echoing through the apartment like the final punctuation of a heated argument. The frustration that had been building up inside her for days now spilled over. Her chest tightened as she stormed through the entryway, her footsteps rapid, each one heavier than the last. She didn't want to be here, didn't want to feel this way, but she couldn't shake the sense of abandonment that had taken hold of her.

She had tried calling Jersey—more than once—but every call had gone unanswered. It wasn't like Jersey to avoid her, to retreat into the chaos of her work and the tangled mess of the company. Mabella knew that Jersey was dedicated, driven, but this was different. This felt like a wall, one that Mabella couldn't breach, no matter how many messages she left or how many calls she dialed.

Why is she doing this to us? Mabella's mind raced as she stepped out into the night. The city streets stretched before her, bathed in the harsh glow of neon lights. The streets were alive, full of people hurrying to their destinations, each wrapped up in their own lives, their own struggles. But Mabella felt isolated, disconnected from the world around her.

She quickened her pace, the sound of her heels tapping on the pavement almost drowned out by the bustle of the city. The further she walked, the more the world seemed to close in on her. She needed to talk to someone. Someone who would listen, someone who would understand. She needed comfort, a break from the constant stress that had taken over her life.

Finally, she reached the modest building she knew so well. The apartment was far from the glitzy, high-rise world that Jersey inhabited, but in that simplicity, Mabella found a strange sense of peace. It was a quiet space, far removed from the corporate jungle, where the noise of the city didn't intrude. She needed this refuge now more than ever.

The door to Vertina's apartment opened before Mabella even had the chance to knock, as if Vertina had been expecting her. Mabella didn't even need to speak for her friend to see the storm brewing in her eyes. Vertina, ever the perceptive one, simply stepped aside, her arms open in welcome.

VERTINA
(concerned, her voice soft but full of understanding)
"What's eating you up, Mabella?"

Mabella stepped into the apartment, the warmth of Vertina's presence soothing her just a little. She sank onto the couch, feeling the weight of the world on her shoulders, her breath coming in shallow bursts as she tried to find the words.

MABELLA
(exasperated, her voice tinged with frustration)
"It's Jersey, Vertina. She's so wrapped up in that company mess, she won't even pick up my calls anymore. It's like she's in a different world."

Her voice cracked with the weight of the emotions she had been holding in, and Vertina moved to sit next to her, offering her a tissue without a word. Mabella wiped at her eyes, trying to hold it together, but the dam had already broken. The frustration, the isolation, the helplessness—it all poured out in a rush.

MABELLA
(continuing, her voice thick with emotion)
"I don't know what's happening between us anymore. She's always so busy. Always involved in whatever drama Onica's family has dragged her into, and I'm just... I'm just here. Waiting. Hoping she'll call me back, hoping she'll remember that we're supposed to be in this together."

Vertina listened intently, not interrupting, just allowing Mabella to vent. She knew how much Mabella loved Jersey, and how deeply this situation had begun to affect her.

VERTINA
(gently, her tone both kind and grounded)
"Maybe she's not just avoiding you, Mabella. Maybe she's feeling overwhelmed by everything. You know how she gets when work takes over—when she gets pulled into something that she thinks is bigger than both of you."

Mabella rubbed her temples, trying to calm the storm inside. She had heard that excuse before—Jersey's passion for the work she did, the way she dove into it with such intensity. But it didn't make Mabella feel any less alone.

MABELLA
(shaking her head, frustrated)
"It's not just work, Vertina. It's *everything*. She's so consumed by it all, she can't even see what's happening to us. I don't know how much more of this I can take. I need her to *be here*. With me."

Vertina placed a hand on Mabella's, her touch firm, grounding.

VERTINA
(calmly, with conviction)
"Then maybe it's time to talk to her, Mabella. You can't keep this all inside. You need to let her know how you're feeling. She might be lost in her world, but that doesn't mean she's forgotten you."

Mabella let out a long, shaky breath. Vertina's words made sense, but the thought of confronting Jersey, of opening herself up to more hurt, felt like an impossible task. Still, she knew that silence would only make things worse.

MABELLA
(softly, almost to herself)
"I guess I have to, don't I? I can't just wait forever."

Vertina nodded, squeezing her hand.

VERTINA
(supportively)

"You don't have to do it alone, Mabella. I'm here. And no matter what, you deserve to be heard. You deserve someone who will be present in your life, just like you're there for them."

Mabella took in Vertina's words, her chest tightening with both relief and apprehension. It wasn't going to be easy, but she knew she couldn't go on feeling invisible in her relationship.

MABELLA
(with a faint, determined smile)
"Thanks, Vertina. You're right. I can't keep hiding from this."

Vertina smiled back, offering her friend a reassuring nod. The weight of the world didn't seem so heavy now. With the support of someone who cared, Mabella knew she could face whatever came next.

As the dim light of the apartment settled around them, Mabella sank further into the couch, her shoulders heavy with the weight of everything she had been holding inside. Vertina, sitting across from her, listened with unwavering attention, her warm gaze never leaving Mabella's face. The steady hum of the city outside the window seemed miles away in this quiet refuge, the noise of the world muffled by the comfort of understanding.

Mabella took a deep breath, her fingers fidgeting with the hem of her sleeve as she began to unravel the tangled mess in her heart.

MABELLA
(her voice fragile, vulnerable)
"It's like... Jersey and I are on different planets now. She's so caught up in the mess with the company and Onica's family that I don't even recognize her anymore. I feel like she's slipping away, and there's nothing I can do to stop it."

Vertina, ever the steady rock in Mabella's life, nodded sympathetically. She could see the pain in her friend's eyes, the frustration that had been building for weeks. She had witnessed Mabella's devotion to Jersey, how deeply she cared for her. And she knew that sometimes, no matter how much love one person gave, it wasn't always enough to bridge the gap created by overwhelming circumstances.

VERTINA
(gently, with a knowing look)
"I get it, Mabella. Relationships can be tricky, especially when work starts to take over. You know, sometimes people get so focused on their careers that they forget the other important things in life. It's like they're in their own world, as you said."

Mabella nodded, her fingers still twisting the fabric of her sleeve, her gaze distant as she reflected on Vertina's words. She had always understood Jersey's ambition, her drive. But it didn't make it any easier to feel left behind, to watch as her girlfriend became increasingly consumed by the chaos of her work. Mabella longed for the connection they once shared, but it felt like Jersey was slipping further away with every passing day.

MABELLA
(her voice quiet, filled with longing)
"Exactly. I know she's under so much pressure, and I want to be there for her, but it's just... It's like I don't even exist in her world anymore. Like... I'm fading into the background, and I don't know where I stand. It's so hard, Vertina. I don't know what to do."

Vertina's expression softened with empathy. She could see how deeply Mabella was hurting, the uncertainty eating away at her. She leaned forward slightly, her voice gentle but firm, offering the kind of advice only a true friend could.

VERTINA
(with quiet conviction)
"Well, maybe you two need to sit down and have an honest conversation about this. Communication is key. Let her know how you're feeling, how her work is affecting your relationship. She might not even realize it, Mabella."

Mabella paused, her brow furrowed as she considered Vertina's words. She had been so wrapped up in her own frustration, so caught up in the loneliness of it all, that she hadn't thought about the possibility that Jersey might not even realize how her actions were affecting her. Perhaps Jersey was so entrenched in her world of deadlines and board meetings that she hadn't seen the toll it was taking on their relationship.

But then there was the phone—Jersey hadn't even picked it up once.

MABELLA
(sighing, her shoulders slumping slightly)
"You're right, Vertina. I *know* I need to talk to her. I just... I wish she'd pick up her phone once in a while. I feel like I'm talking to a wall. I don't know how to reach her anymore. It's like... she's physically here, but emotionally? I'm just a stranger to her."

Vertina's heart ached for her friend. She knew how much Mabella loved Jersey, how much she wanted to make things work, but relationships took effort from both sides. And sometimes, that meant having the difficult conversations, even when the fear of confrontation lingered.

VERTINA
(with a reassuring smile, placing a hand gently on Mabella's)
"I know it's hard, but you have to try. If you don't, how will things ever change? You deserve to be heard, Mabella. You deserve to feel like you matter, too. And Jersey... she loves you. But sometimes, love gets lost in the chaos, and it takes a wake-up call to bring it back."

Mabella nodded slowly, the words sinking into her like a slow, steady tide. She knew Vertina was right, but the thought of confronting Jersey, of laying bare all the hurt and fear she had been holding onto, made her stomach twist. It wasn't easy to admit that something was wrong, that she felt neglected, that she was no longer sure of where she stood in their relationship. But if she didn't speak up, how would Jersey ever know?

MABELLA
(softly, but with a sense of resolution)
"I guess I don't have a choice, do I? I can't just keep waiting around, hoping things will fix themselves. I need to be honest with her. I need to let her know how I feel, even if it's scary."

Vertina squeezed her hand, her expression warm and encouraging.

VERTINA
(smiling kindly)
"You're stronger than you think, Mabella. And if Jersey truly cares about you, she'll listen. You just have to find the courage to speak your truth."

Mabella took a deep breath, a sense of calm settling over her as she looked at her friend. For the first time in days, the weight on her chest felt a little lighter. She wasn't alone. She didn't have to carry this burden by herself.

MABELLA
(with a small but genuine smile)
"Thanks, Vertina. I don't know what I'd do without you."

Vertina smiled back, her eyes filled with warmth and understanding.

VERTINA
(lightly, with a wink)
"You don't have to do anything alone, Mabella. We've got this."

And for the first time in a long while, Mabella felt a flicker of hope. Maybe things could be fixed after all—if only she could find the strength to make that first step.

deliver results that will far surpass the competition. And, Mr. Jones, you won't believe the potential returns on your investment."

Jacob stood up, his laptop open in front of him as he began to walk them through his intricate visualizations, graphs, and predictive models. The room, once filled with tension, was now buzzing with the possibilities that his insights promised. The weight of the data—so well-organized, so precise—was impossible to ignore. Every word he spoke sounded more convincing than the last.

JONES
(nodding slowly, intrigued, his skepticism melting away as he saw the scope of the project unfold before him)
"I have to admit, I was skeptical at first, but this... this is something else. It's not just about delivering; it's about delivering beyond expectations. I like it. I like it a lot."

Jersey exchanged a glance with Levy, their expressions a mixture of relief and triumph. They had known this moment would come—when Jones would finally see the potential of their work. It was exactly what they had hoped for, and now the deal was within reach.

JERSEY
(smiling, her fatigue forgotten for a moment as the excitement of the successful pitch washed over her)
"We knew you would, Mr. Jones. We're here to make this project a game-changer."

Levy, always the pragmatic one, leaned back in his chair, crossing his arms as he turned the conversation back to the financials, sealing their argument with a final, confident statement.

LEVY
(firmly, his voice carrying a sense of finality)
"And the 1.5 million dollars you're offering is a testament to our confidence in the results we'll achieve. We're committed to making this partnership a resounding success."

MY WEDDING CONTRACT TOO   111

Jones nodded, his fingers now still, his gaze focused on the data displayed on the screen. He could see the potential, the clear path forward, and he was ready to take the leap.

JONES
(with a grin, his earlier skepticism gone, replaced by genuine enthusiasm)
"Then let's not waste any more time. I'm in. I'm looking forward to what we can accomplish together."

A wave of relief swept through the room. The team exchanged quick glances, knowing that this deal, this partnership, was going to take them to places they had only dreamed of. Jersey, Levy, and Jacob had just turned a long, exhausting night into a triumph. The work had paid off, and now, with Jones on board, their project would not only succeed—it would surpass all expectations.

The team sealed the deal, shaking hands and exchanging excited words. But amid the jubilation, there was a quiet understanding that this was only the beginning. The real work, the true challenge, lay ahead. And for Jersey, the weight of the day was already beginning to lift, replaced by the exhilarating anticipation of what was to come.

The room, once filled with the tense hum of negotiations, now buzzed with an energy of triumph. Jersey stood at the head of the table, her arms outstretched in a gesture of disbelief and excitement. The moment had come, and they had nailed it.

JERSEY
(grinning widely, almost incredulous)
"Can you believe it, folks? We turned that million-dollar contract into 1.5 million! This project just became the opportunity of a lifetime. Levy, great job, and Jacob, you're a genius!"

The words tumbled out of her, and as they did, the team couldn't help but share in her elation. Levy, always the calm, collected one, couldn't contain the satisfaction in his smile. He had known this moment was possible, but seeing it happen in real time felt like a small victory for his meticulous planning and vision.

LEVY
(with a proud but humble smile)
"I knew we had something special to offer. Thanks to all of you for your hard work and innovative thinking. We're in for an exciting journey!"

Jacob, who had been leaning back in his chair, tapping his fingers against the edge of the table, let out a satisfied breath. It wasn't every day that his unconventional methods paid off so spectacularly. But today, they had.

JACOB
(grinning, full of quiet confidence)
"I'm just glad I could contribute to this fantastic outcome. Let's make this project a game-changer!"

As the team exchanged looks of accomplishment, their spirits lifted by the weight of their success, the room suddenly felt lighter, the air charged with possibility. The tension and sleepless nights were forgotten, replaced by the thrill of potential.

Jersey's gaze swept across her team, feeling the pride swell in her chest. This was what she had worked for—the moment when their combined efforts bore fruit. It wasn't just about the money; it was about proving to herself and to everyone else that they were capable of much more than anyone had originally believed.

The team gathered in a circle, raising their glasses for a celebratory toast. Their faces, lit by the glow of the city skyline outside the windows, reflected a mix of exhilaration and relief.

JERSEY
(with a determined smile, raising her glass)
"Here's to the future—one that just got a whole lot brighter. To making things happen, together."

As the glasses clinked together, the sense of camaraderie was palpable. They had done it. The project, once a distant dream, was now a tangible reality, and they had secured the resources to bring it to life. The possibilities were endless, and the team was ready to meet whatever challenge lay ahead.

Outside, the city seemed to glow brighter, as if it, too, was celebrating their success.

The door creaked open, and Jersey stumbled into the dimly lit hallway, her exhaustion evident in every step. Her shoulders slumped, eyes heavy with fatigue, and her face was drawn with the weight of a long, relentless day. She barely managed a faint smile as she walked through the door, but it quickly faded as she caught sight of Mabella standing there, still dressed in her security uniform, her posture rigid and unyielding.

JERSEY
(whispering, her voice low and tired)
"This is not a good day to talk about something very serious."

Mabella didn't respond immediately. She simply opened the door wider, stepping aside to let Jersey in, but her arms stayed crossed, and her eyes—hard and unreadable—followed Jersey's every move. When Jersey moved toward her, arms outstretched for a hug, Mabella stiffened, stepping back just enough to prevent the embrace.

There was a subtle shift in the air—a quiet resistance. The silence stretched between them, thick with the unspoken tension that had been building for weeks.

MABELLA
(her voice calm but sharp, laced with frustration)
"Did I say we're gonna talk about our wedding or your busy schedule at work? You forgot *us*, Jersey. Our plans... our life."

Jersey stopped, her hand still hanging in the air, awkwardly suspended between them. She could feel the sting of Mabella's words, but her exhaustion weighed too heavily on her shoulders to respond with the same intensity. Instead, she sighed, the weariness in her voice betraying her inner turmoil.

JERSEY
(weakly, with a dry chuckle)
"I can smell the wedding discussion from here."

Mabella's eyes narrowed, her lips pressing into a thin line. Her frustration was simmering just beneath the surface, and Jersey could feel it, even in her half-conscious state.

MABELLA
(with a hint of bitterness)
"Since you became the manager, you've lost interest in our plan to get a proper wedding. Or signing at home affairs. You know, the things that matter to *us*."

Jersey's tired eyes blinked slowly. She wasn't sure if it was the exhaustion clouding her thoughts, but her initial defensive reaction fizzled into something softer—something more uncertain.

JERSEY
(trying to keep her voice steady, though the fatigue in her tone was undeniable)
"Who said I lost interest?"

Mabella shook her head, her expression becoming more exasperated with every passing second.

MABELLA
"Then why are we not setting up a proper date, signing—being properly married? Why does it feel like *everyone* else is moving forward with their lives while we're stuck in limbo?"

Jersey took a deep breath, her shoulders sagging further. She had no energy left to argue. The weight of work, deadlines, and the relentless pressure of her role at the company had consumed her entirely. But the truth was, this moment had been coming for a long time.

JERSEY

(softly, avoiding Mabella's gaze)
"I have a lot to deal with right now at work..."

Mabella's gaze hardened, her arms still crossed, her voice now more resolute.

MABELLA
(firmly)
"I should be part of your worries, not just your work. *I* deserve to be part of your life, Jersey—not just a distant thought you push to the side when things get too overwhelming. I'm not just a checkbox on your to-do list."

The words hung in the air, heavy with unspoken truths. Jersey felt the weight of Mabella's disappointment sinking in, her exhaustion now mixing with guilt. She had been so consumed by everything else, she hadn't even realized how far she'd drifted from the one person who had always been there for her.

Jersey opened her mouth to speak but found no words—no explanations that could undo the quiet rupture she had caused. Mabella stood in front of her, arms still crossed, her eyes unwavering.

In that silence, it became painfully clear.

Jersey, her tired eyes still heavy from the long hours at work, reached into her pocket and pulled out her cell phone. With a few quick presses of the buttons, she sent a transfer. Moments later, a ringtone echoed through the quiet apartment, followed by the familiar beep of an incoming SMS. Mabella, standing near the kitchen counter, caught the sound and glanced over. A small smile tugged at her lips as she saw Jersey's gesture.

JERSEY
(with a hint of satisfaction)
"I transferred it..."

Mabella raised an eyebrow, curious. The phone beeped again, and she glanced at the message.

MABELLA

(laughing softly)
"This is almost my six months' salary money."

Jersey gave her a knowing smile, a mix of reassurance and affection in her eyes.

JERSEY
(gently)
"This is to assure you that we're still one team. Don't worry."

Mabella's expression softened as the tension between them slowly ebbed away, replaced by a warmth that only Jersey seemed able to provoke. Mabella let out a small sigh, a smile creeping onto his lips as he stepped toward Jersey.

MABELLA
(softening his voice, a playful tenderness in his words)
"I can see that, this is my love, my only superwoman."

Jersey chuckled, leaning back in her chair with a relaxed sigh.

JERSEY
"You can do whatever you want while I'm preparing some documents for work."

Mabella, now feeling a bit lighter, gave her one last smile before walking off toward the bedroom. Jersey, intent on finishing the paperwork, opened her laptop and sat down at the dining table. The soft clatter of keys was the only sound for a while, as Mabella returned to the living room with a new air about him. He was dressed differently—neatly, sharply—and the change in attire caught Jersey's eye.

Mabella stood in the doorway, hands casually tucked in his pockets, a grin spreading across his face.

MABELLA
(with a hint of mischief)
"How do I look now?"

Jersey looked up from her laptop, her gaze momentarily distracted by the striking change in Mabella. Her eyes lingered on him, the confidence in his posture, the sharpness of his new clothes.

JERSEY
(with a teasing smile)
"New clothes, you smell like a millionaire."

Mabella chuckled, leaning against the doorframe with a playful smirk.

MABELLA
(grinning, his tone light and teasing)
"My woman's a millionaire now, so what does that make me…?"

Jersey's eyes twinkled with amusement, setting the laptop aside. She stood up and walked toward him, her expression softening. She cupped his cheek in her hand, the affection between them undeniable.

JERSEY
(affectionately)
"You're my partner, Mabella. You're worth more than any money could buy."

For a moment, they stood there, the quiet intimacy of the exchange enveloping them. Mabella smiled back, feeling the weight of Jersey's words more than he had anticipated.

Their world may have been filled with complications and tension, but in this moment, nothing else mattered.

Jersey walked into her home, her body heavy with the weight of the day's accomplishments. The smooth click of the door closing behind her signified the end of another long day. She kicked off her shoes, the soft thud echoing through the quiet house, and her steps led her toward the dining area. The soft lighting and the familiar comfort of her home brought a sense of contentment that settled deep in her chest.

As she stood there, looking over the simple, well-kept space, a smile tugged at the corner of her lips. She couldn't help but chuckle, thinking back on how far they had come. From the sleepless nights to the tense negotiations, everything had finally started to fall into place. But the road ahead was still long, and she knew it would take more than just one victory to secure their future.

Exhaustion crept up on her, sinking into her bones, urging her to give in. She made her way to the couch, letting her body collapse into the soft cushions. Her eyelids grew heavy as the peace of the moment overwhelmed her, and before she knew it, sleep claimed her—deep, restful, and filled with the promise of what lay ahead.

INT. ONICA'S LIVING ROOM - DAY

The stillness of Onica's living room felt unnerving. The air was thick with a sense of unease, the silence only interrupted by the faint hum of the refrigerator in the corner. Onica lay motionless on the couch, her form barely visible beneath the blanket draped over her.

Jersey stood in the doorway, her hand still clutching a wad of cash she had brought with her, the money meant to help her friend with the mounting bills. She hesitated, uncertainty clouding her thoughts as she looked down at Onica. What had she been hoping to accomplish here? Would this gesture—this simple act of kindness—be enough?

JERSEY
(softly, to herself)
"I hope she'll be okay. I just wanted to check on her... help her out a bit."

Her voice faltered as she glanced around the room, the lingering tension thick in the air. There had been so much turmoil between them, so many unanswered questions. Jersey wasn't sure if this was the right thing to do, but she couldn't stand seeing Onica like this, isolated and struggling.

Suddenly, Onica stirred, her body shifting beneath the blanket as she regained consciousness. Her eyes opened slowly, unfocused at first, before snapping to attention. Upon seeing Jersey standing in her living room, the fury in her eyes was immediate.

ONICA
(enraged, her voice sharp)
"You! What are you doing here, JERSEY?"

Jersey flinched, the anger in Onica's voice slicing through the air like a blade. She was caught off guard, unsure of how to respond to the hostility that seemed to radiate from her.

JERSEY
(nervously, trying to explain)
"Onica, I... I just came to see if you're okay. I brought some money to help with the bills."

Before Jersey could finish her sentence, Onica's rage boiled over. In a swift motion, she reached for the kettle on the nearby counter, its contents still steaming. With a swift, violent movement, Onica threw the boiling water directly at Jersey.

JERSEY
(screaming in pain)
"Ahh! Onica, what are you doing?!"

The water hit Jersey with a searing force, the sudden shock of the heat making her gasp. She stumbled backward, her hand instinctively going to her face where the scalding water had splashed. Pain radiated through her, and her heart raced with a mixture of shock and disbelief.

Without another word, Jersey bolted for the door, her movements frantic as she stumbled toward the exit. The pain from the burn was sharp, but the deeper pain—the emotional weight of the betrayal—was far worse. As she reached the door, she glanced back one last time, only to see Onica standing there, her eyes filled with a storm of resentment and anger.

Jersey didn't look back as she fled into the cold air outside, her heart pounding. The door slammed behind her, and the silence that followed felt like a suffocating weight on her chest.

Inside, Onica stood motionless, her body trembling with the aftermath of the outburst. Anger and regret swirled within her, but there was no way to take it back now. As the sound of Jersey's footsteps faded away, Onica was left alone in the bitter stillness of her own making.

The room is still and tense, the quiet punctuated only by Onica's shallow, labored breaths. She sits on the couch, clutching her chest, her face pale and slick with sweat. Her body trembles as though it's fighting something far more insidious than just physical pain.

Dr. Reyes stands beside her, his brow furrowed with concern. His professional demeanor remains steady, but the worry in his eyes betrays the urgency of the situation.

DR. REYES

(firmly)

"Onica, I strongly recommend that you go to the hospital. The pain you're experiencing is severe, and we need to run some tests to understand what's happening."

Onica shakes her head, her breath coming in quick, shallow gasps. The pressure in her chest is growing, but there's a stubbornness to her, a refusal to accept the reality of her condition.

ONICA

(resistant, her voice strained)

"I can't go to the hospital, Doctor. I'll be fine; it's just stress. I've been under a lot of pressure, that's all."

As she speaks, the pain spikes again—sharp, violent—and she gasps, her body stiffening. Her face contorts in agony, and for a moment, she can't breathe. The world feels as though it's closing in around her. Her hand trembles as it presses against her chest, trying desperately to push the pain away, but it lingers.

Dr. Reyes doesn't hesitate. His hand gently but firmly touches her shoulder, his voice steady and unwavering.

DR. REYES
(urgent, his tone rising slightly)
"Onica, we can't take any chances. Your health is the top priority. I can see that you're in tremendous pain right now. We need to act fast."

Onica tries to wave him off, her breath ragged as she fights to maintain control. But the pain is overwhelming, and her vision blurs at the edges. She can feel the tightness in her chest, the thumping of her heart, each beat more erratic than the last.

The moments stretch on in painful silence, the weight of her decision looming. Finally, the pain reaches a crescendo, and she can no longer ignore the reality of her situation. With a weak nod, Onica relents, her voice barely a whisper.

ONICA
(labored, defeated)
"Alright... I'll go. Please, help me."

Dr. Reyes's expression softens with a quiet relief as he helps her to her feet. Her legs wobble beneath her, unsteady from both the pain and the exhaustion, but his steady hands guide her. He leads her toward the door, moving quickly yet carefully, his every step a measure of concern for her well-being.

Together, they make their way out of the apartment, the door closing behind them with a soft click. As they step into the dimming light of the evening, the air is cool against Onica's flushed skin, but it does little to alleviate the growing tightness in her chest. With every step, the pain pulses, but she keeps her focus on the moment ahead—on the hospital that might hold the answers.

The sound of their hurried footsteps echoes in the empty hallway, a stark contrast to the silence that had filled Onica's apartment just moments before.

The soft beeping of machines fills the quiet space, a rhythmic reminder of the fragility of life. Onica lies in the hospital bed, her body tense, every breath a struggle against the dull, persistent pain that clings to her chest. The sterile white walls of the room feel both foreign and suffocating, a stark contrast to the hustle and chaos of her usual world. Her face is pale, her brow furrowed in discomfort as she stirs, finally breaking free from the haze of sleep.

Her eyes flutter open, the light from the window cutting through the heavy silence like a distant memory. She blinks a few times, the world slowly coming into focus. Dr. Reyes is standing by her side, looking down at her with concern, his hands holding her medical charts. He notices the slight movement, his voice soft and reassuring.

DR. REYES
(gentle)
"Onica, you're awake. How are you feeling?"

Her voice is hoarse, barely a whisper, but the frustration in her tone is unmistakable.

ONICA
(strained)
"I'm in pain, Doctor, but I'll manage. I need to get back to work... the readings... there's so much to do."

She tries to sit up, the effort leaving her breathless, but before she can get very far, Dr. Reyes steps closer, his hand gently pushing her back down onto the pillow.

DR. REYES
(calm, soothing)
"I understand your dedication, but right now, your health comes first. You need to rest and recover for a few days before we can consider any readings or work."

Onica's eyes darken with frustration. The thought of falling behind, of losing momentum, gnaws at her. The work—her work—has always been her lifeline, and she can't bear the idea of stepping away from it, even for a short time. But the pain in her chest is undeniable, and even her stubbornness can't ignore the toll it's taking on her body.

She sighs deeply, a mix of resignation and disappointment in her gaze.

ONICA
(reluctantly)
"Alright, Doctor... if it's necessary... I'll rest. But I can't be away for too long."

Dr. Reyes gives her a sympathetic smile, his hand resting briefly on her shoulder as he makes a reassuring adjustment to the IV drip beside her bed.

DR. REYES
(reassuring)
"Don't worry, Onica. We'll monitor your progress, and we'll have you back on your feet in no time. Your health is our priority."

The words are meant to comfort, but for Onica, the weight of them only adds to the pressure. The need to get back to her work, to prove to herself and everyone around her that she's not broken, is overwhelming. She closes her eyes again, trying to will herself into the rest her body demands, but her mind is racing.

Dr. Reyes steps back, making a few notes on her chart. As he moves quietly around the room, Onica feels the softness of the pillow beneath her head and the weight of her fatigue. The pain is still there, but it is manageable now, subdued by the promise of rest. Her eyes flutter closed again, the pull of sleep strong, but her thoughts are anything but peaceful. The world outside, with all its demands, continues to spin, and she can't help but feel like she's slipping further away from it, even if just for a short time.

For now, she will rest. But it's clear that the battle is far from over.

The soft hum of the machines is a constant reminder of the fragility of life. Onica lies in the sterile quiet of her hospital room, her eyes heavy with exhaustion and the weight of the uncertain future hanging over her. Ms. Martin, her lawyer, sits by her side, carefully flipping through some legal papers, but her gaze is frequently drawn to Onica's pale face, the lines of worry etched deep across her features.

Dr. Reyes enters the room, his steps measured and professional. He approaches the bed where Onica and Ms. Martin are seated, a calm but serious expression on his face. He takes a moment to glance at Onica's charts before addressing both of them.

DR. REYES
(professional)
"Ms. Martin, I've reviewed Onica's tests, and her condition is stable for now. However, we're still investigating the cause of her health issues. We need more time to make a conclusive diagnosis."

Ms. Martin nods, her lips pressed together in concern. She glances at Onica, whose gaze is unwavering despite the pain she's clearly enduring.

MS. MARTIN
(concerned)
"Thank you, Doctor. We understand that. But can you give us any insights into what might be the problem?"

Dr. Reyes exhales deeply, the weight of uncertainty still present in the air. He adjusts his glasses, looking from Ms. Martin to Onica before responding.

DR. REYES
(thoughtful)
"It's too early to say definitively. We're considering various factors, including stress and other health-related issues. Further tests will be conducted to get a clearer picture."

Onica, though weakened, interjects with a voice filled with determination, her eyes locked on Dr. Reyes and her lawyer.

ONICA
(resolute)
"Ms. Martin, please make sure everything is in order. I need to fight for my estate. We can't afford to lose any time."

Ms. Martin places a hand gently on Onica's, her tone supportive but firm.

MS. MARTIN
(supportive)
"Don't worry, Onica. I'll handle everything, and we'll fight for what's rightfully yours. Your health is our priority, but your estate will also be protected."

Dr. Reyes looks at them both, his voice gentle but insistent, trying to balance both the legal and medical concerns in the room.

DR. REYES
(emphatic)
"Let's focus on your recovery, Onica. We'll address the legal matters in due course. Your health comes first."

Onica sighs, the weight of the doctor's words settling over her like a shroud. Her eyes close, and for a moment, she simply listens to the rhythmic beeping of the machines, the only constant in the storm of thoughts racing through her mind. As Dr. Reyes and Ms. Martin continue to discuss her condition, Onica drifts back into a restless sleep, her body weary but her mind still racing.

The afternoon light filters through the blinds, casting long shadows on the sterile walls of the hospital room. Onica stirs in her bed, her eyes fluttering open at the sound of footsteps. A figure stands in the doorway, silhouetted by the light—a woman with a mysterious air about her.

Onica's pulse quickens, her eyes narrowing as she recognizes the newcomer. It's Lucy, the stranger who had appeared in her life seemingly out of nowhere, claiming to have information about the marriage certificate mix-up.

LUCY
(mysterious)
"Onica, I've heard about the mix-up with your marriage certificates. It's a terrible situation, but I think I might know something important."

Onica's heart skips a beat, a flicker of hope igniting in her chest. She sits up a little straighter, ignoring the wave of pain that pulses through her body.

ONICA
(hopeful)
"You do? Please, tell me what you know. I need to get to the bottom of this."

Lucy takes a step closer, her expression guarded but still carrying an air of intrigue. Onica leans forward, eager, almost desperate for any information that might unravel the mystery that has plagued her.

LUCY
(vague)
"I suspect that there might have been foul play involved. You see, I overheard the Pastor and Jersey talking in a restaurant just a day before the wedding."

Onica's breath catches in her throat. Jersey. The woman she's been battling to understand, the one who seems to hold all the answers, yet is so elusive.

ONICA
(intrigued)
"What were they talking about?"

Lucy hesitates, a flicker of discomfort passing across her face. Her voice drops to a near whisper.

LUCY
(hesitant)
"I couldn't hear everything clearly, but they seemed awfully friendly, and they mentioned something about documents. I couldn't make out the details."

Onica feels a sinking sensation in her stomach. The brief hope she had felt begins to fade, replaced by a cold realization. The conversation is too vague, the details too scattered for it to hold any weight. She clenches her fists, the frustration bubbling up.

ONICA
(disappointed)
"Lucy, this is important, but we need concrete evidence to prove anything. Without it, I can't fight for what's rightfully mine."

Lucy's face softens with regret, her shoulders slumping slightly.

LUCY
(apologetic)
"I understand, Onica. I wish I could offer more, but this is all I know."

The weight of the moment hangs heavily between them, Onica's gaze fixed on Lucy, trying to piece together what little she has been given. There are no answers here, not yet, but the need to find them is more urgent than ever.

The sterile smell of antiseptic fills the air as Onica sits on the edge of an examination table, her hands trembling slightly as she grips the edge of the paper gown. Dr. Reyes enters the room, his expression grave, and the moment he closes the door behind him, Onica knows this isn't just another checkup.

DR. REYES
(somber, professional)

"Onica, I need to be honest with you. The test results have revealed some serious health concerns. Your blood pressure is dangerously high, and there's a significant issue with your heart. It's not functioning as it should, and that's putting immense stress on your body."

Onica's world seems to slow down, her pulse pounding in her ears. Her hands shake, and she can feel the chill of fear crawl up her spine.

ONICA
(anxiously)
"How bad is it, Doctor?"

Dr. Reyes meets her gaze, his eyes filled with sympathy but also with a kind of quiet certainty.

DR. REYES
(with empathy)
"I won't sugarcoat it. Your heart condition is quite severe, and we've also observed some signs of brain damage, likely due to lack of oxygen. These findings are a matter of great concern."

The room feels smaller, the air thicker. Onica's breath catches in her throat, and for a moment, it feels like the world is collapsing around her. Her mind spins with fear, with all the things she has left to fight for—her work, her estate, her life. But now, none of that matters if she can't hold onto her health.

ONICA
(voice quivering)
"Is there anything that can be done, Doctor? Any treatment or surgery?"

Dr. Reyes places a hand on the counter, his voice steady but filled with the weight of what he must say next.

DR. REYES

(gravely)
"We'll need to bring in a specialist to assess the full extent of your condition. We can explore treatment options, but I won't deny that your situation is complex and challenging."

Onica swallows hard, trying to hold back the tears that threaten to spill. There's a deep sense of helplessness, a realization that the fight she thought she was ready for may be far more difficult than she had imagined.

Jersey walks briskly down the corridor, her heels clicking against the cold floor with a rhythm that matches her thoughts—focused, determined, and moving quickly. She can feel the weight of the day pressing on her shoulders, but she forces herself to push through, knowing the importance of the appointment that lies ahead.

As she approaches Dr. Reyes' office, another figure comes into view, walking just ahead. It's Dr. Elie, her trusted OB-GYN. She smiles politely when she notices Jersey, but there's a hint of concern in her gaze as she takes in Jersey's posture. Dr. Elie pauses, her expression softening.

DR. ELIE
(apologetic)
"Apologies for keeping you waiting."

Jersey doesn't respond immediately. Instead, she exhales deeply, clearly exhausted but trying not to show it.

DR. ELIE
(noticing Jersey's body language)
"You look strained, Jersey. That can't be healthy for the baby."

Jersey gives a small, tired smile but shakes her head lightly.

JERSEY
(exhaling)
"I'm going to try to keep up with your advice, Dr. Elie. I know it's important."

There's a brief pause, and Jersey looks at the ground, her brow furrowing in thought. She gathers herself before continuing, her voice quiet but resolute.

JERSEY
(concerned, looking up at Dr. Elie)
"I'm the only one who understands just how important this pregnancy is."

Dr. Elie's expression softens, understanding the weight behind Jersey's words. She places a hand gently on Jersey's arm.

DR. ELIE
(with a reassuring tone)
"Are you still taking care of yourself? Making sure you're getting the rest you need?"

Jersey looks away briefly, her eyes clouding with a mixture of sadness and determination. She hesitates for a moment before answering.

JERSEY
(murmuring)
"I have to. Even though the baby's father is no longer here... this is a special child. I have to do everything right."

Dr. Elie nods, her eyes filled with empathy. She can see the weight of Jersey's grief mixed with the fierce love she already feels for the child growing inside her.

DR. ELIE
(kindly)
"Let me do a check-up now and see how the baby's progressing. It'll put your mind at ease."

Jersey nods and moves toward the examination table, her movements slightly stiff but determined. Dr. Elie steps aside to close the blue curtains, giving Jersey privacy as she lies down on the bed. The gentle hum of the room fills the air, and Jersey's breath slows as she tries to relax.

As Dr. Elie adjusts the equipment, she glances at Jersey, her hands steady and professional. Jersey looks up at her, her gaze intense with both anticipation and a quiet worry.

DR. ELIE
(smiling gently as she works)
"The baby is looking strong. It's like a magnet, Jersey. Full of life and energy. A little sunshine."

Jersey's eyes widen at the words, and a soft smile tugs at the corner of her lips. It's the news she's been longing to hear, and for the first time in a while, she allows herself to feel a glimmer of hope.

JERSEY
(with a sense of relief, a tear threatening to fall)
"Dr. Elie, this is big news for me. Peter would be so proud. He would have realized we were meant for each other... for this."

There's a moment of silence between them, as Jersey's words linger in the air. Dr. Elie, though professional, can see the depth of emotion in Jersey's eyes. She's holding onto the memory of Peter, her love for him still alive in every beat of her heart, but now there's this new life growing within her.

DR. ELIE
(softly)
"I'm sure he would be, Jersey. And you're doing a wonderful job. You'll be an amazing mother."

Jersey closes her eyes for a moment, letting the words wash over her. The road ahead will be difficult, but for this child, she will carry on, step by step. The future, though uncertain, now feels a little brighter.

Jersey is seated at the sleek, polished conference table, surrounded by her team as she reviews the latest project documents. The air is thick with the hum of high-level business discussions, but Jersey's mind is elsewhere, focused on making sure every detail is perfect. The door to the boardroom creaks open, and a familiar voice cuts through the meeting.

LUCY
(firmly)
"Jersey, we need to talk about what happened with those marriage certificates. I was there, remember?"

Jersey looks up, startled. She hadn't expected Lucy, one of the bridesmaids from her wedding, to be here, let alone confront her in front of her colleagues. Her heart skips a beat, and she immediately feels the tension rise in the room.

JERSEY
(defensive)
"Lucy, I have no idea what you're talking about. Everything was a blur that day."

Lucy stands in the doorway, her posture rigid with determination. The casual demeanor that she normally wears is gone. She steps forward, closing the distance between them, her eyes fixed on Jersey with a mixture of suspicion and frustration.

LUCY
(determined, her voice low but insistent)
"I find it hard to believe that you don't remember. I overheard you and the Pastor talking about documents just a day before the wedding. Now, there's a mess with Onica's marriage certificate."

Jersey's face tightens, her grip on the papers in front of her tightening. She can feel the walls closing in, and suddenly the room feels a lot smaller than it should. She tries to maintain her composure, but Lucy's words sting. She's caught off guard, and it shows.

JERSEY
(exasperated, trying to maintain control)

"Look, Lucy, I can't remember every conversation I had back then. It was a chaotic time. Besides, even if there was a mix-up, it wasn't intentional."

Lucy steps closer, not giving an inch. Her gaze is unwavering, a mixture of concern and disbelief.

LUCY
(skeptical, raising an eyebrow)
"Was it? Because it's hard to ignore the timing of it all."

The weight of Lucy's words hangs heavy in the air, and Jersey can feel her composure beginning to crack. The nagging feeling of doubt that has been creeping in for weeks grows louder. She wants to deny it all, to brush it off as just another misunderstanding, but something about Lucy's persistence makes it hard to shake the feeling that there's more to the story than she's willing to admit.

JERSEY
(nervous, her voice faltering slightly)
"I can't prove anything, Lucy. I just want to move forward and make things right."

Jersey's words hang in the air, but they feel empty, as if they hold no weight. She knows she's not being entirely honest with herself, and that uncertainty gnaws at her. Lucy, sensing the shift in Jersey's demeanor, doesn't back down.

LUCY
(quietly, but with a sense of urgency)
"You can't just brush this aside, Jersey. People's lives are tangled up in this. Onica deserves answers, and so do you."

Jersey's hands begin to tremble slightly, and she looks away from Lucy, her gaze now lost in the blur of the conference room's walls. The sense of unease grows. The power dynamics in her life—work, relationships, and now this lingering mystery—are shifting in ways she doesn't fully understand.

JERSEY

(softly, almost to herself)
"I just don't know what to do anymore."

Lucy's eyes soften, a momentary flicker of compassion crossing her face before the resolve returns.

LUCY
(quiet but firm)
"Then start by telling the truth, Jersey. No more hiding. No more running from it."

Jersey opens her mouth to say something, but the words catch in her throat. She wants to defend herself, to argue that she's done nothing wrong. But in the pit of her stomach, she knows something is off, something she's been trying to ignore. The confrontation leaves her feeling exposed, like a crack in the foundation of her carefully constructed world.

Lucy turns and walks out of the room without another word, leaving Jersey to wrestle with the storm of questions swirling in her mind. The boardroom is silent again, but the tension in the air is palpable. Jersey lets out a shaky breath, realizing that Lucy's visit has stirred up more than just a legal mix-up—it's unraveling the truth that she's tried so hard to bury.

Onica shuffled into the kitchen, her movements slow and weary. The sterile white walls felt like a suffocating reminder of the hospital she had just left behind, and she longed for the warmth of normalcy, even if it was just for a few quiet moments. She reached for the coffee pot, the comforting ritual of brewing something familiar in a world that felt foreign and heavy. The rich scent of the coffee grounds filled the air, and for a brief second, she allowed herself to breathe, to hope for a moment of peace.

But then, a sharp knock at the door broke the fragile silence.

Onica froze, her hand still hovering above the coffee pot. She wasn't expecting anyone—who could be visiting her now? Hesitant, she set the pot down and walked towards the door, feeling the weight of her exhaustion settling deeper with each step. As she opened it, she was met with two young filmmakers, standing on her doorstep with cameras and microphones in tow.

FILMMAKER 1
(enthusiastic, almost gleaming with excitement)
"Hello, Ms. Onica! We're here to interview you about the story of the marriage certificates mix-up. It's a fascinating and thought-provoking tale!"

The words hit Onica like a slap to the face. She blinked, stunned for a moment by the audacity of it all. They were standing there, cameras poised, completely unaware—or worse, completely indifferent—to the pain she had endured.

ONICA
(irritated, her voice sharp and fatigued)
"I don't want to be interviewed."

Her chest tightened, and her grip on the door tightened as well, her fingers feeling the sharp edges of the wood beneath them. "This story has caused enough pain," she continued, her voice rising despite her attempt to stay composed. "It's not a fascinating tale; it's a nightmare. It won't help anyone; it'll just create more depression after losing my husband."

The filmmakers exchanged a look, their enthusiasm faltering in the face of Onica's raw, unfiltered emotion. **FILMMAKER 2** stepped forward, his expression apologetic but still laced with the professional distance that people like him always seemed to carry.

FILMMAKER 2
(genuinely apologetic, but still trying to salvage the situation)
"We didn't mean to upset you, Ms. Onica. We thought it could shed light on the issues surrounding marriage certificates. Something to help others, maybe…"

But Onica was already shaking her head, the weight of the day and the weight of everything she had lost pressing down on her, refusing to let the intrusion slide.

ONICA
(firm, unwavering)
"I appreciate your interest, but I've been through enough. Please leave."

Her words were final, as sharp as the edge of a broken heart, and without waiting for another word, she closed the door with a soft, yet deliberate, click. She could feel the tension in her body, the adrenaline of the confrontation rushing through her veins, but she didn't allow herself to linger on it. She wouldn't. She couldn't.

Inside, her apartment felt quiet again, but it wasn't peaceful. The silence had an almost suffocating quality to it, the way silence often does after an argument or an emotional outburst. But she was done. No more people trying to turn her life into a story. No more strangers poking into the rawest parts of her existence.

Onica turned back to the kitchen, her legs heavy as if weighted with the grief she'd been carrying for far too long. She poured herself a cup of coffee, letting the warmth of the mug seep into her cold fingers, her eyes staring blankly out the window. She would have peace, even if it was just for this moment. For now, that was all she could hold on to.

The tension in Jersey's office was palpable as the two film crew members stood near the door, their cameras hanging like burdens at their sides. Jersey sat behind her polished desk, her posture rigid and her eyes narrowed in frustration. The soft hum of the office was broken only by the eager words of the filmmakers.

FILM CREW MEMBER 1
(enthusiastically, as though they hadn't already sensed the hostility in the room)

"Ms. Jersey, we believe this story has the potential to make a compelling documentary that can shed light on the issues surrounding marriage certificates. It's a story that could really resonate with people."

Jersey's jaw clenched, her fingers pressing into the surface of her desk, her irritation brewing like a storm. Without missing a beat, she shot back.

JERSEY
(voice rising, clearly defensive)

"A documentary? Are you trying to pull my status down by making a film about desperate people?" She leaned forward, her gaze sharp, and her voice low and cutting. "This isn't some feel-good story. It's not something you can spin into entertainment for your audience."

FILM CREW MEMBER 2
(calm, trying to defuse the tension)

"We understand your concerns, Ms. Jersey, but we believe it's essential to raise awareness about the flaws in the system. The public needs to see how these issues affect real lives."

The words felt like they didn't reach her. Jersey's frustration only intensified, her fingers now gripping the edge of her desk as if it were her only anchor in the chaos that surrounded her.

JERSEY
(voice firm, almost biting)

"You won't win this, trust me. If you think you can dig into courtrooms and underground systems and come out with some tidy narrative, you're in for a rude awakening." Her eyes flared with cold fury. "The legal battles are far from over, and you won't have access to what you're looking for. So don't even try."

The film crew members exchanged nervous glances, the resolve they had entered with beginning to waver. They hadn't anticipated such resistance, but Jersey's presence was commanding, her warning sharp enough to pierce through their initial excitement.

FILM CREW MEMBER 1
(cautiously, stepping back from the confrontation)
"We'll consider your words, Ms. Jersey. But our intention is to tell a story, not take sides."

Jersey's lips curled into a thin, controlled smile, though there was no warmth in it—only the unmistakable edge of someone who knew how difficult the road ahead would be for them. She leaned back in her chair, her eyes locked onto them as if daring them to take one more step toward this battle.

JERSEY
(warning, with quiet intensity)
"Just be prepared for what you're getting into. This is no ordinary story. You won't walk away with what you think you will."

The filmmakers stood in stunned silence for a moment, the weight of her words sinking in. They had expected a challenge, yes, but this... this was something far more complex. They glanced at each other, unspoken hesitation settling in.

After a long, quiet beat, **FILM CREW MEMBER 2** nodded, and they both turned to leave. Jersey watched them go, her expression unwavering, as if she'd already won a battle she hadn't even chosen to fight.

As the door clicked shut behind them, she allowed herself a small sigh of relief. Another challenge, another obstacle. But she knew this wasn't over. It was only just beginning.

Onica sat on the couch, the quiet hum of the room only punctuated by the faint ticking of the clock on the wall. The weight of her recent health scare lingered heavily on her, leaving her feeling drained and uneasy. She hadn't been able to focus on much else, and despite the silence of her home, her mind was loud with unanswered questions about what came next.

Suddenly, the sound of the doorbell broke through the stillness, and she frowned, not expecting any visitors. With a hesitant sigh, she rose from the couch, her body still feeling weak from the strain of her recovery. She opened the door, and there he was—her **former boyfriend**, standing on her doorstep, holding a bouquet of flowers in his hands.

A rush of emotions stirred in Onica as she took in his familiar, earnest expression. She hadn't seen him in months, but the sight of him brought back a flood of memories—both good and painful.

FORMER BOYFRIEND
(his voice smooth, almost charming)
"Onica, I've missed you so much. I couldn't stop thinking about us."

Onica's heart skipped a beat, but she quickly masked it with caution. Her hand rested lightly on the doorframe, and her voice was guarded as she responded.

ONICA
(steadily)
"What are you doing here?"

He stepped closer, his eyes soft with hope, the bouquet still extended towards her.

FORMER BOYFRIEND
"I brought you these. I thought you might appreciate them."

Onica hesitated, her thoughts swirling. Despite her better judgment, she reached out and took the flowers, the cool stems a stark contrast to the warmth of his hand. She stepped back, closing the door slightly behind her, her eyes fixed on the arrangement in her hands as if they could somehow give her the right words.

ONICA
(firmly but with an edge of weariness)
"Thank you, but this isn't the right time. I'm still dealing with a lot."

He didn't step back, though. Instead, he shifted slightly, a look of persistence in his eyes.

FORMER BOYFRIEND
(softly, leaning in just a little)
"I understand, Onica. I was there for you before, and I can be there for you now. We can start over, just like old times."

The words hung in the air, and Onica felt the familiar tug of old affection. But she shook her head, setting the flowers on the nearest table. She wasn't about to let nostalgia cloud her judgment.

ONICA
(sharply, her voice hardening)
"Look, our past didn't work out for a reason. I'm not interested in rekindling things right now. I have other priorities."

The words were like a wall she placed firmly between them. She saw the brief flash of disappointment in his eyes, but it was quickly replaced with something else—a stubborn resolve.

FORMER BOYFRIEND
(with a quiet, almost mocking smile)
"Onica, I've been patient. Peter won your heart because of money, but he's gone now. I'm still here, and I won't wait forever. Think about it."

Onica's frustration flared, the sting of his words cutting deeper than she expected. She took a steady breath, the resolve within her growing stronger.

ONICA
(coldly)
"I appreciate your feelings, but this isn't the right time. I need space to figure things out on my own."

He stood there for a moment, his expression unreadable, before he finally seemed to accept her words. He let out a deep sigh, his shoulders slumping slightly as he stepped back from the door.

FORMER BOYFRIEND

(defeated, but with a final, lingering note of hope in his voice)
"Okay, Onica. I'll respect your decision. But remember, I'm not going to be around forever."

With that, he turned and walked away, the soft echo of his footsteps fading as Onica watched him disappear into the distance. The door clicked shut behind her, and she stood there for a long moment, the silence of her home settling over her once again.

Onica glanced at the bouquet of flowers sitting on the table, their vibrant colors a stark contrast to the heaviness in her chest. She wasn't ready for any of this. She needed to sort out her life, her health, her future—and the last thing she needed was the past barging in.

Taking a deep breath, Onica walked away from the door and toward the couch. She sat down, her fingers brushing against the delicate petals, but her mind was already moving forward, focused on what mattered most: her own healing, her own strength, and the future she was going to build—without looking back.

In a quiet and dimly lit kitchen, Onica sits alone at the table, a daunting array of medication bottles spread out before her. The room is filled with an eerie silence, broken only by the soft ticking of a nearby wall clock.

As she gazes at the pills in her hand, her face is etched with profound worry. Onica's fingers tremble as she carefully organizes the various pills. The weight of her recent diagnosis and the uncertain future ahead cast a long shadow over her.

She knows that her health struggles have taken center stage, demanding her immediate attention and concern.

The medications were laid out in front of her on the table, their sterile, clinical bottles a constant reminder of her fragility. Onica stared at them blankly, the weight of her diagnosis pressing down on her chest like an invisible hand. It was a reality she couldn't ignore, no matter how much she wished she could. The thought of the future—what it would hold, what she might lose—was overwhelming.

A gentle knock at the door broke through the haze of her thoughts. Onica blinked, momentarily disoriented, and then slowly pushed herself out of the chair. She felt drained, as though the mere act of moving took more effort than she had left in her body. When she opened the door, Lizer was standing there, a warm smile on her face, but Onica could see the concern in her eyes.

ONICA
(wearily)
"Lizer, it's been a day..."

LIZER
(compassionately)
"I know, my dear. I've been so worried about you."

Onica's heart softened at the sight of her friend. Lizer had been there for her through thick and thin, a steady presence in her life when everything else felt uncertain. She stepped aside to let Lizer in, closing the door gently behind her.

ONICA
(sighing, her voice quiet)
"It's just... everything's so complicated now. My health, the company, the court case... It feels like I'm trapped in a never-ending storm."

Lizer crossed the room and, without a word, placed a hand on Onica's shoulder, a silent gesture of comfort. Onica leaned into it slightly, grateful for the quiet support.

LIZER
(softly)
"You're a strong and resilient woman, Onica. I've seen you overcome so much in the past, and you'll overcome this, too."

Onica blinked back tears, her chest tightening with the weight of her fears. She hadn't allowed herself to break down in front of anyone, not even Lizer, but the floodgates were threatening to open now.

ONICA

(teary-eyed, her voice shaky)

"I'm scared, Lizer. Scared of what's to come, scared of losing everything. I never imagined my life would take this turn."

Lizer's eyes softened, her grip on Onica's shoulder tightening in solidarity. She knew all too well the turmoil her friend was facing.

LIZER

(gently)

"Life can be unpredictable, my friend. But you have a fighting spirit, and you've always found a way through. You're not alone in this. We're all here for you, ready to support you through this storm."

Onica nodded, taking a deep breath as she absorbed her words. The tears didn't fall, but the pressure in her chest eased, just a little.

ONICA

(quietly, a flicker of hope in her voice)

"Thank you, Lizer. I needed to hear that."

Lizer didn't need any more words. She stepped forward, pulling Onica into a tight hug, and for a moment, the world outside melted away. It was just the two of them, sharing a quiet moment of reassurance.

LIZER

(whispering softly into her ear)

"You're stronger than you think, and no matter how tough it gets, we'll weather this storm together. You'll see, brighter days will come."

Onica closed her eyes, letting the warmth of the hug sink into her bones. The storm was far from over, but for the first time in days, she believed maybe—just maybe—she could make it through.

The room is bathed in soft, natural light, its warmth filling the space with a calming aura. A plush couch and two chairs are arranged in a circle, inviting openness and conversation. The atmosphere is serene, a sharp contrast to the tension that lingers between **JERSEY** and **ONICA**. Both women sit on opposite sides, their body language stiff and guarded. Their expressions, a mixture of apprehension and determination, reflect the weight of everything they've been through.

The **THERAPIST**, a calm and empathetic professional, sits in a chair nearby. Her presence is soothing, her demeanor one of quiet understanding.

THERAPIST
(gentle, yet steady)
"Thank you both for coming today. I understand that this has been a challenging journey for both of you. Let's use this space to open up, share your feelings, and work towards resolution."

ONICA and **JERSEY** exchange a wary glance before settling into their seats, the air between them thick with unspoken words. Both take a deep breath, unsure where to begin.

ONICA
(hesitant, her voice barely above a whisper)
"I... I just don't understand how this all happened. It feels like a nightmare, and I'm stuck in it."

The weight of **Onica's** words hangs in the air, and **JERSEY** shifts uncomfortably in her seat, her fingers absently twisting a ring on her hand.

JERSEY
(reflective, but guarded)
"I know, Onica. I never wanted any of this either. It's been a rollercoaster, to say the least."

The **THERAPIST**, sensing the need for deeper introspection, turns her attention to **JERSEY**, her voice encouraging yet neutral.

THERAPIST

"Jersey, why don't you start by telling Onica how you felt when you realized the marriage certificate mix-up?"

JERSEY pauses, the question weighing heavily on her. Her gaze drops to her hands, and for a moment, she seems lost in thought, the memories clearly still fresh.

JERSEY
(guarded, a slight tremor in her voice)
"Well, at first, I was shocked. I mean, I couldn't believe it. But then... I saw an opportunity. I thought maybe I could make the best of the situation."

The air grows tense, and **Onica's** eyes narrow. Her jaw clenches as the words sink in, her hurt evident in the way she holds herself.

ONICA
(hurt, a faint edge of disbelief in her tone)
"You saw an opportunity to take over my husband's company... our life together..."

The vulnerability in **Jersey's** eyes flickers, and she struggles to maintain control. A tear escapes down her cheek, but she doesn't wipe it away, as though letting it fall is part of the unspoken truth she's been avoiding.

JERSEY
(teary, voice cracking slightly)
"Onica, you have to understand that... I was grieving too. I lost Peter, my best friend. I thought maybe we could make something good out of all the confusion."

ONICA
(softening, her voice quieter now, filled with her own pain)
"I know, Jersey. I miss him so much. But this situation... it's been like a second loss. And the way it's torn us apart... I can't bear it."

A thick silence follows, both women lost in their memories of Peter and the fracture their lives had suffered. The **THERAPIST** watches them, her gaze gentle but insistent.

THERAPIST
(encouraging, yet subtle in her approach)
"Remember, you both have a shared history and friendship that's been strained. It's clear that this mix-up has affected both of you deeply. Are there any memories or moments you can hold onto, something positive that might help rebuild trust?"

The room feels quieter now, as if the suggestion has opened a small window for the possibility of reconciliation. **JERSEY** and **Onica** exchange a brief but meaningful glance, something unspoken passing between them as they each begin to sift through their shared history.

JERSEY
(smiling faintly, nostalgia creeping into her voice)
"There was that time when we laughed so hard at Peter's dad jokes during the wedding preparations."

A small smile tugs at **Onica's** lips, the warmth of the memory a stark contrast to the heaviness of the present.

ONICA
(smiling too, a soft chuckle escaping her)
"And when you helped me choose the perfect dress... you were like my sister, Jersey."

The **THERAPIST** observes the subtle shift in their expressions, her gaze focused as she sees the faint traces of something once familiar beginning to resurface. She leans forward slightly, her voice low but firm.

THERAPIST
"It's clear that your bond was genuine. Is there a way you can use that history to rebuild trust and move forward?"

The room grows still again, both women lost in thought. The air feels lighter, though the journey ahead is still uncertain. **Jersey** and **Onica** sit in silence, the weight of their shared past and the possibility of healing resting between them. After a long pause, **Jersey** speaks, her voice more steady, though tinged with uncertainty.

JERSEY
(softly, almost to herself)
"I don't know... but maybe we can try."

ONICA
(quietly, but with a trace of hope)
"Maybe... we can."

They sit together, the road ahead unclear, but for the first time, there's a flicker of hope that maybe, just maybe, they can rebuild what was broken.

The kitchen is dimly lit, the only source of light coming from the window above the sink. **Onica** stands by the counter, holding a boiling kettle, her gaze fixed on the empty cup of coffee sitting on the table before her. She stares at it for a moment, the steam rising from the cup mixing with the tension in the air. The weight of everything seems to settle on her shoulders like a heavy, suffocating blanket.

Suddenly, a sharp pain sears through her chest, just to the left of her heart. She gasps, feeling a deep, radiating ache that takes her breath away. Instinctively, she lets go of the kettle, her hand trembling as it falls to the counter. The kettle continues to hiss, boiling away, forgotten.

Her vision blurs, and a wave of weakness washes over her. Her knees buckle, and slowly, she sinks to the floor, her body unable to withstand the pain. The air feels thick, as though every breath is a struggle. Her pulse pounds in her ears, and she can feel her strength slipping away.

Then, there's a knock at the door.

LIZER
(calling from outside)
"Onica, I'm outside."

Onica tries to respond, but her voice comes out as a whisper, barely audible. Her hand presses against her chest in a futile attempt to alleviate the pain, but it's no use. She doesn't have the energy to rise. She sits on the floor, her back against the counter, eyes fluttering shut in exhaustion.

The door opens with a creak, and **Lizer** steps in, her expression immediately changing from casual to one of alarm when she sees **Onica** sitting on the floor. Her face pales, and without hesitation, she rushes to her side.

LIZER
(panicking, rushing to her side)
"Onica! Oh my God, what's happening?!"

Lizer quickly wraps her arm around **Onica**, helping her to her feet, though she can barely keep her own balance. She guides **Onica** to the couch, her movements gentle but urgent. Lizer sits beside her, trying to calm her, and pours the coffee into the cup, her hands trembling slightly as she sets it before **Onica**.

ONICA
(weakly, her voice a strained whisper)
"I... I can't do this anymore, Lizer."

LIZER
(concerned, setting the cup down)
"This isn't right, Onica. You need some care. You can't keep on fighting for the money and sickness at the same time. This isn't how you get through it."

ONICA
(her voice faint, her face drawn with frustration)
"I have no choice... this is on top of my shoulders. I can't let that *bitch* win over my marriage, over everything Peter and I built. I can't."

Her chest rises and falls unevenly, her breath shallow. She grips the armrest, trying to steady herself, but the weakness still lingers.

LIZER

(gently, but firmly)

"But you need to take it slowly. We don't want to lose you, Onica. Please. You're not well."

A bitter laugh escapes **Onica's** lips, though it's hollow, filled with regret.

ONICA

(softly, her voice carrying a trace of deep sorrow)

"If only I knew Peter was gonna die so soon... I would've taken my former boyfriend back. I'm so... *emotionless*. He watches me suffer from a distance, and he doesn't even know the mistakes I've made."

Tears threaten to spill, but she holds them back, her hands trembling as she clutches the cushion beneath her. **Lizer** leans in, her gaze soft with understanding and concern.

LIZER

(soothingly, but with a quiet conviction)

"But you chose Peter, Onica. You chose him because he was a businessman—he could offer you everything you needed. You made that choice for a reason. The life you built with him is real, even if it's crumbling now."

ONICA

(her voice shaking, frustration seeping through)

"But I'm drowning in this crisis now, Lizer. The money... the company... it doesn't matter when everything feels like it's falling apart. I thought I was doing the right thing, but now... now it feels like I'm just spinning out of control."

Her hands tremble, her head sinking into the couch, as though the weight of her words is too much to carry. **Lizer** sits beside her, a constant presence, her hand resting lightly on **Onica's** arm.

LIZER

(firm but compassionate)

"You don't have to do this alone, Onica. I'm here. We'll figure this out together, but you need to take care of yourself first. You can't fight a battle like this if you're not whole."

ONICA

(tears welling in her eyes, her voice breaking)

"I don't know if I can, Lizer. I'm not sure I have anything left to give."

The room falls into a heavy silence, the sound of the boiling kettle long forgotten. **Onica** leans back against the couch, feeling the weight of her choices, the pressure of her grief, and the overwhelming burden of everything she's lost. The journey ahead is uncertain, but for the first time, **Lizer's** presence offers her a fragile lifeline, one that might just keep her from sinking entirely.

The sun is setting low, casting long shadows across the dusty pavement of the old petrol station. **Former Boyfriend**, dressed in his worn-out petrol station uniform, wipes the sweat from his brow with the back of his hand. His face is tired, but there's a steely determination in his eyes. He glances at the clock on the wall, checking the time as he walks toward the back lot. The summer heat has been relentless, and his uniform clings to his body, damp with sweat.

His steps slow as he approaches an old, beat-up van parked near the edge of the station. The van looks like it's seen better days—its faded blue paint peeling, a few rust spots dotting the body. The door creaks loudly as **Former Boyfriend** opens it, the hinges protesting with a rusty squeal that echoes through the empty lot. He winces, his face tight as the door opens with effort, the sound adding to the weight of the day.

He slides into the driver's seat, the old leather squeaking under his weight. The interior smells faintly of gasoline and the faint scent of stale cigarettes. He reaches over, pulling the door closed with a firm slam. The van groans in protest, a deep rumble coming from the engine as it reluctantly comes to life. The vehicle sputters and coughs, then lurches forward as **Former Boyfriend** puts his foot on the gas pedal.

As he drives away from the station, the engine rattles and shakes, the sound of the old van cutting through the air like a broken record. The tires crunch on the gravel road as the van slowly picks up speed. The windows are down, and the wind rushes through, tousling his hair and bringing with it the scent of exhaust and hot asphalt. The sun casts long, harsh shadows across the road ahead, painting everything with a golden hue that matches the heaviness in his chest.

Sweat drips down his temple as he grips the wheel, his knuckles white against the worn leather. He doesn't glance back, only forward, as the city's skyline grows smaller in his rearview mirror. His mind is elsewhere—on the past, on the choices he's made, and the distance he feels growing between him and the life he once thought he'd have.

The van coughs again, its engine sputtering as it climbs a small hill. He curses under his breath but pushes forward, his eyes narrowing against the setting sun. The world around him is fading into twilight, but inside the van, everything feels stuck—stuck in a moment he can't shake, a moment he doesn't want to face.

With a final groan, the old van surges forward, its tired engine giving one last effort before coasting down the road, taking him further away from everything he knows.

The worn tires of the old van crunched against the gravel as **Former Boyfriend** pulled into the long, winding driveway of a grand mansion. The massive gates creaked as they slowly closed behind him, a soft metallic sound that felt strangely final. He parked the van under the shadow of the towering oak trees that lined the entrance, their leaves whispering in the evening breeze. The mansion loomed ahead, its windows glowing warmly from the inside, a stark contrast to the cold, dark exterior of his own life.

He threw the gear into park with a gruff movement, his hands still stiff from a long day at the station. The van's engine sputtered one last time, groaning in its familiar, mechanical protest. He sat there for a moment, staring at the mansion, his mind clouded with memories of better times and unspoken regrets.

Reluctantly, he opened the door, the old thing groaning and protesting with each twist of the handle. It screeched loudly as he tugged it open, a sound that felt so out of place against the quiet grandeur of the mansion. When he stepped out, his shoes sank slightly into the gravel as he walked around the front of the van. His face was taut, his shoulders heavy with the weight of his own decisions, and the heat of the day still clung to his skin like a second layer.

He reached back to slam the door shut, but the old hinges wouldn't cooperate. He pulled once, then twice, each attempt met with resistance, the door creaking in protest. Sweat beaded on his forehead as he gave the door one final tug, banging it shut with a firm thud that echoed through the still air. His breath came out in a huff, and he wiped his forehead with the back of his hand, his heart beating too fast in his chest.

A faint sound interrupted the silence—a knock on the door of the mansion.

The sharp sound seemed to pierce the heavy quiet, and he froze for a moment, his heart lurching in his chest. His gaze flicked nervously toward the front door, as if he could will away the moment. He hadn't planned on this, hadn't expected this kind of interruption. Yet, the knock came again, more insistent this time.

He squared his shoulders, exhaled, and stepped toward the door, his footsteps slow, deliberate, but with a sense of inevitability.

The sharp click of high heels echoed through the hallway as **Lizer**, an undeniably attractive woman with a confident, almost magnetic presence, moved towards the door. Her figure, graceful and purposeful, was the very definition of allure, and as she opened the door, her lips curled into a smirk upon seeing the **Former Boyfriend** standing there, clad in his petrol station uniform, boots worn from the long hours of labor.

LIZER
(smirking)
"Speak of the devil."
FORMER BOYFRIEND
(humbly)
"Oh, is she around?"
LIZER
(with a sharp edge)
"She just lost her husband. Not in any condition to discuss love-making issues, if that's what you're here for."

Without waiting for a response, Lizer stepped aside, allowing him to enter. He shuffled inside, the creaking of his boots on the wooden floor barely audible over the tension that seemed to hang in the air. His eyes flicked to **Onica**, who sat slumped on the couch, her face pale and drawn with exhaustion. The weight of everything that had happened over the past few weeks seemed to press down on her, her form fragile and vulnerable.

LIZER
(gesturing to Onica)
"You see for yourself. Her health needs more than a couple of thousand dollars to fix. Her legal fees are piling up too—more than you could imagine—just to regain her strength. But nothing in this world comes for free."
FORMER BOYFRIEND
(sympathetic, but with a note of guilt)
"Oh, that's terrible."
ONICA
(softly, barely audible)

"I'm glad you came. My mind is all over the place... Everything is a mess."

The Former Boyfriend stood silently, shifting uneasily. Lizer, ever the observer, sipped her tea, maintaining a careful distance but keeping her ears keenly tuned to their conversation.

LIZER
(cutting in, her tone sharp)
"Do you know anyone who can give her a couple of thousand dollars? Maybe her problems will disappear if someone steps up. And let's not forget about the hospital bills. They need to be paid too."

His face flushed with embarrassment, his lips tight. He remained silent, the weight of his inadequacy settling between them. Lizer's gaze never left him, the faintest smirk curling at her lips as she watched his discomfort.

LIZER
(whispering to herself)
"I knew it... You won't have solutions."

FORMER BOYFRIEND
(looking down)
"I came at..."

LIZER
(interrupting, cutting him off)
"Wrong time, of course. She'll call you... when it's the right time."

The Former Boyfriend could feel the truth of Lizer's words deep in his chest. He was a man without resources, standing in the middle of a storm, and he realized that he was never part of the solution. He wasn't even a part of the journey to fix things. He shifted uncomfortably, stepping back from the conversation as the weight of his poverty and helplessness grew heavier.

Lizer, pacing back and forth, muttered under her breath, the sound of her voice almost drowned by the tension in the room.

LIZER

(whispering)
"Everyone can see that there's no match here. No type, no connection. There's nothing pulling you together, nothing at all."

Suddenly, Onica, already weak from her struggle, let out a sharp cry as another wave of pain hit her, a burning ache in her chest. She fell back against the couch, her face contorting in agony.

ONICA
(shouting, frantic)
"Shut up with your big mouth!"

The Former Boyfriend, seeing her in distress, immediately moved to help. His hands were unsure at first, but he carefully assisted her to lie down. Lizer, startled by the sudden intensity of Onica's pain, ran to her side, spilling her cup of coffee as she rushed to help.

LIZER
(fuming, almost frantic)
"I told you she needs some time to rest! This is really bad timing."

The Former Boyfriend stepped back, the overwhelming weight of the moment sinking in. He looked helplessly between the two women before turning and heading toward the door. His exit was swift, but it felt like a resignation to the harsh truth.

Lizer watched him leave, her expression one of silent disapproval. She turned back to Onica, who lay on the couch, her breathing shallow. Lizer's face softened, but there was no denying the frustration that lingered in her eyes.

With a soft sigh, Lizer muttered to herself, still pacing.

LIZER
(under her breath)
"Sometimes, there's no point in forcing something that was never meant to be."

She turned back to Onica, her voice now more gentle, yet still full of concern.

LIZER

"You need to rest, Onica. Let go of everything for now. We'll figure it out... But you need to take care of yourself first."

The air in the therapist's office had shifted. The tense, guarded atmosphere that had marked the beginning of the session slowly gave way to something more open, more accepting. The soft hum of the room's calming ambiance seemed to mirror the transformation unfolding between **Jersey** and **Onica**. The space that once felt heavy with unresolved pain now felt like a place of possibility.

THERAPIST

(supportive)

"This is a journey, and it won't be easy. But remember, you can choose how to move forward. Is there anything you'd like to say to each other, something that might help you heal?"

For a long moment, there was only silence between **Jersey** and **Onica**. Both women sat on opposite sides of the room, their hands clasped tightly, as if holding onto something deeper than words could express. It wasn't an easy thing, this reaching out after so much distance had built between them. But as their eyes met across the room, a shared understanding passed between them—both carrying a burden of regret, both knowing that something had to give if they were ever going to heal.

ONICA

(teary-eyed, voice barely above a whisper)

"I want to find a way to move forward, Jersey... as friends. To honor Peter's memory, and our bond."

JERSEY

(eyes welling with tears, her voice thick with emotion)

"I'm so sorry, Onica. I didn't want to hurt you. I never meant to bring pain into your life. I want us to find a way to heal... to support each other."

There was something deeply raw in their words, a vulnerability that neither had allowed herself to express before. It was as if a dam had broken, and the flood of emotions that had been held at bay for so long poured out in that single moment of mutual understanding.

The **therapist**, who had remained silent until now, smiled warmly. Her gentle presence was the glue that had held the session together, and now she could see the first stirrings of healing.

THERAPIST
(softly)
"You're taking the first steps towards healing, and that's a significant achievement. Remember, it's okay to seek help when life throws unexpected challenges your way. You're not alone in this journey."

The words felt like a balm, soothing the raw edges of their open wounds. The therapist's encouragement was a reminder that they were not bound to their past mistakes, nor to the weight of their grief and resentment.

JERSEY and **ONICA** exchanged a long, meaningful look. In that brief silence, the tension that had once felt so suffocating between them began to lift. They both knew that this wasn't a magic fix, but it was a start. A fragile, hopeful start.

As they stood up to leave the therapist's office, it was as if a weight had been lifted from their shoulders. Neither of them was naïve enough to think the road ahead would be without difficulty, but for the first time in a long while, they felt something like hope.

They walked out together, side by side, their footsteps in sync. The journey to rebuild their friendship had only just begun, but they both knew that, with time, patience, and support, they could heal. They could move forward.

The room is dimly lit, its shadows stretching long across the walls. The air feels thick, heavy with unspoken words, a tension that clings to the space between them. **Onica** sits on one side of the room, her posture slumped, her face etched with sadness and frustration. Her eyes, red from crying, reflect a deep sorrow that she cannot seem to shake. Across from her sits **Peter's mother**, an elegant yet stern woman whose presence fills the room with an undeniable weight. Her gaze is sharp, unyielding, a judgment carved into every line of her face.

The silence stretches, and **Peter's mother** is the first to break it, her voice cold, each word a cutting reminder of her disdain.

PETER'S MOTHER
(cold)
"You were never the right choice for my son, Onica. I told him from the beginning, but he wouldn't listen."

ONICA
(tearfully, voice trembling)
"I loved him with all my heart, Mrs. Collins. Our marriage was real, our love was real. The mix-up with the marriage certificate was just a cruel twist of fate."

PETER'S MOTHER
(accusatory)
"Fate? Or a sign that this was never meant to be? You brought nothing to this relationship, Onica. No education, no responsibility, no children. What did you offer my son?"

Onica's throat tightens, her words a fragile thread as she fights to maintain composure. Her chest heaves with the effort to explain herself, to make Peter's mother see that her love had been enough, even if it hadn't met her standards.

ONICA
(emotionally, voice cracking)
"I may not be educated, but I loved Peter with all my heart. I supported him in every way I could. When he was stressed about his new contract, I was there for him. He never stopped at the robots that night. It was an accident... a tragedy that took him away."

PETER'S MOTHER
(unyielding, voice rising)
"And what about his sickness? You think I don't know that he suffered because of it? You couldn't even give him a child to carry on his legacy."

The words hit Onica like a physical blow, her eyes welling with fresh tears. She clenches her hands into fists, fighting to keep her composure. She wants to scream, to tell Peter's mother that none of those things mattered—none of them could ever change how much she had loved him.

ONICA
(desperate, voice barely a whisper)
"He didn't care about any of that, Mrs. Collins. He loved me. He wanted a life with me. I was willing to give him a family, but fate had other plans."

Peter's mother looks at her with cold, unwavering eyes, her face a mask of stoic judgment. There's no softness in her gaze, no flicker of understanding. **Onica** feels small beneath her gaze, but she refuses to shrink away completely.

PETER'S MOTHER
(stubborn, harsh)
"You'll have to prove your love in court, Onica. I refuse to be a character witness for you. I've told my husband the same. You were never the one for my son, and I won't change my stance now."

Onica's tears spill over, her heart breaking under the weight of the woman's words. The room feels like it's closing in on her, the walls pressing down, suffocating her in the rawness of her grief and rejection.

ONICA
(heartbroken, voice shaking)

"I understand your feelings, Mrs. Collins, but please, try to remember the love we shared. I need your support now more than ever, for Peter's memory."

But Peter's mother remains unmoved, her expression as hard as stone, her heart as closed as the door she has firmly shut between them. Onica's chest tightens with the realization that she may never find the solace she seeks in this woman's eyes.

The tension in the room continues to simmer, the silence growing more oppressive with each passing moment. Neither of them speaks, but the weight of their words lingers in the air like a storm on the horizon, unspoken, unresolved.

And in that silence, **Onica** feels the crushing weight of loss once again. Not just the loss of Peter, but the loss of any chance of reconciliation, of the one person who should have understood her pain.

Onica stepped out of **Jersey's** house, the door closing behind her with a soft click that seemed to echo in the quiet night air. Her hands, cold despite the warmth of the evening, gripped the fabric of her coat tightly as if it could hold her together. Her breath came in shallow, uneven gasps, and each step she took down the pathway felt heavier than the last. She was overwhelmed, consumed by a deep, suffocating grief that seemed to have no end. The weight of her situation—of everything she had lost, and everything she was still fighting for—pressed down on her chest, threatening to crush her.

The streets outside were eerily calm, the hum of the city distant, as though it were happening in another world entirely. In this moment, there was only the crushing silence inside her mind and the relentless ache in her heart. She could feel the weight of **Peter's** family's rejection still lingering in her bones. His mother's words, harsh and unyielding, cut through her like a knife, leaving a wound that no time would seem to heal.

Her steps faltered, and she paused for a moment to steady herself, the cold wind biting at her face as it swept through the empty street. It didn't matter how much she tried to hold herself together; the tears came anyway, pooling in her eyes and blurring the world around her. Her entire body trembled with the strain of it all—her health, the court case, the emotional toll of losing **Peter**, and now, this cruel rejection from the one family who should have stood by her. It felt as though everything she had ever known had crumbled beneath her feet, leaving her standing in the wreckage of a life she could no longer recognize.

She wiped her eyes quickly, the cold of her fingers against her skin sharp and grounding. There was no time for weakness. She couldn't afford to fall apart, not now. But the reality was that she felt as if she were already broken. Every part of her—her heart, her mind, her very soul—was shattered into pieces that no amount of trying could put back together.

As she made her way down the street, her feet moving automatically as if they knew the path, she couldn't help but replay the conversation in her mind. **Jersey** had tried to comfort her, had offered words of support, but nothing could change the fact that the woman who had once been her closest friend was now so far removed from her pain. There was no magic solution, no easy fix to what she was going through. Everything felt too big, too complicated.

She could feel the sting of the rejection from **Peter's family**, the weight of their disapproval pressing down on her like an invisible hand. She had loved him—truly loved him—but now, that love seemed like a distant memory, something that had been torn apart by fate and the unforgiving cruelty of the world. And in its place, there was only the harsh reality of a life she no longer recognized.

By the time she reached her car, her legs felt like lead, and she slumped against the door, taking a moment to steady herself before getting inside. She closed her eyes briefly, allowing herself the smallest flicker of a reprieve from the turmoil swirling within her. But the peace was fleeting, like sand slipping through her fingers. She couldn't escape this—this weight, this grief, this suffocating uncertainty.

With a heavy sigh, she started the engine and pulled away from the curb, her mind a whirlwind of fractured thoughts and emotions. The road ahead was dark, and the future felt as uncertain as the night sky stretching out before her. All she could do was keep moving forward, even if she didn't know where that path would take her.

One thing was clear: nothing would ever be the same.

Onica sat on the park bench, her hands folded tightly in her lap, feeling the cool breeze brush against her skin. The sky overhead was clouded, a dull gray that mirrored the uncertainty in her chest. She looked around, trying to keep herself distracted, but her thoughts kept spiraling back to the conversation she was about to have. Her heart raced, and she could feel the weight of her decisions bearing down on her.

The sound of footsteps approached, and Onica turned her head, her breath catching in her throat. **Former Boyfriend** was walking toward her, his familiar presence a mix of comfort and unease. They locked eyes for a brief moment, and despite the tension between them, he gave her a cautious smile.

ONICA
(anxious)
"Thanks for coming."
FORMER BOYFRIEND
(gentle)
"Of course, Onica. I'm here."

He took a seat beside her, the space between them full of unspoken words. For a long moment, neither of them spoke. The air felt thick, heavy with everything they hadn't said yet. Onica glanced at him briefly, unsure how to start, and then looked away, her fingers tracing the edge of the bench.

ONICA
(after a long pause, vulnerable)
"I've been thinking about what you said, and I want to understand your perspective. But I need you to understand something too."

FORMER BOYFRIEND
(listening attentively, his gaze softening)
"Go ahead. I'm listening."

Onica took a deep breath, her chest tightening as she tried to find the right words. This was harder than she'd imagined. She wanted to explain, to make him understand the chaos swirling in her life right now, but she wasn't sure how.

ONICA
(her voice trembling slightly)
"I know my past choices weren't perfect, and I see how patient you've been. But right now, I'm dealing with a lot. Peter's business, my health... everything feels like it's falling apart. I need time and space to figure things out. I can't give anyone—or anything—my full attention right now."

She could feel the tears pressing at the back of her eyes, but she fought them back. She had cried so many times already, and she didn't want to break down in front of him. Not now, not when she needed to be strong.

FORMER BOYFRIEND
(his tone gentle, understanding)
"Onica, I respect that. I never meant to rush you into anything. I just want you to know that I care about you. No matter what happens, I'm here—for whatever you need."

Onica nodded slowly, her heart aching as she processed his words. She had always known he cared for her, but in that moment, she realized just how much she'd taken his patience and support for granted. She had pushed him away so many times, and now, she was asking him to wait again. She didn't know if that was fair.

ONICA
(softly, grateful but conflicted)
"Thank you for understanding. I don't want to close the door on the possibility of a future... but it has to happen in its own time. Can we start as friends again? Just... friends?"

He turned to look at her, his eyes warm, though tinged with a hint of sadness. He hesitated for a moment, as though weighing the request, but then he gave her a small, genuine smile.

FORMER BOYFRIEND
(smiling warmly)
"Of course, Onica. Friends sounds like a great place to start."

Onica exhaled slowly, feeling a mix of relief and sorrow. She didn't know if this was the right path, but for the first time in a long while, it felt like the only one she could walk. She wasn't sure what the future held, but for now, she had taken the first step toward rebuilding something with him, however small.

As the two of them sat there, the silence between them felt less charged, more like a moment of shared understanding. Onica wasn't sure where things would go from here, but for now, it was enough to know they were taking it one step at a time. And that, she realized, was the only thing she could promise herself.

Jersey crouched low behind the thick trunk of a towering oak tree, her eyes sharp and focused on the scene unfolding before her. Onica and her former boyfriend were seated on a park bench, talking quietly, their laughter drifting through the air like an unspoken secret. Jersey's thumb hovered over her smartphone's screen as she snapped picture after picture, each one capturing the two of them in the midst of their seemingly innocent conversation.

She clicked once more, her eyes narrowing as she observed the way they leaned in slightly, the familiarity between them unmistakable. A wave of satisfaction washed over her, and she whispered under her breath, a small smirk tugging at her lips.

JERSEY
(whispering to herself)
"This should show everyone that Onica's not as innocent as she seems."

The wind rustled through the leaves, but Jersey's gaze never faltered from her target. She'd been waiting for the right moment, and now, it seemed like she had it.

Hours later, Jersey found herself seated in a quiet corner of a nearby café, the tension in her shoulders palpable. She tapped her fingers anxiously on the table, waiting for Mrs. Collins and the lawyer to arrive. Her heart pounded as she pictured the fallout—she could already hear the disapproving murmurs when she revealed the pictures. This was her chance to show that Onica wasn't the grieving widow she portrayed herself to be.

The door jingled as the lawyer and Mrs. Collins walked in. They spotted Jersey at the table and made their way over, Mrs. Collins still looking somber as always, while the lawyer's sharp eyes gleamed with a certain calculated interest.

Without wasting any time, Jersey pulled her phone from her bag and slid it across the table, showing the photos she'd so carefully taken. She leaned back in her chair, her arms folded with a satisfied smirk on her face.

JERSEY
(smirking)
"Look at this! Onica's not as devastated as she claims. She's meeting her former boyfriend. This is proof she's not the grieving widow she wants everyone to believe she is."

The lawyer leaned forward, eyes scanning the images, his expression hardening as he took in the details. Mrs. Collins' face, however, remained unreadable at first, until she looked up at Jersey with a hint of concern.

LAWYER
(surprised, impressed)
"This could be vital evidence, Jersey. It suggests that Onica might not be entirely truthful about her intentions. This could work in our favor."

Jersey's heart skipped a beat. She'd expected them to be shocked, but hearing the lawyer's approval made her feel a surge of triumph.

But Mrs. Collins, whose emotions had always been so tightly guarded, lingered on the images for a long moment before slowly meeting Jersey's gaze. Her expression was far more conflicted than Jersey had anticipated.

MRS. COLLINS
(concerned, her voice low)
"We need to consider what this means carefully. It's important not to jump to conclusions."

Jersey's excitement faltered slightly. She had hoped for full support, but Mrs. Collins' hesitation was a reminder of the complex web they were entangled in. Still, she wasn't about to back down.

JERSEY
(determined, her tone hardening)
"I just want everyone to see the truth. Onica's been playing all of us, pretending she's fallen apart, but she's out there with him, looking perfectly fine."

The lawyer leaned back in his chair, folding his arms. He glanced from the photos to Mrs. Collins, waiting for her to respond. The tension in the room thickened.

Mrs. Collins sighed, her fingers gripping the edges of the table as though weighing the consequences. She was torn—her maternal instincts pulling her one way, while the weight of what had happened between Onica and Peter tugged her in the other direction.

Finally, she spoke, her voice softer than before, but still resolute.

MRS. COLLINS
(quietly)
"We need to be careful, Jersey. If we act out of anger, if we push too hard... we could make things worse. For everyone."

Jersey bit her lip, her brow furrowing. She wasn't used to this kind of restraint. She wanted action, but Mrs. Collins' caution reminded her that not everything was as simple as it seemed.

But Jersey wasn't backing down. This was the moment she'd been waiting for. She couldn't let Onica slip away from the consequences of her actions. She'd made her choice, and Jersey was determined to make sure the world saw who Onica truly was.

JERSEY
(firmly)
"I don't care about the consequences. Onica's been playing the victim for too long. It's time the truth came out."

And with that, the atmosphere in the café shifted. Mrs. Collins' uncertainty lingered in the air, while Jersey, fueled by a sense of justice (or perhaps revenge), felt the first stirrings of a plan beginning to take shape. Whatever happened next, she was ready to see it through.

The tension in the room was palpable as Mrs. Collins entered Jersey's home. The elegant woman moved with the grace of someone accustomed to command, but her composure didn't mask the intensity of the moment. Jersey, seated on the couch, shifted uneasily, her eyes flickering between Mrs. Collins and the door, as if trying to read the situation before them.

MRS. COLLINS
(calmly, but with a firm tone)

"Jersey, I didn't come here to fight with you. I believe it's in our best interest to find a way to resolve my son's legacy and accommodate you as a mother."

Jersey's posture stiffened slightly, her defenses still up, but she held her ground. She'd heard this kind of rhetoric before, but it was hard to ignore the sincerity that seemed to weigh in Mrs. Collins' words. She listened attentively but remained cautious, her eyes narrowing in suspicion.

JERSEY
(guarded)
"I appreciate your willingness to talk, Mrs. Collins, but what kind of plan are you suggesting?"

Mrs. Collins took a moment to consider her words, her fingers lightly brushing against the edge of her handbag. The air between them crackled with the weight of their shared history, the tension that had built up over months of fighting for control. Still, Mrs. Collins' demeanor remained steady, her voice never wavering from its calm, practiced tone.

MRS. COLLINS
(thoughtful)
"I'm suggesting that we work together to find a solution that allows you to continue pushing the company forward while preserving my son's legacy. I'm not here to take everything away from you. I just want peace."

Jersey hesitated, her eyes narrowing as she weighed the offer. There was a vulnerability in Mrs. Collins' eyes that seemed genuine, but Jersey knew better than to trust too quickly. Yet, there was something in her proposal that gave Jersey pause. A glimpse of cooperation, of shared purpose, that had been lacking in their previous interactions.

JERSEY
(hesitant, still cautious)

"What kind of solution are you thinking of, Mrs. Collins?"

A faint smile tugged at the corners of Mrs. Collins' lips, and for the first time, Jersey saw a hint of warmth in her otherwise composed expression.

MRS. COLLINS
(with a small smile, more assured now)

"Well, I would like to be involved in the company's decision-making, especially regarding my son's legacy. But I'm willing to let you continue to run the business. After all, you have the expertise."

Jersey's guard lowered slightly, the weight of her own ambition momentarily overshadowed by the possibility of an arrangement that could preserve both her control and Mrs. Collins' involvement. It wasn't a perfect solution, but it could be a step toward something more manageable, something that wouldn't lead to an all-out war.

JERSEY
(cautiously, but more open now)

"I need full control of the company, but I'm willing to discuss a plan that accommodates both of our interests. Can we ensure that Onica is not part of this, though? She's been causing so many problems."

Mrs. Collins' gaze sharpened, her eyes darkening with resolve.

MRS. COLLINS
(determined)

"I assure you, I have no intention of supporting Onica. We can work out the details and present a united front against her in the legal battle. And there's something else I want to share."

Jersey raised an eyebrow, curious despite herself. The conversation had taken an unexpected turn, and she could feel the stirring of cautious hope.

JERSEY
(curious, leaning forward slightly)

"What is it?"

Mrs. Collins' expression softened, her voice losing some of its usual steel, replaced with something more personal, more vulnerable.

MRS. COLLINS
(excited, her tone shifting)
"I'm going to be a grandmother. You're carrying my son's child, and that means a lot to me. It's a part of him that I want to see continue. We can ensure that the child has a bright future within this legacy."

The words hung in the air like a heavy secret. Jersey felt her chest tighten, a mixture of shock and emotion sweeping over her. She hadn't expected this revelation, hadn't expected Mrs. Collins to pull her into her family's circle in this way. It felt like a quiet shift in the power dynamics between them, a softening of the edges that had once seemed so jagged.

JERSEY
(emotional, her voice wavering slightly)
"I... I didn't expect that. It changes things."

Mrs. Collins placed her hands gently on the table, her eyes locked with Jersey's, her expression sincere.

MRS. COLLINS
(reassuring, with a small, encouraging smile)
"I hope it can be a unifying factor, Jersey. Let's work together for the sake of Peter's memory and our shared future."

Jersey's heart pounded, a surge of new emotion flooding her chest. The thought of Peter's child—her child—being part of his legacy, part of something that could give her the future she never thought possible, left her momentarily speechless.

She swallowed, then nodded, her voice softer now, more reflective.

JERSEY
(softly, her voice steadier than before)

MY WEDDING CONTRACT TOO 171

"Let's find a way to make this work, Mrs. Collins. For Peter, and for our future."

And with that, the two women, once enemies in their fight for Peter's legacy, began to craft a delicate, uncertain alliance. The road ahead would be difficult, fraught with challenges and compromises, but in that moment, there was a shared understanding between them. A glimmer of hope.

The soft light filtering through the window seemed to warm the room as Mrs. Collins and Jersey sat across from each other, the weight of their previous animosity finally lifting. The air between them, once charged with tension, now carried a sense of calm, the tentative beginnings of a partnership taking root.

MRS. COLLINS
(smiling, her voice warm but steady)
"I'm glad we're on the same page, Jersey. I believe this partnership can honor my son's memory and ensure a bright future for his child."

Jersey, for the first time in a long while, allowed herself to smile back, feeling an unexpected sense of camaraderie between them. The path ahead wasn't going to be easy, but it was beginning to feel like it could be navigated together.

JERSEY
(nodding, her smile matching Mrs. Collins')
"I agree, Mrs. Collins. It's essential that we protect Peter's legacy and provide for our child. We'll need to be strong together."

Mrs. Collins' eyes softened, a glimmer of pride reflecting in them as she regarded Jersey. There had been a time when she viewed this woman with suspicion, even disdain. But now, she saw a strength in Jersey—a strength that could carry them both through the turbulent waters ahead.

MRS. COLLINS
(her voice firm with conviction)

"Absolutely, and as you continue to run the business, I'll be there to support you in decisions related to Peter's legacy. We can navigate this complex situation."

Their eyes met, and for a moment, the weight of everything—Peter's death, the business, the legal battles—seemed to vanish. All that was left was the sense of unity they had just formed. Slowly, tentatively, they reached out and clasped hands, the physical gesture marking the beginning of their new alliance.

JERSEY
(her voice full of sincerity)
"Thank you for your understanding and willingness to work together, Mrs. Collins."

MRS. COLLINS
(with a soft but resolute smile)
"Thank you for carrying my grandchild and keeping Peter's memory alive. We can do this, Jersey."

There was a quiet moment between them, a shared silence that held the weight of both their gratitude and their resolve. It wasn't perfect, and it wasn't without its complications, but it was a start—a start that felt stronger than either of them had expected.

The road ahead would not be without its hurdles, but for the first time in a long while, both women felt the comforting certainty of having found a common purpose. Together, they would face whatever came next—no longer divided by grief or ambition, but united in their desire to honor the man they had both loved in their own way, and to build a future for the child who would carry his name.

The conference room was still, the air thick with an unspoken tension as Onica and Jersey sat across from each other, the weight of their history and their shared ties to Peter hovering between them. It was a strange moment—one where both women, despite their differences, knew that for the sake of the company, they would have to find a way to work together.

ONICA
(her voice steady, but her eyes sincere)
"Jersey, I understand your legal claim, and I'm willing to compromise."

Jersey's posture stiffened, her expression still guarded, but she gave Onica a cautious glance, waiting for her to explain. The offer hung in the air, uncertain and precarious.

JERSEY
(slowly, with suspicion lingering in her tone)
"What are you suggesting, Onica?"

Onica took a deep breath, her gaze unwavering as she met Jersey's eyes. There was a quiet determination in her that Jersey hadn't expected, and for a moment, Jersey could see the woman she had once known, the woman who had been part of Peter's life, who had loved him just as fiercely.

ONICA
(with quiet resolve)
"Let's share control of the company. I'll still hold the majority, but you'll have a significant stake. And we can find a position for you in the company."

The words settled between them, a proposal that was both generous and calculated. Jersey didn't respond immediately, her mind turning over the offer, weighing the pros and cons. She hadn't expected this kind of solution—something that wasn't all about dominance or victory, but rather a chance for both of them to carve out a role in Peter's legacy.

Jersey leaned back slightly in her chair, her fingers drumming the surface of the table, her eyes narrowing as she processed the offer. Onica was right about one thing—this was about Peter, and if she were honest with herself, Jersey had always wanted to be part of the company, to keep his vision alive.

JERSEY
(reluctantly, but with a sigh of acknowledgment)
"I don't love the idea, Onica, but I can't deny that the company is our connection to Peter."

Onica's eyes softened at Jersey's words, a flicker of understanding passing between them. It wasn't easy, but it was necessary. The tension that had held them both in its grip was slowly beginning to unravel.

ONICA
(softening, her voice almost pleading)
"We can make this work, Jersey. For Peter's memory and the success of the company. It's not about us—it's about him, and the future we both need to build."

Jersey's gaze lingered on Onica for a moment longer, studying her face, the sincerity in her words. Slowly, the walls she'd built around herself seemed to lower, just a fraction. There was still mistrust, but the possibility of peace was beginning to take root.

JERSEY
(nods slowly, her voice quieter now, more open)
"Alright, let's try. For Peter."

Onica gave a slight nod in return, the tension between them now easing, replaced by the fragile beginnings of a partnership. It wasn't the resolution either of them had expected, but it was a start—a way forward.

As they began to outline a plan, their voices became less strained, more collaborative. The future was still uncertain, but they both knew that if they wanted to honor Peter's legacy and ensure the company's survival, they would need to work together. And in that moment, despite everything that had happened, both women could see the possibility of something new.

The boardroom was sleek, polished, but the atmosphere inside felt anything but. The tension between Onica and Jersey was palpable, the silence between them like an unspoken storm waiting to break. Papers and business plans were spread across the table, but neither woman seemed able to focus on anything other than the mounting strain of their partnership.

Onica sat with her arms crossed, her gaze fixed on Jersey. There was a resolve in her eyes, a decision that had been building for days. The frustration of trying to balance their conflicting visions was finally pushing her to a breaking point.

ONICA
(concerned, her voice steady but firm)
"Jersey, I've been giving it a lot of thought. Our cooperation has been rocky, and it's affecting the company. We can't keep going like this."

Jersey's eyes narrowed, the defensiveness creeping into her posture as she shifted slightly in her chair. She knew this conversation was coming, but that didn't make it any easier to hear.

JERSEY
(defensive, her voice rising with a touch of irritation)
"I'm doing my best, Onica. But I won't deny that we have our disagreements. You're not making it easy either."

Onica let out a small, controlled breath, choosing her words carefully. She didn't want to escalate things, but she could feel the weight of the situation pressing down on her. Their differences had become too big to ignore, and they were starting to affect the very foundation of Peter's company.

ONICA
(resolute, her gaze unwavering)
"I think it's time we make a final decision. Either we find a way to work together harmoniously, or I'll have to consider legal action to remove you from the company."

Jersey stiffened, her face tightening as Onica's words landed like a heavy blow. The thought of losing everything she'd fought for was suddenly all too real. She hadn't expected Onica to be so blunt, but the urgency in her tone was undeniable.

JERSEY
(anxious, her voice faltering for a moment)
"Onica, I don't want it to come to that. I really don't. But we need to find common ground, or this will never work."

Onica held Jersey's gaze, her own eyes hardening with a sense of finality. She wasn't backing down—not now. Too much was at stake, not just for the company but for her and Peter's legacy.

ONICA
(determined, her voice cutting through the tension)
"I agree. Let's give it one last chance to make this partnership work. But it has to be our final attempt. No more compromises, no more second chances."

The weight of Onica's words settled heavily in the room. Jersey, for a brief moment, felt the pull of defeat. But then, something inside her shifted—a flicker of resolve. She wasn't ready to let go of everything she had worked for, not yet.

JERSEY
(softly, but with a new determination)
"Alright, Onica. One last try. For the company, for Peter."

The two women shared a brief, strained look before turning their attention back to the table before them. The decision had been made, but it was clear that the road ahead would be anything but easy. Both were now tethered to each other, bound by a fragile truce and the promise of one final chance.

And as the silence lingered in the air, the tension between them shifted—neither of them knew what the future would hold, but they both understood one thing: this was their last chance.

The room is cold and sterile, the hum of fluorescent lights overhead adding to the tense atmosphere. At the head of the long conference table, JERSEY and LEVY sit, both staring down at the financial reports spread before them. JERSEY's brow furrows in concentration, her fingers tapping rhythmically on the edge of the table as she scans through the figures. The numbers don't add up. There's something off, something she can't quite put her finger on.

JERSEY
(concerned, frustrated)
"Levy, our financials are a mess this quarter. I can't figure out what's going on. This could jeopardize our deal with Jones."

LEVY leans forward, his expression a mix of determination and frustration. He's been looking over the same numbers and knows what's coming. The unease has been building for days, but now it's becoming a palpable threat to everything they've worked for.

LEVY
(decisive, but with a touch of anger)
"Jersey, I think I know what's happening. It's Jeff—one of our employees. He's been causing financial losses intentionally."

JERSEY
(shocked, disbelief in her voice)
"What? Why on earth would he do that?"

LEVY shifts uncomfortably in his seat, the frustration in his eyes clear. He's been following Jeff's behavior for a while now, and it's only gotten worse.

LEVY
(with a hint of regret)
"He's been unhappy for a while, feels underappreciated. I think he's trying to sabotage us. He's angry about not getting the recognition he thinks he deserves."

JERSEY's face hardens, her hands clenched into tight fists. The thought of someone inside the company actively working against them is infuriating.

JERSEY
(through gritted teeth, voice rising with anger)
"We can't let this slide, Levy. This jeopardizes everything we've worked for. The Jones deal, the future of this company—he's playing with fire."

LEVY nods in agreement, his jaw tightening. The situation is more than just a few bad numbers; it's a betrayal.

LEVY
(resolute)
"I agree. We need to confront him, warn him, and if this doesn't stop, we may have to let him go. We can't afford this kind of behavior."

They share a look, understanding the gravity of what needs to be done. It's not just about financial losses anymore—it's about maintaining control of their company and the future they've built.

The office feels even colder now as JERSEY and LEVY corner JEFF in a secluded corner of the building, away from prying eyes. Jeff, looking disheveled and uncomfortable, stands nervously under their gaze. He knows this meeting is coming. The tension in the room is palpable, and the weight of his actions is finally catching up with him.

JERSEY
(firm, cutting through the silence)
"Jeff, we've noticed the irregularities in the financial reports. We know you're behind it. Why?"

JEFF looks down at the floor, his guilt written all over his face. He knows there's no way out now.

JEFF
(mumbles, voice shaky)

"I... I was frustrated. I didn't think anyone would notice."

LEVY steps closer, his voice sharp and unforgiving. He's not in the mood for excuses.

LEVY
(stern, with authority)
"This behavior is unacceptable. You've put the company at risk, Jeff. If it continues, we'll have no choice but to terminate your employment. Do you understand?"

Jeff swallows hard, the weight of the consequences finally sinking in. He's not used to being held accountable, and the severity of the situation hits him like a wave.

JEFF
(apologetic, eyes wide with regret)
"I'm sorry. I was frustrated, but I won't do it again. I didn't mean to hurt the company."

JERSEY's face remains stern, but there's a flicker of something softer in her eyes. She doesn't want to fire him, but she can't let this kind of behavior slide.

JERSEY
(cold but with a hint of pity)
"You've already put the company at risk, Jeff. We're giving you one last chance. If anything like this happens again, you're gone. Do you hear me?"

Jeff nods quickly, his eyes wide with fear. He's seen the determination in their eyes. This isn't a warning he can afford to ignore.

JERSEY and LEVY leave the room, their footsteps heavy with the weight of their decision. They know they've given Jeff a final opportunity, but the line has been drawn. If he crosses it again, there will be no coming back.

As the door closes behind them, they exchange a silent understanding. The stakes have never been higher, and the future of the company hangs in the balance.

The room is sterile and cold, its neutral tones and minimalist decor offering no comfort. Onica sits across from her attorney, MORGAN, the weight of the situation pressing down on her shoulders. The legal battle for the company has drained her, and she's come to him for advice on how to secure her future. But as Morgan opens his mouth, she senses the unease in his posture, the hesitation in his eyes. It's not a good sign.

MORGAN
(hesitant, his voice soft)
"Onica, I've been thinking... we're facing an uphill battle with Jersey in control. To secure your full control of the company, we might have to consider a drastic option."

Onica's heart skips a beat. She leans forward, her eyes narrowing with concern. She already knows this conversation isn't going to be easy, but the way Morgan is speaking makes her uneasy.

ONICA
(concerned, but trying to mask her growing anxiety)
"What do you mean, Morgan?"

Morgan shifts in his seat, his gaze drifting away for a moment as if trying to gather his thoughts. His hands are clasped tightly, a nervous habit that betrays his calm demeanor.

MORGAN
(cautiously, his voice low)
"I suggest we make it appear as though Jersey died naturally. That way, she would be out of the picture, and you'd regain full control of the company without any legal hurdles."

The words hang in the air, their gravity almost suffocating. Onica freezes, her heart racing. Her blood runs cold as the implication of

Morgan's suggestion sinks in. For a moment, she can't process it. She looks at him, her eyes wide with disbelief.

ONICA
(shocked, her voice trembling)
"You're talking about... eliminating her?"

Morgan meets her gaze with an expression that's almost too calm, his eyes hardening, as if he's weighed the decision and believes it's the only way forward.

MORGAN
(rationalizing, his tone still detached)
"I'm not saying it lightly, Onica. But legally, it might be our only way out of this mess. If Jersey's gone, the company is yours, without any resistance."

Onica's mind races, her thoughts colliding with each other. The idea of taking someone's life—of crossing that line—feels foreign and abhorrent. It's not who she is. But the desire to regain control of the company, to reclaim her position, gnaws at her. The weight of her responsibilities, the loss of Peter, and the pressure from all sides have pushed her to the brink.

ONICA
(struggling, her voice barely a whisper)
"Morgan, I can't do that. I won't be a part of something like that."

Her chest tightens as the words leave her lips. The moral weight of what he's suggesting overwhelms her. No matter how tempting the prospect of control is, this isn't a price she's willing to pay.

Morgan lets out a long breath, his expression softening. He clearly sees the internal battle playing out in her eyes. He leans back in his chair, clearly thinking it over.

MORGAN
(understanding, his voice gentler now)
"I understand, Onica. It's a difficult decision. But we need to find another way, and quickly. If Jersey stays in control, we'll lose

everything. You need to be prepared to fight, but we have to be smarter than this."

Onica stares at him, the reality of her situation settling in. She knows he's right. She knows that fighting Jersey—legally, morally, or otherwise—will require more than just determination. But taking that dark path is something she can't reconcile with herself. She needs another solution. And time is running out.

The room falls into a heavy silence as Onica stares at the papers in front of her, her mind swirling with thoughts of what could be, what should be, and the person she's trying desperately not to become.

Onica sits alone at her dining table, the soft glow of the afternoon sun streaming through the window. Her fingers gently trace the rim of her tea cup, the warm liquid offering comfort as she gazes out at the quiet street. The sound of birds chirping outside fills the space, and for a brief moment, the world feels still. The tension that has consumed her for so long has started to ebb away, replaced by a rare sense of peace. Her shoulders, once burdened by so much, feel lighter now. A small smile plays at her lips as she breathes in the calmness that surrounds her.

Suddenly, her phone buzzes on the table, interrupting the tranquility. Onica reaches for it, her thumb hovering over the screen before she answers. It's Morgan. She straightens up in her seat, anticipation building in her chest.

MORGAN *(on the phone, his voice steady)*

"Onica, the court has ruled in your favor. You now have full control of the company, and the restraining order against you has been lifted."

For a heartbeat, Onica is silent. The words sink in, her mind struggling to process the reality of it. Full control of the company. No more legal battles, no more fear. She takes a slow breath, her heart swelling with gratitude and relief.

ONICA *(softly, almost whispering)*
"Thank you, Morgan. It's been a long and difficult journey."
MORGAN *(his tone warm, filled with pride)*
"You've shown remarkable strength throughout this process, Onica. I'm glad justice has prevailed."

A rush of emotion fills her chest, and she closes her eyes for a moment, allowing herself to savor the feeling. All the late nights, the sleepless hours spent preparing her case, the uncertainty of it all—it has all led to this. She's won.

ONICA *(a contented smile forming, her voice steady now)*
"I can finally move forward and honor Peter's memory."
MORGAN *(encouragingly, his voice carrying a note of optimism)*
"And you have a bright future ahead of you, Onica. Use this opportunity to make the company thrive."

Onica nods, even though Morgan can't see it, the conviction settling in her bones. The path ahead is clear now. She knows what she has to do—not just for the company, but for herself, for Peter's legacy. She will rebuild, reimagine, and lead the way forward.

ONICA *(with quiet determination)*
"I will, Morgan. I'll make sure Peter's legacy lives on."

As she ends the call, Onica takes a long, steadying breath, her gaze drifting once more to the outside world. The sun is lower now, casting a golden hue over everything, and for the first time in what feels like forever, she can see the future with hope. The weight of the past has been lifted, and she's free—free to create, to rebuild, and to honor the man she loved.

She looks around the room, the familiar surroundings of her home suddenly feeling more like a sanctuary than it ever has. The emptiness that once threatened to swallow her now feels like a space filled with potential.

Onica takes another sip of her tea, her heart at ease for the first time in a long while, ready to step into a new chapter. The future is hers.

The courtroom is thick with tension as the evidence is presented. The large screen flickers to life, displaying the series of photographs that have suddenly become the focus of the trial. The pictures show Onica and her former boyfriend sitting together, speaking intimately, a stark contrast to the grief-stricken widow everyone had assumed Onica to be.

MORGAN, the magistrate, leans forward, his brow furrowed in confusion. He had been following the case closely, but this new evidence takes him by surprise. He shifts uncomfortably in his chair, glancing at Onica, who sits stiffly beside Mrs. Martin, her face pale and drawn.

JERSEY'S LAWYER *(his voice firm, confident)*
"Your Honor, we have undeniable evidence that calls into question the sincerity of Mrs. Martin's claims. These pictures were taken after her husband's passing, suggesting that she was not grieving as deeply as she pretends. Her actions here speak volumes about her true intentions."

A murmur ripples through the courtroom, and Mrs. Martin, sitting next to Onica, mutters under her breath, her eyes wide with concern.

MRS. MARTIN *(whispering, visibly upset)*
"Oh no, this isn't good."

Onica's body tenses beside her mother-in-law, her fingers tightening on the armrest. She had known this moment would come, but the reality of it—the cold, clinical nature of the accusations—still strikes her like a blow to the chest.

Jersey's lawyer presses on, his eyes narrowing as he turns back to Onica. His voice, cold and deliberate, cuts through the room.

JERSEY'S LAWYER *(intense, addressing Onica)*

"Mrs. Martin, can you clarify the nature of your relationship with this man? Were you dating him before your marriage, during your marriage, or right after your wedding?"

Onica feels the room grow smaller, suffocating, as the eyes of the courtroom turn toward her. She feels the heat rise in her cheeks, a rush of anxiety flooding her system. The question feels like a trap, each word twisting around her, tightening its grip.

Her throat is dry, and for a moment, she can't speak. The photographs, flashing on the screen, feel like a mirror reflecting every mistake she's made. She tries to gather her thoughts, to form a coherent response, but her mind is blank.

ONICA *(nervous, voice shaking)*
"I... we... it wasn't during the marriage, but..."

Her voice falters, and her words trail off, the pressure mounting as she struggles to find the right thing to say. She feels the eyes of the entire courtroom on her, the weight of judgment crushing down on her. The walls seem to close in.

Before she can finish her sentence, the strain becomes too much. Her vision swims, the room tilting dangerously, and she feels a sharp, dizzying sensation in her head. She opens her mouth to speak but can't form the words. The world around her spins faster and faster, and she collapses forward, her body crumpling to the floor in an uncontrollable heap.

MORGAN *(shouting, voice filled with authority)*
"Order in the court!"

Chaos erupts as people jump to their feet. A hush falls over the room, and the sound of feet scrambling across the polished floor fills the air. The paramedics rush in, pushing past the onlookers to get to Onica's side.

Onica's world becomes a blur of noise and motion as she's gently lifted and carried out of the courtroom. The last thing she hears is Morgan's voice, distant and concerned, calling for a recess.

MORGAN *(calling out to the room)*
"We'll recess for the day. Everyone, please remain calm."

But Onica isn't listening anymore. Her vision fades, and she sinks into unconsciousness, the weight of the courtroom's judgment still heavy on her shoulders.

Onica sits alone in her dimly lit apartment, the weight of her actions pressing down on her like a suffocating cloud. The evening light filters through the blinds, casting long shadows across the room. She stares at a family photo on the coffee table, her eyes tracing the smiling faces of Peter and their child. Once, this image had been a symbol of a life she cherished, a future she believed in. Now, it feels like a cruel reminder of what she's lost—both in the world and in herself.

ONICA *(softly, to herself)*
"What have I done? Was it worth it?"

Her voice is barely a whisper, as if the question itself is too painful to ask aloud. The silence in the room is deafening, the only sound her shallow breathing and the ticking of the clock on the wall. Her hands tremble slightly as she picks up the photo, holding it close to her chest.

ONICA *(guilt-ridden, almost pleading)*
"Eliminating Jersey... to regain control... I never thought it would feel like this."

Her gaze drifts to the window, where the world outside seems unaware of the storm raging within her. The city is quiet, but in her mind, everything is in chaos. She tries to justify her actions, to convince herself that it was the only way to secure her future, but the weight of the choices she's made feels heavier with each passing second.

ONICA *(whispering, to herself)*
"I've sacrificed my principles. And Peter... I wonder if he would be proud of me."

The thought of Peter, his unwavering moral compass, sends a pang of pain through her heart. She had promised him, on their wedding day, that she would always choose the right path. But now, standing at the edge of this dark place, she isn't so sure what the right path even is anymore.

A knock at the door interrupts her reverie, the sharp sound cutting through the heavy silence. Startled, Onica stands up quickly, wiping away the tears that have begun to fall. She takes a moment to steady herself before walking to the door, unsure of what to expect. When she opens it, Morgan, her attorney, stands on the threshold. His face is etched with concern, his usual confidence replaced by a somber expression.

MORGAN *(gently, his voice soft)*
"Onica, I can see you're tormented by what we did."

Onica's breath catches in her throat, and she steps back, allowing him to enter. She doesn't have the strength to hide her emotions anymore. Her walls have come down, and all that's left is the raw truth of what she's done.

ONICA *(voice trembling, tearful)*
"Morgan... it's not just about the company. It's about the choices I made. I don't know if I can live with this."

Her words hang in the air between them, a confession she's never said aloud. She had been so focused on the end goal—on securing the company and her future—that she hadn't stopped to consider the cost of those decisions until now. Now, as she faces the consequences of her actions, the guilt and doubt threaten to consume her.

Morgan sighs and sits beside her, his presence a quiet comfort in the storm of her emotions.

MORGAN *(supportive, yet pragmatic)*

"We made difficult choices in difficult circumstances. Sometimes, the path to justice isn't clear-cut. But Onica, you did what you thought was necessary."

She shakes her head, not convinced by his words. The weight of the truth lingers, heavy and unforgiving.

ONICA *(torn, voice barely audible)*

"But what's the cost of those choices? The moral consequences... I can't ignore them anymore."

Morgan watches her closely, his expression thoughtful, before he speaks again, his tone gentle but firm.

MORGAN *(wise, reassuring)*

"Onica, life is filled with gray areas. The important thing is what you do next. How you use this second chance."

His words hang in the air, giving her something to hold on to. She isn't sure if it's enough, but it's a start. She still feels the sting of what she's lost—her sense of self, the values she once held dear—but she knows deep down that her story isn't over yet. There's still time to make things right.

Onica exhales slowly, as if releasing some of the tension that has built up in her chest. She looks back at the family photo, her mind swirling with thoughts of the future. It won't be easy, and she isn't sure where to begin, but for the first time in a long while, she feels a flicker of hope.

Perhaps there is still a way to rebuild, to find redemption and peace. It's not going to be simple, but she's ready to try. For herself. For Peter. For the future she wants to create, not out of fear or greed, but out of the strength to choose what is right.

The air is thick with tension as Onica and her attorney, Morgan, stand before the judge. The courtroom has been silent for what feels like an eternity, the evidence they've presented still hanging in the air like a dense fog. Onica's heart pounds in her chest, every beat a reminder of the long, exhausting journey she's endured to get to this moment.

The judge, a seasoned figure of authority, flips through the final pages of the case file. Her gaze sharpens as she assesses the weight of the evidence before her.

JUDGE
(impressed, authoritative)
"After reviewing the evidence and conducting a thorough investigation, it is clear that Ms. Onica is the rightful wife of the late Peter. The marriage certificate was incorrect."

A wave of relief washes over Onica, her hands trembling slightly as she tries to steady herself. This battle, the one that has consumed her every waking hour, is finally coming to an end. She can hardly breathe, the tension in her body starting to dissipate as the judge continues.

JUDGE
(with finality)
"Ms. Onica, you now have full control over your late husband's company, and the restraining order against you is lifted."

Onica can barely process the words. The world around her seems to slow as she hears them—her body flooding with a rush of emotion. It's over. It's really over. The fight for Peter's legacy, for her place in it, has been won.

ONICA
(grateful, barely above a whisper)
"Thank you, Your Honor."

She turns her head, her eyes catching the framed photo of Peter that sits on a nearby shelf in the courtroom. The sight of him, smiling and proud, stirs something deep within her. It's as though he's right there beside her, reassuring her that everything has led to this moment—that she has done right by him.

Morgan stands beside her, his face glowing with pride as he watches the judgment unfold. He had always believed in her, even when Onica herself had begun to doubt.

MORGAN
(proudly)
"This is a victory for justice, Onica."

ONICA
(with quiet emotion)
"It's been a long and difficult journey, but we did it."

As the courtroom clears and the weight of the decision settles in, Onica and Morgan exchange a silent moment of understanding. The battle has been hard-fought, but they've come out victorious.

INT. ONICA'S LIVING ROOM – MORNING

The sun streams through the large window, casting warm light across the room. Onica sits at her dining table, the scent of tea in the air, the cup cupped between her hands. She gazes out of the window, lost in thought, her mind drifting over everything that has transpired. It's as though the world has been restored to some semblance of balance, and for the first time in a long while, she feels at peace.

Her phone rings, breaking the quiet of the room. Onica's heart gives a small flutter, her fingers instinctively reaching for it. The caller ID reads *Morgan*.

ONICA
(answering, with a soft smile)
"Hello, Morgan."

MORGAN
(on the phone, with pride)
"Onica, the court has ruled in your favor. You now have full control of the company, and the restraining order against you has been lifted."

Onica leans back in her chair, the weight of Morgan's words sinking in. Her breath comes easier now, and a smile tugs at the corners of her lips.

ONICA
(relieved, sincere)
"Thank you, Morgan. It's been a long and difficult journey."

MORGAN
(proud, with warmth in his voice)
"You've shown remarkable strength throughout this process, Onica. I'm glad justice has prevailed."

A soft laugh escapes Onica's lips, the release of tension almost palpable. She places her cup of tea down gently on the table, her eyes tracing the path of sunlight across the room. It's as though the world itself is acknowledging her victory.

ONICA
(content, looking out the window)
"I can finally move forward and honor Peter's memory."

The words feel like a promise, a new chapter unfolding before her.

MORGAN
(encouraging, with quiet conviction)
"And you have a bright future ahead of you, Onica. Use this opportunity to make the company thrive."

Onica nods, her heart filled with a renewed sense of purpose. There will be challenges ahead, no doubt, but she feels ready to face them. Peter's legacy will continue through her, and with her own hands, she will build something that honors the love and dedication they once shared.

ONICA
(determined, with clarity)
"I will, Morgan. I'll make sure Peter's legacy lives on."

As Onica ends the call, she sits back in her chair, her gaze drifting around her living room. It's not just the physical space that has shifted; it's her entire sense of self. The weight of the past has lifted, and with it, a new sense of hope fills her.

She is no longer just Peter's widow. She is Onica Martin, the woman who will shape the future of the company, and she is ready to take the first step forward.

Onica stood at the front of the courtroom, her hands clasped tightly in front of her. Her heart raced, the anticipation hanging in the air like a heavy fog. Morgan, her attorney, stood beside her, his posture confident yet knowing the stakes. The room was silent, all eyes on the judge, who had been reviewing the evidence they'd painstakingly presented. Every moment felt like a test of endurance, the weight of years of struggle and sacrifice pushing down on her shoulders.

The judge, a woman with a sharp gaze and a commanding presence, scanned the documents in front of her one last time. She adjusted her glasses, looking up at Onica with an expression that betrayed neither sympathy nor judgment—just the cold precision of the law.

JUDGE
(impressed, but firm)
"After reviewing the evidence and conducting a thorough investigation, it is clear that Ms. Onica is the rightful wife of the late Peter. The marriage certificate was incorrect."

A shiver ran through Onica at the words, a mixture of relief and disbelief surging through her veins. Her body seemed to freeze for a second as the gravity of the moment sank in. This was it—the moment she'd fought for, the moment that would define the course of her life.

JUDGE
(authoritative)

"Ms. Onica, you now have full control over your late husband's company, and the restraining order against you is lifted."

Onica's breath caught in her throat. Her entire body sagged with the sudden release of tension, and the pounding of her heart began to slow. She had won. She had *finally* won. The road to this victory had been long, tangled with pain, lies, and obstacles that seemed insurmountable, but here she was—on the other side of it.

She whispered a quiet "Thank you, Your Honor," the words almost lost in the weight of her emotions. She wanted to say more, wanted to express how much this moment meant, but the lump in her throat made it impossible.

Her eyes instinctively sought out the framed photo of Peter on the wall nearby. It was a picture of them together, smiling, carefree—a time before everything had gone awry. Onica silently thanked him for his love, for the life they'd shared, and for giving her the strength to fight for what was rightfully hers.

MORGAN
(with pride, his voice warm)
"This is a victory for justice, Onica."

ONICA
(grateful, with a soft sigh of relief)
"It's been a long and difficult journey, but we did it."

The words felt both hollow and full, as if they had taken an eternity to come out, yet still couldn't fully encapsulate the enormity of the battle she'd fought. But now, in the quiet aftermath, she allowed herself a moment to savor the victory.

The morning light spilled softly into the room, the golden glow settling over the furniture like a blanket. Onica sat at her dining table, her cup of tea still warm in her hands. She gazed out the window, her mind far away, replaying the events of the past days and weeks in flashes. Her thoughts were as scattered as the sunlight across the floor—distant yet comforting.

Her phone rang, breaking the stillness of the moment. Onica reached for it absently, recognizing the number before she even looked.

ONICA
(answering with a calm, steady voice)
"Hello, Morgan."

MORGAN
(on the phone, his voice full of pride)
"Onica, the court has ruled in your favor. You now have full control of the company, and the restraining order against you has been lifted."

The words hit her like a wave crashing over a shoreline, and for a moment, she simply stared at her phone in disbelief, as though the reality of it all still hadn't fully settled. But then, the rush of gratitude and relief came pouring in. She could hardly believe it—it was finally over.

ONICA
(softly, grateful)
"Thank you, Morgan. It's been a long and difficult journey."

MORGAN
(with genuine warmth)
"You've shown remarkable strength throughout this process, Onica. I'm glad justice has prevailed."

A smile tugged at the corners of Onica's lips as she placed the phone on speaker, her hand trembling slightly as she took a sip of her tea. The weight of everything she'd endured, every sleepless night, every argument, every setback, seemed to drain from her in that moment.

ONICA
(content, her voice filled with quiet resolve)
"I can finally move forward and honor Peter's memory."

She felt a strange calm wash over her—like a weight lifting from her chest, leaving room for something new to grow. The past had been heavy, but now, there was space for the future.

MORGAN
(encouraging, as though speaking to a friend)
"And you have a bright future ahead of you, Onica. Use this opportunity to make the company thrive."

The words were a promise, a challenge. Onica could feel the weight of them, but this time, it didn't feel burdensome. It felt like something to aspire to, something that could finally be within reach.

ONICA
(determined, her voice firm)
"I will, Morgan. I'll make sure Peter's legacy lives on."

As Onica ended the call, she set the phone down gently, her eyes wandering around her living room. It was the same room she'd sat in countless times, in moments of doubt and worry. But now, it felt different—brighter, somehow, as though the light had come back into the space.

With a deep breath, she stood up and walked over to the framed picture of Peter, placing a hand on the glass. "I'll do it for you," she whispered, a sense of peace settling over her like a warm embrace.

For the first time in a long time, Onica felt ready. Ready to take back control. Ready to honor her husband's memory. Ready to carve out a future that was truly her own.

The hum of the office filled the air as Onica and Jersey sat side by side at the long conference table, papers and laptops spread out before them. The atmosphere was different now, quieter, yet charged with a sense of shared purpose. It hadn't always been this way—only a few months ago, the tension between them had been palpable, a bitter rivalry clouding every decision. But now, there was a calm that neither of them had expected, an understanding that had grown out of necessity, and, perhaps, something deeper.

Onica glanced over at Jersey, who was reviewing a financial report with a focused expression. A small, contented smile tugged at the corners of Onica's lips. They had come a long way from the days of distrust and conflict, the weight of their struggles now behind them.

ONICA
(smiling softly)
"Jersey, it's been a challenging journey, but I think we're finally finding our rhythm."

Jersey looked up, meeting Onica's gaze. Her grin was wide, genuine—a far cry from the guarded expression she used to wear whenever Onica spoke to her.

JERSEY
(grinning)
"It hasn't been easy, Onica, but I think we're making it work."

There was an unspoken understanding in her voice. Despite the bumps along the way, despite the hurdles they'd both had to overcome, they had found a way to work together. The past was still there, hovering like a shadow, but it no longer defined them. Their collaboration had become something far more productive than either of them had ever imagined.

Their eyes drifted to the framed photo of Peter on the wall—his smile frozen in time, a reminder of everything they'd both lost, and everything they had to gain. The picture was more than just a tribute to Peter; it had become a silent symbol of their journey together.

ONICA
(reflective, her voice softening)
"I think Peter would be proud of what we've accomplished."

Jersey's gaze lingered on the photo for a moment before she nodded, her expression thoughtful. There was a deep sincerity in her eyes as she spoke.

JERSEY

(nodding, with quiet conviction)
"I'd like to think so. We're honoring his legacy."

A comfortable silence settled between them, one that felt different from the tension that had once ruled their interactions. They had both changed—shaped by the trials they had faced, but also by the mutual respect that had slowly taken root. There was no longer the need to fight for control, no need to prove who was right. They had both come to understand that their success depended on working together, on finding common ground, and on keeping Peter's memory alive in the work they did.

Onica reached for a document, her fingers brushing against Jersey's as they both reached for the same page. They shared a brief smile, and in that small gesture, there was more understanding than words could express.

ONICA
(with a small chuckle)
"Looks like we're finally in sync."

JERSEY
(laughing lightly)
"About time."

Their laughter faded, but the lightness remained. It was a rare moment of peace, one they both cherished. As they returned to their work, their movements were more in tune, their decisions more aligned. The future of the company seemed brighter now, not just because they had achieved success, but because they had learned to trust each other.

The journey had been hard, and the scars of the past would always linger, but now, as they worked side by side, Onica and Jersey both knew that they had finally found something worth fighting for—together.

Onica sat alone at Peter's old desk, papers and business plans scattered in front of her. The once-familiar space now felt colder, haunted by memories of her late husband and the weight of the responsibility that had fallen on her shoulders. Her fingers traced the edges of a document, her thoughts drifting as she considered the future of the company—Peter's legacy.

Suddenly, the door to the office creaked open, and Onica's attention snapped back to the present. She looked up, startled, as Jersey stepped into the room. The suddenness of her appearance took Onica by surprise.

JERSEY
(firm, eyes sharp)
"Onica, we need to talk."

Onica's heart skipped a beat. She hadn't seen Jersey since the accident, and now, here she was, walking into the very heart of Peter's empire like she owned it.

ONICA
(startled, standing up)
"Jersey, where have you been? You disappeared after the accident."

Jersey didn't falter. Her gaze was unflinching, her presence commanding as she walked into the room. She stood tall, her posture resolute.

JERSEY
(confident, almost defiant)
"I've been dealing with personal matters. But I'm back now. And I want my share of the company."

Onica's breath caught in her chest. She hadn't expected this. Jersey's words hung heavy in the air, carrying a sense of finality that made Onica's pulse quicken.

ONICA
(hesitant, searching for her bearings)
"Jersey, I legally have full control of the company now. You're not a part of it anymore."

Jersey's eyes narrowed, and the air between them grew tense. She crossed her arms, standing her ground.

JERSEY
(demanding, unyielding)
"Onica, I'm still legally married to Peter. And I want a share of what's rightfully mine. I won't let this go."

The words hit Onica like a blow. A part of her wanted to argue, to remind Jersey of all the work she had put into this—how she had taken control, made difficult decisions, and fought for the company's survival after Peter's death. But Jersey's presence in the room was like a shadow, reminding Onica that no matter the legalities, Jersey had a claim—a connection that couldn't be dismissed so easily.

ONICA
(conflicted, her voice wavering)
"But I've worked hard to make the company thrive. I can't just give it away."

Jersey stepped closer, her expression hardening as she stood before Onica, unwavering in her resolve.

JERSEY
(insistent, voice low but firm)
"And I need job security. I want a position in the company, too."

Onica's mind raced, torn between the legal victory she had fought so hard to achieve and the undeniable truth that Jersey still had rights—rights tied to her marriage to Peter. The room felt smaller now, the space between them charged with the weight of unspoken history.

Onica's hands shook as she clenched them into fists, the papers on the desk now a blur in front of her. She didn't want to back down, didn't want to give up what she had worked so tirelessly to build.

ONICA
(struggling, her voice soft but determined)

"Jersey, let's find a compromise. We can work together, but I can't just hand over everything."

Jersey's gaze never wavered. There was no trace of doubt in her eyes, no sign of hesitation. She had come for what she believed was hers, and she wasn't about to back down.

JERSEY
(resolute, her voice unwavering)
"I won't back down, Onica. We share a history with Peter, and we both deserve a place in his legacy."

The words lingered in the room, the challenge clear. Onica felt the weight of them press against her chest. She had been prepared to fight for control of the company, but this was different. This was a battle not just for business but for the memories and the legacy of a man who had once brought them together.

For the first time in a long while, Onica wasn't sure what the future held.

The night was heavy with silence, the kind of silence that felt too thick, too suffocating. Onica stood, her fingers trembling as she clasped her hands together, the weight of what they were about to do pressing heavily on her chest. Morgan stood beside her, his face hard, his eyes scanning the empty street ahead. He didn't look nervous. But Onica could feel his tension—an almost palpable electricity in the air.

The plan was simple: manipulate, deceive, and make sure Jersey would never threaten her claim on the company again. The stakes were higher than ever. Once they set this in motion, there was no going back.

MORGAN
(whispering, his voice low)
"Remember, Onica, once this is done, there's no turning back."

Onica nodded, but her heart was pounding so loudly in her ears she could barely hear him. She swallowed hard, trying to steady her breath, to calm the whirlwind inside her. She wasn't sure what scared her more—the fact that she had come this far or the dangerous road ahead.

ONICA
(nervous but resolute, her voice tight)
"I know, Morgan. This is the only way."

The headlights of a car suddenly pierced the darkness, its approach growing louder. The car that had been expected. Jersey. Onica felt a strange flicker of guilt but shoved it down—this wasn't about feelings anymore. This was about securing her future, her place in the company Peter had built.

As the car neared, Onica pulled out her phone and dialed Jersey's number. Her fingers felt stiff, but she managed to press the buttons, her pulse racing. The phone rang three times before Jersey picked up.

JERSEY
(on the phone, her voice laced with concern)
"Onica? Where are you?"

Onica hesitated for a fraction of a second, pretending she was out of breath, her panic building. She had to make it believable.

ONICA
(feigning panic, her voice quivering)
"Jersey, I need your help. I'm stranded on this dark road. I don't know what to do."

There was a brief pause, and Onica could almost hear Jersey's brain working through the possibilities. Would she fall for it? Would she come?

JERSEY
(concerned, a hint of urgency in her tone)
"I'm almost there. Just stay put. Don't move."

Onica's eyes darted to the headlights in the distance. The moment was coming, and it was all she could do to keep her composure. She felt the weight of her actions like an iron anchor pulling her down, but there was no turning back. Not now.

As Jersey's car neared, a dark figure stepped out from the shadows, the driver of the other car—Morgan's accomplice—swerved into the path of Jersey's vehicle. The sudden maneuver was deliberate, the crash timed perfectly.

A deafening collision rang through the night, followed by the sickening screech of metal grinding against metal. Onica's stomach twisted, but she forced herself to watch, her breath held, her heart racing in her chest.

JERSEY
(panicking, her voice trembling)
"Oh my god! What just happened?"

From where Onica and Morgan stood, hidden in the shadows of the alleyway, they could see the chaos unfold. The smoke from the crash began to rise, and Jersey stumbled out of her car, disoriented, shaking, trying to make sense of the accident. Her hands gripped the door frame for support, her face pale in the dim glow of the streetlights.

MORGAN
(whispering to Onica, his voice low and cool)
"This is it, Onica. Our plan is in motion."

Onica nodded, her eyes locked on Jersey's every move. She could feel the tension in her own body, an almost sick satisfaction bubbling beneath her skin. Jersey, now helpless, was the final piece in their plan. She had to be.

They watched in silence as Jersey stumbled, her movements slow and disoriented. The woman who had once been a formidable adversary, a threat to everything Onica had fought for, was now at her mercy. The staged accident was playing out just as planned.

Onica's breath escaped in a soft sigh as she turned to Morgan. Their plan was unfolding perfectly—too perfectly. And yet, the sense of dread that hung over her like a shroud refused to lift.

She watched as Jersey tried to gather herself, her eyes darting in every direction, her confusion clear. But Onica wasn't there to help her. She wasn't there to save her.

Not anymore.

The soft hum of the afternoon settled over the house, but a sudden knock at the door shattered the calm. Onica's heart jolted, and she set down the cup she had been holding, her fingers still lingering on the edge of the porcelain. She wasn't expecting anyone.

With a deep breath, she opened the door, and standing in front of her was a man she'd never seen before—tall, with a confident, almost imposing air about him. His eyes, though, held an intensity that made Onica instinctively take a step back.

JAMES
(with a firm tone)
"I'm James, Peter's cousin. I've come to discuss my rights in the family business."

The words hung in the air, heavy and unexpected. Onica's stomach tightened, the weight of the moment sinking in. She stared at him for a long moment, her mind racing.

ONICA
(defensive, her voice steady but laced with disbelief)
"What rights are you talking about? This is my late husband's business, and I'm the legitimate heir."

The audacity of this man standing at her doorstep, claiming a stake in Peter's legacy, took Onica by surprise. She felt a flare of anger rise in her chest, a fire that had been smoldering for months finally igniting.

James met her gaze with a confident smile, one that didn't reach his eyes. His calm demeanor only deepened her unease.

JAMES
(insistent)
"You may be the one holding the reins now, but the family has a right to be involved. Peter and I were close, and I believe I'm entitled to a say in what happens with the business."

The audacity. The nerve. Onica's pulse quickened. She needed advice. **Now.**

Without another word, she stepped back from the door and grabbed her phone. She quickly dialed her lawyer, Morgan. The line clicked and then connected, his voice immediately answering with an unmistakable firmness.

MORGAN
(on the phone, authoritative)
"Onica? What's going on?"

ONICA
(frustrated, barely holding her composure)
"Morgan, a man named James just showed up at my door claiming to be Peter's cousin. He says he has rights to the business. What do I do?"

MORGAN
(calm, yet stern)
"James claims what? The legitimacy of his rights? I would advise him to challenge those claims in court, Onica. You've already proven your position. You have nothing to worry about."

Onica's hand tightened around the phone, but her gaze remained fixed on James, who was still standing there, waiting, unbothered by her silence. She could feel her blood boiling.

ONICA
(growing agitated, her voice sharp)
"I don't care about his claims! This is my husband's business, and I've worked for it—sacrificed for it. Who the hell does he think he is?"

MORGAN
(firmly reassuring)
"You're in the clear. Stay strong, Onica. He has no legal standing. Don't let him intimidate you."

Onica didn't need to hear any more. She was done with this conversation. She hung up the phone with determination, her grip still tight. Then, without warning, she turned back to James, who was still standing at the door, as though he were waiting for an invitation.

ONICA
(her voice low, cold with fury)
"Listen, I don't know who you are, but I suggest you leave. There's no place for you here."

James' smile faltered, but he didn't move. His stance remained unchanged, as if testing her.

Onica didn't hesitate. Her frustration reached a boiling point. She didn't have time for games, for idle threats, for anyone who thought they could take what belonged to her. She grabbed the nearest object she could reach—a kettle of hot water, still steaming from when she'd boiled it for tea earlier—and waved it toward him, her voice rising.

ONICA
(furious, her eyes burning with resolve)
"Get out of my house. Now."

James flinched, taken aback by her sudden aggression. Onica took a step forward, the kettle still raised, making her intentions clear. She wasn't backing down.

James held up his hands in mock surrender, his earlier confidence wavering for a moment. "Alright, alright, I'm going," he said, a small smirk playing at the corner of his mouth, though it didn't reach his eyes.

But Onica didn't stop there. She watched him closely as he turned to leave, making sure he knew she meant business. When the door finally slammed shut behind him, she leaned against it, breathing heavily, trying to calm the storm of emotions swirling inside her.

She'd defended her ground—her territory. But she knew this wasn't over. James would be back, of that she was certain.

ONICA
(whispering to herself, a cold edge to her voice)
"This isn't over, James. Not by a long shot."

Onica stealthily tails James, her late husband's supposed long-lost relative, to his residence. As she shadows him through the winding streets of the city, the suspense builds.

The dimly lit surroundings and the purr of her car's engine add to the overall sense of tension. Upon reaching James' home, Onica's car remains parked nearby as she closely observes his every move. Her unyielding determination is evident in her eyes as she waits for the opportune moment to strike.

Finally, as James enters his home, Onica makes her move.

Swiftly and silently, she enters his residence, her every step calculated and deliberate.

She clutches a small, silenced gun tightly in her hand, her finger poised on the trigger.

The air is thick with anticipation. As she approaches James, who is seemingly oblivious to her presence, she takes aim and, with a single gunshot, extinguishes any potential threat he posed to her late husband's business and her own future.

James crumples to the ground in a shocking and irreversible turn of events.

The room hums with energy as Alex's words hang in the air, igniting something within each of the employees gathered. Their faces, once etched with uncertainty, now reflect a collective resolve. The dissatisfaction that had been simmering for months is finally bubbling to the surface, and Alex has become the catalyst for change.

ALEX (cont'd)
(earnestly)
We've been sidelined for too long. But we are the backbone of this company. Without us, none of this runs. They can't ignore us forever.

The employees glance at one another, a sense of solidarity beginning to form. There's a palpable shift in the room. Where there was once doubt, there is now a shared sense of purpose.

EMPLOYEE 1
(agitated)
They've been treating us like we're invisible. It's not right. We work just as hard as anyone else in this company, and they should start recognizing that.

EMPLOYEE 2
(nods)
I've been passed over for promotions year after year. Enough is enough.

Alex paces slowly, drawing the room's attention with their every move. Their voice is steady, unwavering, as they continue to rally the group.

ALEX
(urgent)
This isn't just about pay or recognition. It's about respect. If we don't stand together, they'll continue to trample over us. But if we unite, if we make our voices heard, we'll force them to listen.

EMPLOYEE 3
(energized)
So we're doing this, huh? We're really going to take it to them?

ALEX
(grinning)

Absolutely. But we'll do it smart. A peaceful protest, right in front of the top management. We'll show them just how powerful we are when we stand together. It's time for us to take back control.

The air in the room crackles with the energy of possibility. One by one, the employees exchange looks of determination, ready to follow Alex's lead. The decision has been made, and there's no turning back now.

EMPLOYEE 4
(determined)
This is it. We're not backing down. Let's do this.

ALEX
(supportive)
Together, we're unstoppable.

As the employees nod in agreement, the sense of unity is almost tangible. Alex looks around the room, their gaze meeting each person's, and knows that this is just the beginning. The protest will be the first step, but the real challenge lies ahead. They've lit a spark, and now they're ready to watch it blaze.

The charismatic leader has sparked a rebellion within the company, and the employees are ready to fight for their rights and bring about change.

The atmosphere in the office has shifted. What began as a simple conversation about protesting for better treatment has now evolved into something more urgent, more significant. The air is thick with a mixture of uncertainty and resolve as Sarah stands before her coworkers, holding their attention like a magnet.

SARAH
(voice steady, though trembling slightly)
I know this isn't easy to hear, but we need to know the full truth. The company has been hiding a lot from us—things that could change everything.

EMPLOYEE 1

(skeptical, narrowing their eyes)

What do you mean, Sarah? What kind of things are we talking about?

Sarah takes a deep breath, her hands gripping a folder she's brought with her, the papers inside shaking slightly from her clenched fingers. The buzz in the room grows quieter as her words begin to sink in.

SARAH

(quietly, with conviction)

There's been financial mismanagement—big discrepancies in the books. But that's just the tip of the iceberg. I've also uncovered unethical practices. We're talking about shady deals with vendors, skimming off the top, and a complete lack of transparency with our dealings. This company is not the place we think it is.

A heavy silence falls over the group. The employees exchange glances, their faces a mixture of disbelief and dawning concern. Sarah's words have landed, and the weight of her revelation begins to settle into their minds.

EMPLOYEE 2

(softly, incredulously)

Are you serious, Sarah? That... that sounds insane.

SARAH

(urgently, nodding)

I've been watching this for months. Keeping a record. And I can prove it. I'm not making this up.

EMPLOYEE 3

(nervously)

But if we go public with this—if we blow the whistle—what happens? Are we just going to lose our jobs? We're talking about exposing some heavy stuff here. It could backfire badly.

Sarah's gaze hardens, her voice stronger now, filled with the kind of resolve that had been missing from their conversations about protests.

SARAH
(firmly)
I know the risks. Believe me, I've thought about them. But we've been complicit in letting this go on for far too long. If we don't stand up now, we'll be part of the problem. This is bigger than us—and I'm not going to sit back and do nothing while they line their pockets with our hard work.

The employees fall into a tense silence, the weight of Sarah's words hanging in the air. No one speaks immediately. It's clear that while they want change, the stakes are higher now, and the consequences far more dire.

EMPLOYEE 1
(quietly, but with growing conviction)
I'm with you, Sarah. We can't ignore this anymore. We've been here too long, watching things get worse. If we've got the proof, we can't keep pretending it's not happening.

EMPLOYEE 2
(sighing deeply)
This is insane. But you're right... it's now or never.

EMPLOYEE 3
(uneasily)
But what do we do with this information? How do we make sure we're not left holding the bag when it all goes down?

SARAH
(determined)
We take it to the authorities. We go public, with the right evidence. We're not doing this for revenge; we're doing it because it's right. I've already contacted a lawyer to help us with the next steps. We won't go in blind.

There's a collective sigh, some of the employees looking toward one another, their faces tight with uncertainty, but also a sense of purpose. What started as a conversation about standing up for their rights has transformed into a bold, dangerous stand against the very company they've worked for.

A quiet resolve settles over the group. They know the road ahead will be treacherous, but there's no turning back now.

ALEX
(stepping forward, voice strong)

Sarah's right. We can't stay silent anymore. If we don't take action, nothing will change. We need to expose this—and together, we'll make sure they hear us.

The others nod in agreement, their voices murmuring, a wave of collective action slowly building in the room. The decision is made. They will fight for what's right, no matter the cost.

As the tension begins to lift, a sense of unity forms among them. They're no longer just employees, fighting for pay raises or recognition. They're crusaders, now united by a common cause—bringing the truth to light, no matter the consequences.

The employees gather at a discreet location to discuss their options, knowing that their decision to blow the whistle could forever change their lives and the company's fate.

The boardroom was charged with an electric tension, the air thick with the simmering frustrations of the employees who had gathered in force. At the head of the table, Onica sat, her hands clenched tightly in front of her as she tried to maintain an air of authority. Beside her, Morgan and her legal team sat in tense silence, their eyes flicking nervously between the employees and their increasingly volatile demands.

At the front of the room stood the Employee Leader, his presence commanding attention, his voice steady but filled with undeniable resolve.

EMPLOYEE LEADER
(firmly)
We've had enough of this mismanagement! It's time for a change!

The murmurs of agreement spread like wildfire through the room, escalating in volume as the employees nodded vigorously, their faces etched with frustration.

EMPLOYEE 1
(angry)
We've been suffering long enough under this leadership!

EMPLOYEE 2
(shouting)
We need someone who knows what they're doing to take charge!

EMPLOYEE 3
(demanding)
We demand a say in the future of this company!

Onica's stomach churned. She straightened in her chair, her breath shallow, as the voices of dissent began to fill the room. She had never felt so vulnerable in her own space, surrounded by the people whose loyalty had once been the backbone of the company. She opened her mouth to speak, but the words caught in her throat.

Her hands trembled slightly as she tried to appear composed, but the cracks in her confidence were beginning to show.

ONICA
(pleading)
Please, I understand your concerns, but we're working on improving the company. We've been taking steps behind the scenes. Just give us some more time.

The Employee Leader didn't flinch. His eyes remained locked on hers, unyielding.

EMPLOYEE LEADER
(determined)

Words aren't enough. We want action! We've heard enough promises. What are you going to do about it?

Morgan, ever the calm voice of reason, leaned forward, his tone measured and controlled, a stark contrast to the rising tension in the room.

MORGAN
(calmly)

We're in the process of considering various options, but we need time to evaluate them thoroughly. Rushed decisions won't solve anything.

But his words were met with harsh skepticism.

EMPLOYEE LEADER
(skeptical)

Time? We've given you enough time. This is about our jobs, our futures. You don't get to keep us waiting indefinitely.

A new voice joined the fray, a female employee standing up, her voice rising in a mixture of frustration and accusation.

EMPLOYEE 4
(accusing)

Our livelihoods are at stake, and we can't wait any longer!

Onica's heart thudded painfully in her chest as the room buzzed with angry voices. The weight of their dissatisfaction, their fear of losing everything, pressed in on her, suffocating the air from her lungs.

ONICA
(desperate)

I promise we'll do everything we can to address your concerns. Just give us a little more time, please. We're working on it, I swear.

Her voice cracked slightly, the strain of the moment breaking through her usually composed exterior. She could feel the eyes of the room on her—judging, weighing, and seeing through her fragile attempts at control.

The Employee Leader exchanged glances with the others, his jaw tightening as he measured his next words carefully.

EMPLOYEE LEADER
(measuring)
We'll give you a bit more time. But we're watching closely. If things don't change soon, you'll see what happens.

The threat was implicit, hanging heavily in the air.

Onica exhaled a shaky breath, her body sagging with the weight of his words. There was no mistaking the seriousness of their stance. The rebellion was simmering, and she could feel it edging ever closer to the point of no return.

ONICA
(relieved)
Thank you. We'll do our best to make things right.

With that, the employees began to file out of the room, their murmurs still echoing in the hallways. The tension lingered long after they left, hanging in the air like a storm cloud that refused to disperse.

Onica remained at the head of the table, staring at the empty space where they had stood. Her mind raced, her thoughts scattered, and her hands still trembled slightly. She could feel the gravity of the situation in every fiber of her being. She had won this round, but the battle wasn't over—not by a long shot.

Morgan and the rest of her legal team exchanged worried looks, knowing that they were walking a razor-thin line. This wasn't just about her position anymore; it was about the company's survival.

As the last of the employees left the building, Onica stood up, her gaze lingering on the empty chairs. She had to fix this. She had no choice.

But the clock was ticking. And the future of the company—her future—hung in the balance.

The rhythmic hum of the office was disrupted by the sound of raised voices near the entrance. The usual murmur of typing and phone calls faltered as employees glanced nervously at one another, unsure of what was happening. Onica sat in a conference room, her brow furrowed as she discussed ongoing matters with Morgan and their legal team, when the ruckus reached a boiling point.

VENGEFUL EX-EMPLOYEE

(shouting)

You thought you could get rid of me, huh?

The sound of his voice was unmistakable—loud, angry, and filled with bitter malice. The door to the office flew open, and the ex-employee, a man Onica recognized immediately, stormed inside. His face was twisted in fury, and his eyes burned with an unmistakable desire for vengeance.

Employees froze in place, some hesitating, others too shocked to move. A few peeked from behind cubicles, trying to get a glimpse of the chaos unfolding. Onica's heart skipped a beat as she exchanged a quick, alarmed glance with Morgan.

ONICA

(calmly)

What's going on here? How did you get in?

The ex-employee's sneer deepened as he stood in the middle of the office, his posture rigid with defiance. He was wearing a scornful grin as he turned his eyes to her.

VENGEFUL EX-EMPLOYEE

(mocking)

Oh, Onica, you should have known that you can't just cast me aside. You really thought I'd disappear quietly?

Morgan shot up from his seat, his expression hardening into a mask of controlled authority. His voice was firm, the kind of tone that left no room for argument.

MORGAN
(firmly)
Security, please call the authorities.

The command was sharp, and two security personnel moved quickly toward the phone to make the call. The office had erupted into whispers, employees exchanging nervous glances, unsure of what would happen next. Onica, though outwardly calm, could feel the tension curling in her chest.

ONICA
(pleading)
Please, we can talk about whatever issues you have. There's no need for this chaos.

The man's face twisted with anger at her words. He took a few steps toward her, his hands clenched into fists.

VENGEFUL EX-EMPLOYEE
(agitated)
Talk? You should have thought about that before you fired me!

His voice grew louder, and it was clear he was beyond reason. He made his way toward the central meeting area, pushing past desks and knocking over stacks of paperwork. The sound of papers scattering across the floor added to the chaos.

EMPLOYEE 1
(whispering to Employee 2)
What's going on? Who is that guy?

EMPLOYEE 2
(whispering back)

I heard he used to work here, but he got fired. I don't know the details, but it doesn't look good.

MORGAN
(shouting)
Stay away from those documents!

The ex-employee ignored Morgan's command, snatching up a handful of files and waving them in the air. His face contorted with rage, his eyes wild as he threatened to destroy the documents.

VENGEFUL EX-EMPLOYEE
(snarling)
I'll make sure everything you've built goes up in flames, Onica!

Onica's heart raced, her mind scrambling for a way to diffuse the situation. She stepped forward, her voice shaking with the mix of fear and desperation.

ONICA
(desperate)
Please, stop! We can work this out. Just put the documents down. This isn't the way to handle things.

The ex-employee ignored her, his focus solely on the chaos he was creating. But just as things were about to escalate further, the sound of approaching sirens grew louder, and within moments, security and the authorities burst into the room.

A security officer, his tone unwavering, stepped toward the ex-employee, handcuffs at the ready.

SECURITY OFFICER
(firmly)
You're under arrest for trespassing and causing a disturbance.

The ex-employee spat on the floor, his eyes glaring at Onica one last time with a fierce, bitter hatred.

VENGEFUL EX-EMPLOYEE
(viciously)
This isn't over!

With that, he was led away, his struggles futile against the officers who restrained him. As the door slammed shut behind them, the office was left in stunned silence. Employees returned to their desks, their movements hesitant, as if unsure whether they were safe to continue their work.

Onica stood frozen, her breath shallow, as she watched the scene unfold. Her relief was palpable, but so too was a deep, unsettling sense of unease. She could feel the eyes of her employees on her, some with pity, others with distrust. The disturbance had shaken them all, and though the immediate threat had been neutralized, the damage was done.

As the office slowly returned to its normal rhythm, Onica exchanged a quiet glance with Morgan, both of them understanding the gravity of the situation. This was only one battle in an ongoing war. The unrest was still there, simmering beneath the surface, and the future of the company—her future—remained uncertain.

But for now, at least, the storm had passed.

Onica sat at her desk, her fingers lightly tracing the edges of the papers in front of her, though her mind was far from focused. The weight of the past few months seemed to press down on her with every passing moment. Her eyes wandered to the framed picture of Peter, her late husband, that rested on the corner of the desk. It had once been a symbol of pride, a reminder of their shared dreams, but now it felt like an anchor, holding her to a future she wasn't sure she could bear.

Morgan, seated across from her, spoke in a calm, measured voice, the steady rhythm of his words a stark contrast to the chaos she felt inside.

MORGAN
(softly to Onica)
Onica, this is Mr. Thompson. He's a billionaire investor, and he's shown significant interest in acquiring the company.

The man seated beside Morgan stood up, extending his hand to Onica. He was dressed sharply in a tailored suit, his presence commanding despite the gentle way he spoke. *Mr. Thompson*—a name that seemed to carry a weight of its own—was nothing if not patient. Onica couldn't help but feel a twinge of skepticism in the back of her mind, but she forced herself to smile and shake his hand.

ONICA

(weary)

I've heard the complaints from our employees, and I've seen the company's financial struggles. I don't want to be a hindrance anymore, Morgan.

Her voice was barely a whisper, the words heavy with the defeat that had been mounting inside her for months. The company, her company, her husband's legacy, was slipping through her fingers. She couldn't keep pretending she had the strength to fight for it any longer. She was too tired—physically, emotionally, mentally.

MR. THOMPSON

(sympathetic)

Onica, I understand that this has been a challenging time for you. He paused, his gaze softening, as though he truly understood the gravity of her situation. *I've reviewed the company's financials, and I believe I can help turn things around. I want to see the company thrive again, and with the right resources, I think it can.*

Onica's shoulders slumped. She had heard this before—promises of a turnaround, of new beginnings—but the words had started to ring hollow.

ONICA

(deep sigh)

I'm not sure what the best decision is anymore. I've been fighting for the company and Peter's legacy, but my health is deteriorating.

Her voice cracked, and she quickly looked away, as though the simple acknowledgment of her exhaustion would somehow make it all too real. But there was no avoiding it. The constant pressure, the sleepless nights, the relentless worry—it was all taking its toll. And no matter how much she loved Peter's vision, she couldn't carry it alone anymore.

Morgan, who had been quietly listening, leaned forward slightly, his voice gentle but firm.

MORGAN
(supportive)
Onica, Mr. Thompson has proposed a fair deal. It would secure your financial future and provide a fresh start for the company.

Mr. Thompson nodded, his expression sincere as he added in a low voice.

MR. THOMPSON
(reassuring)
I'm willing to make this transition as smooth as possible. We'll ensure the employees are taken care of, and you'll be able to focus on your health and well-being. You won't have to worry about the company's future anymore.

Onica met his gaze, searching for any sign of insincerity. But there was none. He seemed genuine. Still, the weight of the decision felt unbearable. Letting go of something that had been so entwined with her life, with Peter's life—it was almost too much to contemplate.

She took a shaky breath, her fingers still resting on the desk, and finally spoke, her voice barely audible.

ONICA
(softly)
I never imagined it would come to this, but if it's for the best... I'll agree to the sale. I just hope it's the right decision.

A silence settled over the room, thick with the enormity of her words. Morgan's face softened, a rare show of emotion as he placed a reassuring hand on her shoulder.

MORGAN
(gentle)
It's a difficult choice, Onica, but your health is what matters most. We'll ensure that this transition is handled with care.

Mr. Thompson smiled then, his expression warm, as though he recognized the significance of the moment.

MR. THOMPSON
(smiling)
Thank you for your trust, Onica. Together, we'll find a way to rejuvenate this company.

Onica nodded, her hands shaking slightly as she signed the agreement in front of her. The decision was made. It felt like the end of an era, but it was also a new beginning. She looked up at Mr. Thompson, then at Morgan, and for the first time in what felt like a long while, a faint glimmer of hope flickered in her chest.

As the papers were signed, Onica felt the weight she'd been carrying for so long begin to lift. For the first time, she allowed herself to believe that maybe—just maybe—this was the right decision.

Onica sat at her desk, her fingers hovering over the keyboard, though her thoughts were miles away. The company had been through so much lately, and her mind was heavy with the decisions she had made. The silence in the office was broken only by the faint hum of the air conditioning, but then, unexpectedly, the shrill ring of her phone shattered the calm.

She glanced at the screen and froze. The name *Mr. Rogers* flashed in bold letters across the display. Her stomach twisted. She hesitated for a moment, her hand hovering over the receiver, but then picked it up, trying to steady her breath.

ONICA
(nervous)
Hello? Mr. Rogers?

A pause on the other end of the line, then a low, mocking chuckle.

MR. ROGERS
(threatening)
Onica, we have some unfinished business. You remember the secrets I hold about the illegal profits Peter made and the tax evasions, right?

Her heart skipped a beat. She hadn't heard from him in months, but she knew exactly what he was referring to. The secrets he claimed to possess were dangerous—damning enough to bring the company, and everything she'd fought for, crashing down.

ONICA
(worried)
Mr. Rogers, I don't want any trouble. We can discuss this calmly.

She could hear the cruel smile in his voice as he spoke again.

MR. ROGERS
(smirking)
Oh, I'm sure you don't want trouble. Well, here's how we can avoid it. You pay me a hefty sum, and I'll keep those secrets to myself.

Onica's pulse quickened. A part of her wanted to reach through the phone and strangle the man who was holding her company's future hostage, but she knew better than to act on impulse. She needed to think. Fast.

ONICA
(desperate)
Mr. Rogers, I can't just hand over that kind of money. It's not that simple.

The line went silent for a moment, and Onica's grip tightened on the phone. She could almost feel the weight of his smirk on the other end of the line as he spoke again, his voice cold and calculated.

MR. ROGERS
(cold)

That's your choice. If you're not willing to pay, I'll make sure those secrets find their way into the wrong hands.

The threat hung in the air, chilling and final. Onica's mind raced, her thoughts swirling with all the ways this could spiral out of control. The company. Her late husband's legacy. Everything was at risk. She had no choice but to act.

She took a slow breath, trying to steady her shaking hands, and then forced herself to speak calmly.

ONICA
(nervous)
Let me talk to my attorney about this. We'll find a way to settle this.

There was a pause, and for a moment, she thought he might refuse. But then his voice came back, smooth and mocking.

MR. ROGERS
(smiling)
Wise choice, Onica. But don't take too long. I have a lot of patience, but not that much.

With a final chuckle, he hung up, leaving Onica sitting there, frozen, her heart hammering in her chest. She felt trapped, her back against the wall. There was no easy way out of this. If the information Mr. Rogers held ever saw the light of day, it could ruin everything.

Without wasting another second, Onica grabbed her phone and dialed Morgan's number. The call rang through, each tone reverberating in her chest like the beat of a drum. She needed answers, and she needed them fast.

MORGAN
(voice calm, professional)
Onica? What's going on?

Her voice was barely above a whisper, her anxiety palpable even through the phone.

ONICA
(panicked)

Morgan, it's Mr. Rogers. He's threatening to expose Peter's illegal profits and the tax evasions unless I pay him. He wants a hefty sum, and I don't know what to do.

A brief silence followed, but then Morgan's voice came through, steady and reassuring.

MORGAN
(serious)
We'll deal with this. I'll take care of it. Don't make any decisions without me. I'll need to talk to him and figure out how to handle this legally. Stay calm, Onica. We'll get through this.

Her breath caught in her throat, but she forced herself to nod, even though he couldn't see her.

ONICA
(faintly)
Thank you, Morgan. Please, hurry. I don't know how much longer I can keep him at bay.

She ended the call and sat back in her chair, her mind racing. Mr. Rogers' threat was more than just a demand for money—it was a weapon, and one she wasn't sure how to defuse. All she could do now was trust that Morgan could find a way to make this right.

Onica sat across from Morgan, her hands trembling as she clutched the edge of the desk. Her eyes, usually sharp and calculating, were clouded with anxiety. The weight of her conversation with Mr. Rogers hung heavily on her mind, and she could feel the pressure mounting, threatening to crush her.

ONICA
(anxious)
Morgan, you won't believe what just happened.

She took a deep breath, steadying herself before continuing.

Mr. Rogers, the ex-employee, is threatening to expose Peter's illegal profits and tax evasions.

Morgan's expression darkened as he listened, his fingers tapping lightly on the surface of the desk as he processed the information. He leaned forward, his tone shifting to one of concern.

MORGAN
(concerned)
This complicates things, Onica. We need to act carefully. If we agree to a settlement, it should be on our terms. We can't let him have the upper hand.

Onica closed her eyes for a moment, feeling a cold knot form in her stomach. The thought of the company, her late husband's legacy, being destroyed by a vengeful ex-employee was almost too much to bear. She didn't know how much more she could handle.

ONICA
(worried)
I don't want any legal troubles, Morgan. Please help me figure out a way to deal with this.

Morgan's jaw tightened. He was always the professional, always thinking three steps ahead, but even he knew this was a delicate situation. He had never liked Mr. Rogers, and now the man was holding the company—and everything Onica had worked for—hostage.

MORGAN
(determined)
I'll talk to Mr. Rogers and negotiate a settlement that protects your interests. We'll try to keep this as low-profile as possible. We can't let him drag this into the public eye.

Onica exhaled slowly, the tension in her shoulders easing just slightly. She knew Morgan would take care of things, but there was still a deep sense of dread that gnawed at her.

ONICA
(grateful)
Thank you, Morgan. I just want all of this to be over.

Morgan nodded, his eyes softening as he gave her a reassuring smile. He had been her rock for so long, through every legal battle and every challenge that came her way. She didn't know what she would do without him.

MORGAN
(supportive)
We'll do our best, Onica. You've been through a lot, and we'll get through this, too. You're not alone in this.

Onica gave him a small, grateful nod, her gaze lingering on him for a moment longer. She was fortunate to have someone like Morgan by her side, someone who always knew how to handle the impossible situations that seemed to find their way into her life. But even his reassurances couldn't shake the worry that clung to her like a shadow.

With a final sigh, she stood up, her movements slow and deliberate. Morgan didn't waste another second. He rose to his feet, ready to face Mr. Rogers, knowing the gravity of what was at stake. There was no room for mistakes now—not when everything Onica had worked for, everything she held dear, was teetering on the edge of collapse.

He gave her one last look, a silent promise in his eyes. He would fix this. He had to.

The boardroom was unusually quiet, a heavy silence hanging in the air. Onica sat at the head of the table, her fingers tightly gripping the edge, her face a mixture of frustration and exhaustion. Jacob, sitting beside her, wore a look of concern, his eyes darting to the papers scattered in front of him. Morgan, as always, was calm and composed, though his eyes betrayed the same urgency as the others.

JACOB
(worried)
This is a disaster, Onica. Our company's reputation is taking a serious hit.

He leaned forward, his voice tense. *We need a plan, and we need it fast.*

Onica's gaze shifted to Jacob, but her mind was elsewhere. The pressure was mounting, the weight of the crisis threatening to swallow them whole. How had things spiraled so quickly? She could barely keep up with the whirlwind of accusations, media scrutiny, and public backlash that had followed the latest scandal.

MORGAN
(agrees)
The media is having a field day with this. We need to address it immediately.

He folded his arms across his chest, his expression grave. *The longer we wait, the more control we lose. We can't afford that.*

ONICA
(frustrated)
I can't believe this is happening now. We have enough on our plate already.

Her voice was a mixture of anger and disbelief, as though the universe had conspired to throw every possible obstacle in her path at once. The company was barely holding itself together after the internal chaos and external pressure, and now this?

She ran a hand through her hair, eyes glinting with both frustration and determination. *This couldn't have come at a worse time.*

JACOB
(grim)
But we can't ignore it. The public is demanding answers.

His voice dropped to a near whisper, but the tension in the room was palpable. *If we don't do something now, the damage could be irreversible.*

Onica stared out the window for a long moment, the weight of the situation pressing on her chest. She was caught between her desire to protect what was left of the company and the need to confront this crisis head-on. Time was slipping through her fingers, and she knew every second wasted was another opportunity for the situation to spiral even further.

MORGAN
(firm)
Onica, we need to respond swiftly and transparently. We must take control of the narrative.

His voice had an edge of finality to it, like a man used to facing down tough decisions. *The public isn't stupid—they can sense when something's being hidden. If we own up to it, if we show them we're taking action, they'll respect us more for it.*

Onica looked at Morgan, his steady eyes locking with hers. She knew he was right. They couldn't hide from this. Not anymore. The world was watching, waiting for the next move, and whatever it was, it had to be decisive.

She sat up straighter, feeling the weight of her role as the leader of this company. It was time to take charge.

ONICA
(resolute)
Alright, let's do this. We'll address it head-on, and we'll make it clear that we're committed to fixing this. But I need every one of you to be on the same page. No more secrets, no more delays.

Her voice was sharp now, the frustration replaced with a hardened resolve. *We clean this mess up, and we do it fast.*

Jacob nodded, Morgan's gaze remained focused, and Onica felt the flicker of hope rekindle in her chest. It wouldn't be easy, and there would be more battles ahead, but they had no other choice but to face it together.

The storm was far from over, but for the first time in a while, Onica felt ready to fight.

The office was dimly lit, the only sound the hum of phones and the frantic tapping of keyboards. Onica sat at the head of the sleek conference table, surrounded by her PR team, each one focused, their brows furrowed as they worked through the mounting pressure. A large whiteboard at the front of the room was covered in notes, half-finished ideas, and scribbled bullet points, a testament to the intensity of the crisis they were facing.

PR SPECIALIST
(focused)
We need to issue a statement addressing the concerns and promising a thorough investigation. We can't afford to be vague—this needs to be direct and reassuring.

The PR specialist was an older woman with sharp eyes, her voice steady, though there was an unmistakable urgency in it. She had been in the industry long enough to know the weight a single word could carry when the public was watching, and she knew the eyes of the world were on them now.

Onica was quiet for a moment, her fingers drumming lightly on the table as she weighed the words she wanted to say. The tension in the room felt suffocating, but her resolve was unwavering.

ONICA
(determined)
I want it to be clear that we're committed to upholding our values and the trust our customers have in us.

Her voice rang with a conviction that surprised even her. For weeks, she had felt like a passenger in her own life, swept up in a tide of complications, one after another. But now, as the weight of the company's future rested squarely on her shoulders, she felt a flicker of clarity. This wasn't just about salvaging the company; it was about proving to herself that she could lead, that she could overcome this.

The room fell into a moment of stillness as everyone processed her words. The weight of the situation was far from over, but Onica had made it clear—this would be their fight, and they would face it head-on.

PR SPECIALIST
(nodding)
We'll craft a message that emphasizes our dedication to transparency and outlines the immediate steps we're taking. It'll have to be sincere—people are looking for honesty right now, not just another corporate spin.

ONICA
(softening)
I know. This is about more than just our image. We need to rebuild trust, not just with the public, but with our employees, too.

A murmur of agreement ran through the team as they began discussing the finer details—how to phrase their commitment to integrity, how to make sure the statement felt authentic rather than rehearsed. Every word mattered. They knew that once they went public with their response, there would be no going back. The world would judge them not only on the crisis itself but on how they handled it.

PR SPECIALIST
(assured)
We'll make sure the investigation is thorough. We'll bring in external auditors and share the process with the public as we go along. Transparency will be key.

ONICA
(nods)
Good. And make it clear that we're taking responsibility. No excuses. This company will own up to its mistakes.

As the team continued to fine-tune the statement, Onica felt a sense of purpose solidify within her. This was the first step. The first moment of reclaiming control. She was still uncertain about what the future held, but at least for today, she was taking the reins.

She stood up from the table, her gaze steady and determined as she addressed the group.

ONICA

Let's make this count. We need to restore confidence, and we need to do it right.

The room buzzed with energy, each person feeling the weight of the task ahead. Onica knew the road to recovery wouldn't be easy, but she was ready. For the first time in weeks, she felt the stirrings of hope—perhaps, just perhaps, they could weather this storm.

In the press conference, Onica stands at the podium, facing a room full of reporters.

ONICA
(confident)

I want to address the recent concerns about our company's practices. We take these matters seriously, and we will be conducting a thorough investigation to ensure transparency and accountability.

The reporters fire questions, and Onica responds with poise and clarity, vowing to resolve the crisis.

The days since the statement had been issued felt like a blur to Onica. The tension had lifted somewhat, but the weight of the crisis still hung in the air like a storm cloud, never fully dissipating. The phone calls and meetings had been relentless, but slowly, the company's reputation began to stabilize. The public, though still wary, had begun to respond to their commitment to transparency and accountability.

Onica sat at her desk, looking out the window at the gray sky. She hadn't slept well in days, but there was a quiet fire in her eyes now. The crisis wasn't over—she knew that better than anyone—but they had taken the first steps toward healing. She could feel it.

Morgan entered the office, holding a stack of papers in her hands. Her sharp eyes softened as she saw Onica lost in thought, but she didn't waste time with pleasantries.

MORGAN
(relieved)
It's a start, Onica. The worst is hopefully behind us.
The words were measured, cautious. Morgan had been with Onica through every storm, and while the road ahead was still uncertain, she could sense the shift in the air. The worst of the fallout from the crisis was starting to recede. The media had begun to focus less on the company's missteps and more on the measures they were taking to make things right.

Onica's fingers drummed lightly on her desk. She wasn't one to celebrate prematurely. There was still so much work to be done, so many loose ends to tie up, but there was a shift—subtle but unmistakable.

JACOB
(optimistic)
We'll get through this, stronger than before.
He stood by the door, his broad shoulders relaxed for the first time in days. Jacob had been by Onica's side from the very beginning, his loyalty unwavering even in the darkest moments. His optimism was a welcome balm, though Onica knew he, too, understood the challenges that still lay ahead.

She turned to look at him, offering a small smile. The fight wasn't over, but it was a fight they could win.

ONICA
(determined)
We have to. Our company's future depends on it.
Her voice was steady, unwavering. It was the same resolve that had carried her through the toughest moments—the same drive that had pushed her to make the tough decisions, even when it seemed like there was no way forward.

The future still felt uncertain, like a bridge they had yet to cross, but for the first time in weeks, Onica could see the faint outline of something beyond the horizon. A future where the company could rebuild, stronger and more resilient.

Morgan and Jacob exchanged a glance, their expressions a mix of relief and resolve. They knew that Onica's strength was the key to everything—her ability to make hard decisions and see them through.

The storm hadn't passed entirely, but it was beginning to lose its intensity. And with each day, the company took one more step toward recovery.

Onica sat at her desk, her eyes bleary, staring at the endless stack of papers before her. Each one felt heavier than the last. Her body ached, her head throbbed, and her mind seemed to be spinning in a million directions. Legal battles with Mr. Rogers, the company's internal turmoil, the mounting pressure of the media—all of it pressing down on her with an unrelenting weight. And as much as she tried to push through, to keep going, her strength was fading.

I can do this... just a little more... she whispered under her breath, trying to summon the willpower to carry on. But deep down, she knew her body was reaching its limit.

The world around her seemed to blur, the words on the papers becoming a haze. She felt dizzy, a sudden wave of exhaustion sweeping over her. Her breath hitched as she struggled to steady herself, but it was no use. Before she could even brace herself, her vision darkened, and she collapsed to the floor with a sharp thud.

Jacob, who had been quietly working in the corner of the office, heard the noise and spun around. His heart skipped a beat when he saw Onica crumpled on the floor.

JACOB
(panicking)
Onica! Are you okay?

He rushed to her side, his hands trembling as he gently tried to lift her, but Onica's body felt limp in his arms. Her face was pale, and though her eyes were open, they were unfocused.

JACOB
(concerned)
Don't try to get up. You need help.

Onica struggled to breathe, her chest rising and falling unevenly. She nodded weakly, but her body betrayed her. Every attempt to sit up only left her feeling weaker. Her head swam with dizziness, and she could barely keep her eyes open.

At that moment, the door to her office opened with a soft creak, and Dr. Anderson stepped in, his gaze immediately landing on Onica's frail form on the floor. His face shifted from neutral to alarmed as he rushed over.

DR. ANDERSON
(urgent)
What happened here?

JACOB
(frantically)
She just collapsed, doctor. I don't know what's wrong with her.

Dr. Anderson dropped to his knees beside Onica, his practiced hands moving quickly as he took her pulse, checking her vitals with an efficiency that only came from years of experience. He murmured to himself, his brow furrowing as he examined her.

DR. ANDERSON
(concerned)
Onica, can you hear me?

Onica's eyes fluttered, her weak attempt to focus on him failing. She managed a faint nod, her voice barely a whisper.

ONICA
(struggling)
Yes... I'm... I'm just...

DR. ANDERSON
(gently)
It's alright, Onica. Let's get you the help you need.

He motioned for Jacob to assist him as he carefully helped Onica into a seated position, supporting her fragile frame. The concern in his eyes was palpable, and he spoke in soothing tones as he ordered Jacob to bring the medical kit.

Onica wanted to reassure them, wanted to tell them she was fine—that she just needed a few moments to catch her breath. But the truth was, her body was telling her a different story. She felt the weight of her responsibilities pressing down on her, but now, in the face of her own exhaustion, she realized she could no longer carry it alone.

The door to her office clicked open once more, and in that moment, the bustling world outside faded away. She wasn't the strong, unshakable leader she had once been. She was just a woman, worn down by the weight of too many battles.

DR. ANDERSON
(firmly)
Onica, you're not going anywhere. We need to get you to a hospital.

Onica wanted to protest, wanted to tell him she was fine, but the words caught in her throat. She felt too weak to argue. She closed her eyes and surrendered, trusting the steady hands of the doctor and the concern in Jacob's eyes.

For the first time in a long while, Onica let go.

Onica lay in the sterile hospital bed, her body frail, her face pale. The rhythmic beep of the heart monitor was the only sound that filled the room, a stark contrast to the chaos that had engulfed her life for weeks. Her once sharp, determined eyes now looked tired, as if the weight of the world had taken a toll she could no longer ignore. Every breath seemed a little harder, each movement a little more labored. She was physically drained, the exhaustion from her mental and emotional battles finally catching up to her.

Dr. Anderson stood at the foot of her bed, his expression grave. He had just completed some preliminary tests, but there were still many questions to be answered. Jacob and Morgan were both there too, standing nearby, their concern evident in their eyes. Jacob paced near the window, his brow furrowed, while Morgan stood close to the bed, offering silent support.

DR. ANDERSON
(serious)
Onica, I've conducted some initial tests, and your health is in a critical condition. We need to run more tests to determine the cause.

Onica's eyes fluttered open at his words, but the weight of his diagnosis seemed to press down on her. She had known something was wrong for a while now, but hearing it so plainly made it feel real—too real. She exhaled slowly, trying to steady her racing thoughts.

ONICA
(weakly)
I've been so stressed, Doctor. It's everything—the legal battles, the company's troubles... I can't handle it all.

Her voice was barely above a whisper, yet it carried the rawness of everything she had been holding inside. The thought of all the unresolved issues she had been grappling with—the accusations, the mounting pressure from her employees, and her failing health—had become too much to carry.

Morgan moved closer, her hand gently resting on Onica's. She looked down at her with a soft, understanding gaze, a quiet reassurance in her touch.

MORGAN
(supportive)

We'll make sure you get the best care, Onica. Your health is the priority now.

Dr. Anderson nodded, his professional demeanor unwavering. His eyes softened slightly as he turned back to Onica, trying to offer her some comfort amid the storm of uncertainty.

DR. ANDERSON
(determined)
We'll get to the bottom of this, Onica. You have a team of experts looking after you.

Onica wanted to believe him, to trust that everything would be okay. But deep down, a nagging fear lingered. She had spent so much time fighting for the company, for her late husband's legacy, that she had neglected her own well-being. Now, faced with the consequences, it was hard not to wonder if it was all too late.

ONICA
(grateful, weak)
Thank you... all of you. I just want to get better and put all of this behind me.

Her voice trembled as she spoke, her gratitude sincere but tinged with the weight of uncertainty. She didn't want to dwell on the stress and the battles anymore. She just wanted a moment of peace. A chance to heal.

DR. ANDERSON
(reassuring)
We'll do our best to make that happen, Onica.

As the conversation continued, a quiet resolve settled in the room. There were no easy answers yet, no promises that everything would be fine. But for the first time in what felt like ages, Onica allowed herself to rest—to trust in the care of those around her. The battle for her health had just begun, but with the support of her team and the dedication of the doctor at her side, she felt, if only for a moment, that she might finally be able to breathe again.

The road ahead was uncertain, but for now, Onica could close her eyes and rest, allowing herself the space to recover.

Onica sat at her desk, the weight of her world pressing heavily on her shoulders. The soft hum of the office around her barely reached her ears as she stared blankly at the papers scattered in front of her. Every document, every number, seemed to blur together in a haze of exhaustion and uncertainty. Her thoughts swirled as she tried to focus, but the mounting pressures of her failing health, the company's struggles, and the constant conflict with her employees had become too much to bear.

Morgan, her trusted attorney, sat across from her, speaking softly to a man Onica had never met. Mr. Thompson, a billionaire investor, had recently shown interest in acquiring the company. His reputation preceded him—a man known for turning failing businesses around, but at a price. Onica had listened to Morgan's assurances, but the idea of handing over control of everything Peter had built felt like a betrayal.

MORGAN
(softly to Onica)
Onica, this is Mr. Thompson. He's a billionaire investor, and he's shown significant interest in acquiring the company.

Onica nodded faintly, her eyes briefly meeting Mr. Thompson's. He was a man of few words, his demeanor calm and collected, but his presence filled the room. He understood the stakes, and from his expression, it was clear that he wasn't here to play games.

ONICA
(weary)
I've heard the complaints from our employees, and I've seen the company's financial struggles. I don't want to be a hindrance anymore, Morgan.

Her voice barely rose above a whisper, the toll of the last few weeks making it hard to speak with conviction. Every word felt like an admission of defeat, but deep down, Onica knew she couldn't continue fighting the losing battle alone. She was tired—physically and emotionally. The company was crumbling, and her health was deteriorating in tandem.

MR. THOMPSON
(sympathetic)
Onica, I understand that this has been a challenging time for you. I've reviewed the company's financials, and I believe I can help turn things around.

Onica exhaled slowly, rubbing her temples as if trying to clear the fog that had settled in her mind. The fight for the company, the legacy Peter had left behind, seemed like an impossible task now. The weight of it all was too much for her to carry.

ONICA
(deep sigh)
I'm not sure what the best decision is anymore. I've been fighting for the company and my late husband's legacy, but my health is deteriorating.

Her voice cracked slightly, the emotion she had been holding in for so long finally breaking through. She had poured everything into this company—her energy, her passion, her life. And now, in the face of everything crumbling, she felt like she was letting it all slip through her fingers.

Morgan, ever the steady presence, leaned forward, her tone gentle yet firm.

MORGAN
(supportive)
Onica, Mr. Thompson has proposed a fair deal. It would secure your financial future and provide a fresh start for the company.

Mr. Thompson nodded, his expression sincere as he spoke.

MR. THOMPSON
(reassuring)

I'm willing to make this transition as smooth as possible. We'll ensure the employees are taken care of, and you'll be able to focus on your health and well-being.

Onica looked at him, her eyes tired but searching for something—hope, perhaps, or reassurance. She didn't know if she could trust him fully, but the alternative felt unbearable. She had fought so long and so hard, but what was left to fight for? The company she loved was falling apart, and her body was giving out beneath her.

She swallowed hard, feeling a tightness in her chest as she spoke the words that felt like an irreversible decision.

ONICA
(softly)
I never imagined it would come to this, but if it's for the best... I'll agree to the sale. I just hope it's the right decision.

Her voice was barely a whisper, as though speaking the words aloud might make them real. She didn't feel like she had much choice left, but the weight of the decision still hung heavily in the air.

Morgan placed a hand on Onica's, offering silent support. Her eyes were soft but unwavering, a small flicker of relief in her gaze. This was the right choice, she knew. It wasn't just about saving the company anymore—it was about saving Onica.

MORGAN
(gentle)
It's a difficult choice, Onica, but your health is what matters most. We'll ensure that this transition is handled with care.

Mr. Thompson smiled, a slight but reassuring expression that suggested he was genuinely invested in making this work for everyone involved.

MR. THOMPSON
(smiling)

Thank you for your trust, Onica. Together, we'll find a way to rejuvenate this company.

As Onica nodded, the weight of the decision seemed to lift slightly, though the uncertainty of what came next remained. She had handed over the reins, and in doing so, she hoped she was giving the company the best chance to survive. For her husband. For herself.

The room was quiet as they all absorbed the gravity of the moment. Onica's mind was still clouded with doubts, but one thing was clear: the future of the company would no longer be her responsibility. Whether that was a relief or a regret, only time would tell.

Onica sat in her living room, surrounded by a mountain of paperwork—company files, medical records, legal documents—each one a reminder of the overwhelming weight on her shoulders. The dim light from a single lamp cast long shadows across the room, highlighting the dark circles under her eyes and the weariness that seemed to seep into every part of her. Her mind was a blur, bouncing between the failing company she had inherited from her late husband and her deteriorating health. It felt like everything she had worked for, everything she had fought to protect, was slipping through her fingers.

As she shuffled through the papers, the doorbell rang. Its sharp chime cut through the quiet of the room, jolting Onica from her thoughts. She sat up, blinking in confusion as if the sound was an intrusion on her fragile peace. Slowly, she stood, her body stiff and aching, and made her way to the door.

She opened it to find a middle-aged woman standing on her doorstep. The woman looked nervous, fidgeting with her hands as she gazed up at Onica, uncertainty written all over her face.

ONICA
(confused)
Can I help you?

ANNA
(nervously)
Are you Onica?
ONICA
(eyes narrowing, still cautious)
Yes, I am. Who are you?
ANNA
(nervous, yet determined)
My name is Anna. I need to talk to you about something very important.

Anna took a tentative step closer, her face a strange mixture of anxiety and something else—something that looked like a burden she could no longer carry. Onica stepped back instinctively, her eyes scanning Anna's face for any hint of deception. But nothing about this woman suggested anything but sincerity, albeit mixed with a palpable nervousness.

ONICA
(guarded)
What's this about?
ANNA
(hesitating, then speaking in a rush)
I don't know how to say this... but I was married to your late husband, Peter.

Onica froze, her body stiffening as the words struck her like a blow to the chest. The air in the room seemed to suck out of her lungs, and for a moment, she couldn't move. She blinked, trying to process what she had just heard.

ONICA
(incredulous)
What? That's impossible! Peter and I were married. We have the marriage certificate to prove it.

Anna took a shaky breath, her hands trembling as she clasped them in front of her, as if trying to steady herself.

ANNA
(desperate)
I know this sounds unbelievable, but we got married in secret. I didn't have the chance to tell anyone, and Peter kept it hidden. I found out about his death, and I had to come forward.

Onica's mind whirled with confusion, her pulse quickening as anger began to rise in her chest. Her thoughts collided in a storm of disbelief and rage.

ONICA
(angry)
You expect me to believe this now? After he's gone?

Anna's eyes filled with tears, her voice breaking as she spoke.

ANNA
(pleading)
I understand your anger, but I swear it's the truth. I have the marriage certificate and other evidence to prove it. I can't keep this secret any longer.

Onica's eyes narrowed as her skepticism deepened.

ONICA
(skeptical)
Evidence? What kind of evidence?

ANNA
(nervous, voice trembling)
Letters, photos, messages... all hidden away in a box in our house. I didn't want to share this burden with you, but now, with Peter gone, I can't stay silent.

The words hung in the air like a heavy fog, and Onica felt her chest tighten. The world felt as if it were tilting, spinning in a way she couldn't control. Her emotions were a whirlwind—anger, confusion, betrayal, all tangled together in a knot she couldn't untangle.

ONICA
(teary-eyed, voice shaking)
I need to see this evidence.
Anna's face softened with relief, her eyes welling up with fresh tears as she spoke quietly.
ANNA
(softly)
I'm willing to show you everything, Onica. I didn't know about you until now. I never meant to hurt anyone.
Onica stood there for a long moment, her thoughts racing. She wanted to close the door, to shut out the stranger standing on her doorstep and pretend that this conversation had never happened. But something in Anna's eyes stopped her. Something raw and desperate, as if this woman was carrying a truth so heavy, it had nearly broken her. Onica's heart was torn between disbelief and a painful, gnawing curiosity.
ONICA
(shaky, voice barely above a whisper)
Just give me a moment to think.
ANNA
(nodding)
Of course.
With a final glance at Anna, Onica retreated back into the house, the door clicking shut behind her. Her steps were slow and deliberate as she crossed the room, the weight of the conversation pressing down on her chest. She sank into her armchair, her head spinning as she tried to process what she had just heard. Peter—her husband—had kept this secret from her? Another woman? Another life, hidden in the shadows of their marriage?

Her hands shook as she reached for the papers on the table in front of her, but they blurred in her vision. The idea that her marriage, the very foundation of everything she had believed in, might have been a lie was almost too much to bear. But Anna's sincerity echoed in her mind. The tears, the trembling hands—they didn't seem like the actions of someone who was lying.

Onica closed her eyes, trying to steady her breathing, but the weight of these revelations felt like a storm breaking inside her. Could she trust this woman? Could she ever understand what Peter had hidden from her all these years?

She didn't know. But she knew one thing for certain: her world had just been irrevocably changed. And what came next was a path she would have to walk, no matter how dark it might be.

Onica returned to the door with a deep sigh, her mind a storm of conflicting emotions. The weight of everything that had happened—her declining health, the company's struggles, the mounting pressure from every direction—had already begun to take its toll. Yet now, as she stood in the threshold of her own home, faced with Anna's revelation, it felt as if another layer of her life was about to be ripped open, exposing hidden truths she was not prepared for.

She squared her shoulders, trying to steady her breath. The last thing she needed was another distraction. But this, whatever this was, couldn't be ignored.

Her voice was low but firm as she addressed Anna, who had been standing there, eyes fixed to the ground, waiting for the next move.

ONICA
(resolute)
Okay, Anna. Show me this evidence.

Anna's face softened with a mix of relief and apprehension. She nodded, her hands trembling ever so slightly as she reached into the bag slung over her shoulder. Onica's heart thudded in her chest. She didn't know if she was ready to hear whatever secrets lay hidden in those old papers, those photographs. But she didn't have a choice. The truth was no longer something she could hide from.

The envelope that Anna pulled from the bag was worn at the edges, as if it had been handled and shuffled through many times. It was stained in places, the kind of wear that only comes from years of being tucked away and guarded. Onica hesitated for just a moment before accepting it.

ANNA
(softly)
I never meant for any of this to come to light, Onica. But you deserve to know... you deserve to understand the truth.

Onica didn't respond, her gaze fixed on the envelope in her hands. She opened it carefully, as if afraid that even the slightest wrong move might tear apart the fragile walls of her life. Inside were several folded papers, their edges creased and yellowed with time. Letters, she assumed, written by Peter himself, perhaps to Anna.

The first letter she unfolded was brief, and yet every word burned into her soul like an accusation. Peter's familiar handwriting, the same script she had seen on their wedding invitations, was scrawled across the page. But the words were different—colder, more distant.

Anna, I think of you every day, but the life we're building, the life I'm trying to create with Onica... it's taking everything from me. I don't know how to break free of this double life, how to live the way I want to without destroying everything I hold dear.

Onica's hands trembled as she held the letter, her heart pounding against her ribs. The words felt like a knife twisting inside her. How long had Peter been hiding this? How much of their life had been a lie?

ONICA
(softly, to herself)
Why didn't he tell me?

Anna, sensing the pain in Onica's voice, took a cautious step forward. She had known the hurt this would cause, but she could not bear the silence any longer. She had to let the truth be seen, no matter the consequences.

ANNA
(gently)
I know this is hard, Onica. But Peter... he was torn. I never wanted to take him from you, but he was a part of my life, too. And now, with him gone, all I have left are these pieces. These fragments of a man I thought I knew.

Onica's throat tightened, the words of the letter swimming in front of her eyes. She fought to keep her composure, her emotions teetering on the edge of something uncontrollable. The reality of what she was holding in her hands was starting to break through the fog of disbelief.

ONICA
(struggling)
I need to see everything. Show me the rest.

Anna nodded and handed over a bundle of photographs. As Onica flipped through them, she felt the ground beneath her shift. Peter, younger in these images, smiled with a woman Onica had never seen before—Anna. They were happy in these photos, in a way that Onica had never seen Peter smile. A life that had been hidden away, locked in a box, just waiting to be unearthed.

Her fingers trembled as she turned the next photo over, only to find a picture of Peter and Anna standing together at a beach, arms around each other, their faces alight with a joy that felt foreign. The last photo was of Peter, alone, his eyes distant and sad, as if he were carrying a burden he could no longer bear.

ANNA
(voice cracking)
I never wanted to hurt you. I didn't know how to tell you. But now, you need to know the truth, Onica. You need to know who he really was... the man behind the man you thought you knew.

Onica sat down heavily, the world spinning around her. This wasn't just a betrayal. It was an unraveling of everything she had believed about her life, about her marriage, and about the man she had loved. It was as if the fabric of her reality had begun to fray, and now there were only pieces—pieces of Peter's life, pieces of her own heart.

For a long moment, neither woman spoke. The silence was thick, almost suffocating, as Onica took in everything she had learned. The secrets. The lies. The love Peter had kept hidden from her, and the life he had lived outside of their marriage.

Finally, Onica looked up at Anna, her face weary but resolute.

ONICA
(quietly)
We'll figure this out, Anna. We'll figure out what happens next. But right now, I need to process all of this.

Anna nodded, her face pale and tear-streaked, but there was no shame in her eyes—only a quiet understanding. She had done what she had to do. Now, the future was uncertain for both of them, bound by the tangled threads of Peter's secrets.

Anna stepped into the living room, the weight of the old, weathered box she carried almost matching the heaviness in her heart. She placed it gently on the coffee table, her hands trembling slightly as she settled it before Onica. The box, once a repository of private memories, now held the key to unraveling the tangled secrets of the man they had both loved.

Her eyes met Onica's, a mixture of hope and apprehension clouding her gaze.

ANNA
(nervous)
This is everything, Onica. Every memory I have of the time I spent with Peter.

Onica stood silent for a moment, her gaze locked on the box. Her heart felt tight in her chest, the weight of the revelation pressing down on her. She had suspected there were things about Peter she didn't know, but nothing had prepared her for this. The betrayal, the secrecy, the life he had hidden from her—it was all contained within that simple box.

ONICA
(somber)
I never knew about any of this. He kept it all a secret.

The words hung in the air, thick with the sting of pain and disbelief. She could barely bring herself to touch the box, as if afraid that simply opening it would shatter the last of the illusions she had clung to about her marriage.

Anna's face crumpled, and for a fleeting moment, she looked as if she might fall apart. Her voice quivered, thick with emotion.

ANNA
(teary-eyed)
I only found out the truth after he disappeared from my life. I never meant to hurt you, Onica.

Onica didn't respond immediately. Instead, she took a deep, shuddering breath, and then, as if guided by some unspoken force, she slowly lifted the lid of the box. The scent of old paper and dust filled the room as she began to sift through the contents—photographs, letters, postcards. Each item was a tangible piece of a life she hadn't known existed. Peter, smiling with Anna in photographs taken on vacations, on holidays, in moments of joy. The evidence of a love so deep, so secret, that Onica had never been allowed to see it.

Her fingers brushed against a pile of letters, carefully folded and yellowed with age. Her eyes scanned the words written in Peter's familiar script, the ones that seemed to tell Anna a story that Onica had never been a part of. A chill ran through her as she read the words of affection, the longing in every sentence.

ONICA
(whispered)
He was leading a double life.

The realization hit her like a blow to the chest. The man she had loved, the man she had built her life around, had been living another life with Anna—hidden, separate from everything they had shared. Her hands shook as she flipped through more photos, more letters. There were vacations Onica never knew about, moments of laughter and intimacy she had been entirely excluded from.

ANNA
(softly)
It was never my intention to disrupt your life, Onica. But Peter was a part of my life too.

The words hung in the room, a fragile apology that only deepened Onica's grief. She wanted to be angry, wanted to lash out, but the sadness was suffocating. The man she had known, the man who had stood by her through thick and thin, had kept secrets so profound that even now, after his death, they seemed impossible to untangle.

Onica let the box sit before her, her fingers trembling as they sifted through the letters, the photographs, the mementos of a life she had never been invited into. Anger bubbled up, but it was quickly replaced by sorrow, a sorrow that seemed deeper than anything she had ever felt before.

ONICA
(teary-eyed)
He left me with so many questions... so many lies.

Anna sat silently beside her, her heart aching for the woman whose world had just been shattered by the secrets of a man they had both loved. She understood the pain, the confusion, the betrayal.

The pieces of Peter's life they had shared were now laid bare, exposing the fragility of what Onica had believed was true.

ANNA

(compassionate)

I know it's hard to accept, but we both loved him. I just want some closure, and maybe... something to remember him by.

The words were soft, filled with a kind of quiet understanding, and Onica's chest tightened even more. She had spent years loving a man who had kept a part of himself from her. And now, this woman who had once been a part of Peter's life was asking for the same closure that Onica so desperately needed.

ONICA

(shaky)

I understand, Anna. I don't know what this means for us, but I appreciate your honesty.

The words felt inadequate, like an attempt to bridge a gap that had only widened with each new revelation. Onica closed the box with a soft click, the weight of everything that had been revealed sinking into her bones. She wasn't sure where this new knowledge would take her—whether it would change everything or nothing at all. But for now, all she could do was sit in the quiet, the room heavy with the secrets of the past and the uncertainty of the future.

Anna nodded, her eyes reflecting a sadness that matched Onica's. Neither of them had the answers yet, but the road ahead was bound to be anything but easy.

Morgan arrived at Jersey's house, his expression set, his mind focused on the legalities of the situation. He had hoped that this would be a straightforward visit, but the tension in the air was palpable. He could see Mabella sitting on the couch, her fingers nervously twisting the fabric of her sleeve. The weight of the situation was clearly taking its toll on her.

MORGAN

(firmly)
Mabella, I'm here with a court order and a restraining order.
Mabella's eyes widened as she looked up, her anxiety deepening.

MABELLA
(nervous)
What's this about, Morgan?
He didn't waste any time. Morgan reached into his briefcase and pulled out the thick stack of documents, placing them carefully on the coffee table. He watched her hands tremble slightly as she picked them up, her eyes scanning the words.

MABELLA
(shocked)
You're asking me to leave the house within 48 hours?
Morgan's voice remained calm but resolute.

MORGAN
(serious)
Yes, Mabella. After Jersey's passing and the recent court decision, the property legally belongs to Onica. You can't stay here any longer.
The words hit Mabella like a punch to the gut. She looked down at the papers again, hoping, praying it was a mistake, but the facts were clear. Jersey was gone, and the law had decided the house belonged to someone else—someone she barely knew. She felt a tightness in her chest, like the walls of the room were closing in.

MABELLA
(frustrated)
But I have nowhere to go! This is my home too!
She stood up, her voice rising in a mix of panic and anger. This was more than just a house to her; it was a place filled with memories, a life she had built with Jersey. The idea of losing it felt like losing everything.

MORGAN
(apologetic)

I understand, Mabella, but the court's decision is final. You must leave the property within the given time frame.

Morgan's words were firm but carried a note of sympathy. He wished there were another way, but he knew he had no choice. The law had spoken, and it was his duty to enforce it, no matter how painful it was for the people involved.

Mabella's eyes filled with tears as she crumpled the papers in her hands, clutching them to her chest as if they might offer some sort of comfort.

MABELLA
(teary-eyed)
I can't believe this. Jersey would never have wanted this.

Her voice was a broken whisper, her face a mix of disbelief and grief. She couldn't reconcile the reality of the situation with the memories of the man she had loved. Jersey's death had already ripped apart her world, and now, this—this cruel final blow—was forcing her to face a future she wasn't prepared for.

Morgan's expression softened, and for a brief moment, he wanted to reach out and offer her reassurance. But he knew the truth. There was nothing he could say to change what had been decided.

MORGAN
(compassionate)
I know it's difficult, but we have to follow the law. I can help you find temporary accommodation if needed.

Mabella didn't respond at first, her eyes distant as the reality of her situation set in. She stood still, tears streaming down her face as she slowly began to gather her belongings. Every movement seemed mechanical, as if her body was acting before her mind could catch up with the chaos inside her. The house that had once been filled with love and laughter now felt like a cage. Every corner, every room, was taunting her with memories of Jersey.

Morgan watched her, his own heart heavy. He understood her pain, but the law had spoken, and there was no turning back. He could offer assistance in finding a place to stay, but that didn't ease the weight of her loss.

Mabella wiped her eyes, took a deep breath, and continued packing. The room was silent, save for the sound of items being placed into boxes—pieces of a life being packed away, one heartbreaking memory at a time.

Onica stood in the center of the living room, her hands trembling slightly as she held out a set of keys. The weight of the moment hung thick in the air. Mrs. Collins, Peter's mother, stood across from her, her face a mixture of sorrow and barely contained anger. Her eyes were red from hours of silent grief, and her hands were clenched at her sides, as though holding herself together by sheer force of will.

ONICA
(softly)
Mrs. Collins, I want you to have these keys. This was your son's home, and I know he would have wanted you to have it.

Mrs. Collins stared at the keys for a moment, the weight of the gesture sinking in. She reached for them reluctantly, her fingers brushing against Onica's as she took hold of them. But there was no smile, no acknowledgment of gratitude—just a deep, aching sorrow reflected in her tear-filled eyes.

MRS. COLLINS
(teary-eyed)
This is not what Peter would have wanted. He wanted this to be our home, ours and his family's.

Her voice cracked as she spoke, her words a mixture of sorrow and regret. Onica felt a pang of guilt, though she knew it wasn't her fault. Still, the tension in the room was palpable, and her heart ached for the woman who had lost so much.

ONICA
(sympathetic)
I understand, Mrs. Collins. I never meant for things to turn out this way. I want to assure you that you will be compensated fairly.

Mrs. Collins' eyes hardened, her lips pressed into a thin line. She lifted the keys, turning them over in her palm as if they were a reminder of everything she had lost.

MRS. COLLINS
(gritting her teeth)
Compensation can't replace the memories in this house.

Onica closed her eyes for a moment, taking in the weight of Mrs. Collins' words. There was no amount of money, no gesture, that could undo the pain she was feeling—the pain of losing her son, of having her home taken away. Onica stepped forward, her voice gentle, though she knew the pain she was causing was inevitable.

ONICA
(gentle)
I know, and I'm truly sorry for the pain this has caused you.

Mrs. Collins turned her gaze away, looking out the window as if the world outside might somehow offer a semblance of escape. She swallowed hard, struggling to maintain her composure.

MRS. COLLINS
(looking away)
It's not your fault, Onica. It's the circumstances.

Onica nodded slowly, understanding that Mrs. Collins' anger wasn't directed at her personally. It was the weight of everything—the loss, the betrayal of a life's plans—manifesting in grief-stricken fury. There was nothing Onica could say to make it better, but she could offer comfort, even if it felt small in comparison to the depth of pain in the room.

ONICA
(compassionate)

I just hope that, with time, wounds can heal, and we can find a way to move forward.

Mrs. Collins glanced back at Onica, her expression softening just slightly. Her shoulders drooped as the tension in her body loosened, though the sadness remained ever-present in her eyes. She wiped at her eyes, trying to regain some measure of composure.

MRS. COLLINS
(softly)
Thank you for the keys, Onica. I'll decide what to do with the house in due time.

Onica nodded, feeling the weight of the decision hang between them. She didn't want to rush Mrs. Collins, didn't want to add to her grief in any way.

ONICA
(sincere)
Take all the time you need, Mrs. Collins. And if there's anything I can do to help, please don't hesitate to reach out.

For a moment, they both stood there, in the stillness of the room, neither knowing quite how to bridge the chasm of loss and grief between them. Mrs. Collins gave a small, grateful nod, her lips trembling as she whispered her thanks again. The exchange wasn't one of resolution or healing, but it was a start—a quiet acknowledgment of the complicated and emotional journey that lay ahead for both of them.

As they stood there, their gazes met—two women bound by the same man, now facing the consequences of his secrets and the harsh realities of his death. Neither of them had asked for this, but it was the path they now had to walk. The future felt uncertain, but they both knew that, somehow, they would have to find a way forward.

The room was filled with the soft rustling of paper and the occasional sigh as Onica and Anna sifted through the contents of the old box. Each item that surfaced seemed to carry its own weight—photographs, letters, trinkets from places long forgotten. The once-vibrant memories of Peter were now reduced to these tangible fragments, scattered across the coffee table between the two women.

Onica picked up a photograph, its edges worn and faded. It was of Peter, smiling, standing on a beach with his arm around Anna. The picture seemed so out of place in the room now, where tension and grief hung like a heavy fog. She studied the photo for a long moment before glancing up at Anna, whose eyes were fixed on the image, her lips trembling slightly.

ONICA
(softly)
He never spoke much about the times before we were together. But I see it now... the joy in his face. He looked happy, truly happy.

Anna's voice was quiet, almost apologetic, as she nodded in agreement. She pulled another photograph from the pile, this one of Peter holding a baby. A child, his child, her child. Anna's gaze lingered on it, as if trying to reconcile the love she had shared with Peter and the life she had never fully known.

ANNA
(softly)
We had dreams, you know. He and I. There was a time when... when I thought it was just us against the world.

Onica's heart tightened at the words. She felt the undeniable pull of sympathy for Anna, for the woman who had once been the center of Peter's life, just as Onica had been. For a brief moment, there was no animosity between them, just the shared ache of loss.

ONICA
(whispering)
I never knew, Anna. I didn't know he had this life... with you. It feels like there's so much I didn't understand about him. About us. I thought we were building something, a future...

Anna's voice cracked, but she quickly regained composure. She hadn't meant to bring more pain to Onica, but she couldn't help herself. It was the truth, and it hung between them like a shadow. The secret life Peter had led was now an open wound that neither of them could ignore.

ANNA
(quietly)
I know. I know how hard this must be for you. It's not what I wanted, not at all. I didn't want to hurt you, Onica. I just wanted... I wanted him to have his truth.

Onica looked at Anna, her own grief pooling in her chest, mixing with a strange understanding. They both loved him, in different ways, yet the man they had known was not the same. Peter had kept parts of himself locked away from both of them, as if fearing that revealing too much would break what they had.

ONICA
(teary-eyed)
It hurts to think about it, to think that he was living this double life. But... I also can't deny it. He wasn't just mine, was he?

Anna shook her head, her voice barely above a whisper.

ANNA
No, Onica. He wasn't. And I'm sorry you had to find out this way. I never wanted to cause you pain. But I also wanted you to know... the truth.

For a moment, neither of them spoke. The silence was heavy, but there was something in it that felt almost like understanding—like the quiet recognition that both women had been deceived, both had loved the same man, and both now had to rebuild their lives in the aftermath of his secrets.

Onica picked up another letter from the box, its paper yellowed with age, the handwriting delicate and familiar. It was from Peter, written during a time when things had seemed simpler, before everything had unraveled. She read it aloud, her voice breaking as the words sank in.

ONICA
(reading aloud)
I'm always here for you, Anna. No matter the distance, no matter the circumstances, we'll find our way back to each other. I promise you, my love, I'm not going anywhere. Always yours, Peter.

Anna's eyes welled with tears as she listened, the words both a comfort and a torment. She had cherished those promises, held on to them for so long, only to have them fade into the past. She let out a soft sob, her hand trembling as she wiped away the tears.

ANNA
(softly)
He kept saying that. He said it all the time, even when we were apart. But in the end... in the end, he wasn't here to keep his word.

Onica reached across the table, her hand resting gently on Anna's. She didn't know what to say—how could she? But in that moment, they shared something more than grief. They shared a bond, fragile and raw, forged by the love they had both once held for Peter and the pain they now faced together.

ONICA
(whispering)
He wasn't here for any of us, Anna. But we are. We're here now. And we'll find a way to heal... even if it takes time.

Anna nodded, her breath shaking as she leaned into the comfort Onica offered. The box lay between them, filled with pieces of a man they both thought they knew. But now, as the truth spilled out, they were left with the pieces of their own lives to rebuild—together, and yet apart.

As the room grew quieter, the women continued to sift through the mementos of the past, their shared grief mingling with a slow, tentative understanding. The journey ahead was uncertain, but for the first time, Onica and Anna didn't feel completely alone.

Did you love *My Wedding Contract Too*? Then you should read *Her Lover is Gone*[1] by Branny Smith!

Have you ever imagined that your partner was involved with someone or married to someone that never existed? Have you ever asked yourself questions on why we never see partners of our friends or family members? Why are they hiding their partners and is it important that they should continue doing what they are doing? Hence this book is written to check who are these secretive partners, maybe they are very romantic, we hope to meet them one day. Love is amazing, and it can change the world, only if we can get it, grab it with our two hands then walk with it.

---

1. https://books2read.com/u/3yJ2rZ

2. https://books2read.com/u/3yJ2rZ

About the Author

The author is a well known filmmaker/producer and a scriptwriter of feature films and documentaries, and he has experience as an investigative journalist. He is now working as a Holistic Therapist and he has passion in Addiction Treatment as part of his focus treatment. In his path as a communicator, and media public relations manager in the creative sector he has learned a lot about interacting with different people. His focus in film is also on psychological thrillers, psychoanalytic approach stories and romantic drama. Branny Mthelebofu as an author he has been teaching Nutrition on radio part of his journey to help patients with weight and nutritional challenges. He has just released a lounge and dance music album .